Bring Me the Head
of Ryan Giggs

Also by Rodge Glass

Fiction

No Fireworks

Hope for Newborns

Dougie's War: A Soldier's Story (co-written with Dave Turbitt)

Non-fiction

Alasdair Gray: A Secretary's Biography

BRING ME THE HEAD OF RYAN GIGGS

Rodge Glass

Tindal
Street
Press

A complete catalogue record for this book can
be obtained from the British Library on request

First published in 2012 by Tindal Street Press

First published in this edition in 2013 by Tindal Street Press
an imprint of Profile Books Ltd
3A Exmouth House
Pine Street
London EC1R 0JH

ISBN 978 1 90699 445 7
eISBN 978 1 90699 487 7

Designed and typeset by Tetragon, London

Printed and bound by CPI Group (UK) Ltd, Croydon CRO 4YY

10 9 8 7 6 5 4 3 2 1

For Tim

This is a work of fiction. Although facts concerning Manchester United Football Club are used for the sake of authenticity, the names of public figures have been used throughout the story in a purely fictitious way. All other characters, incidents and dialogue are imaginary, and any reference to actual persons living or dead is purely coincidental.

FIRST HALF

THE REPUBLIK OF MANCUNIA

'I do not wish to hide my origins, nor do I seek to make it a subject of conversation. I am what I am.'

Ryan Giggs

Summer 1991. July the seventeenth. The beginning.

The Great Man was well early, so when the bell went I wasn't ready and I swear to God I went fuckin *mental*. I started legging it round the house, not knowing where to go. I could have run right up the wall, onto the ceiling and back down again, I had that much energy. I could have taken a bite out of the couch. I jumped over one of the chairs and jumped right back. I ran round it then round it the other way. Mum battered me with a tea towel and said, *Stop it, do you want him to think you're a hamster?* But she was bouncing too. She kept staring out the window at his Merc. (We were thinking that if he left it there too long, it'd probably get nicked.) Then Mum screamed. *Well get the door then! What are you waiting for?* So I opened it, smiled and said, *Hello, Mr Ferguson, come on in!* As if that was a thing I said every day. His first words to me were, *Son, if ye can get up the wing as fast as ye get round your front room, ye'll do just fine. There's no question aboot that. No question aboot that at all.*

Ooh, hhhellooo, said Mum, showing him into the lounge where she'd laid out a plate of biscuits. Then she asked, *How doo yoo like yaw tee?* Like he was a lord or something, and she was his maid, at his service. While he picked up and crunched a digestive I just stood there, thinking. Thinking that he looked pretty small compared to what I expected, and then thinking that he had this funny little red nose, how it didn't look that red on the telly interviews after the games, and then thinking *fuckin hell Alex Ferguson is sitting on my mum's couch, about to drink her tea.* As I stood there, staring, staring, staring at that nose, the manager of Manchester United chatted away about the weather, smiling and nodding whenever Mum spoke. Then he said, *You must be very proud of your boy, Mrs Wilson,* and she laughed that bit too hard, snorting, like she'd just heard a filthy joke and forgot to pretend she didn't think it was funny.

The whole thing was over quick. It must've only lasted twenty minutes and Alex Ferguson hardly touched his drink. (I gave him the United mug, the one that said *European Cup Winners' Cup 1991* on it. He smiled when he saw that.) I reckoned he'd be round ours for half the day, maybe stay for tea, watch a film with us or something. Thought he might come down the park for a bit of a kickabout and a swig from a bottle of cider. When I got the call saying he was coming over, I'd imagined us sitting up all night talking by torchlight, under the duvet, about the great United teams of the past. Eating sarnies and talking about our favourite players. Thinking up Best Ever United XIs and plotting together how we were going to – as he put it years later – *knock Liverpool off their fucking perch*.

But there was none of that. He just told Mum I had a *very promising career in the making, Mrs Wilson, if he works hard, and I'll make sure he does, don't you worry about that*. Well, Mum couldn't stop herself. *Could you make him tidy his room as well, Mr Ferguson? That'd be smashing*. The Great Man didn't laugh. He just turned to me, face straight like he was saying something important and told me, *Son, be good to your mother. She brought ye into the world and she can take ye back out just as easy.* (Was that a joke? Was he joking? Did Alexander Ferguson make jokes?) Then he thanked Mum for the tea, got up and smiled. At the door he said, *I don't usually do home visits, son. I've only done it once before.* He rubbed his thumb and forefinger together. Looked out of the window. Perhaps checking his car was still there. Then he said, *Have you seen Ryan Giggs play, Mike?* I was too numb to answer with words so I just nodded, once, all tight. *Some talent, that boy*, said Alex Ferguson. *Some talent. You could do worse than learn from him. Be at the Cliff for nine on Monday and we'll see what we can do about making a player out of ye.* Then he touched me softly on the shoulder and left. Didn't ask if I had an agent. Never even mentioned City or asked me how much they'd offered. Didn't matter, did it?

After he went, I danced in the kitchen. No music, no need – just danced and danced like a spastic, arms and legs everywhere, till I'd forgotten why I started. Then I fell onto the couch *he* had sat on with *his* arse – the same one he sat in the dugout with – and grinned so hard my cheek muscles ached. But Mum grabbed those cheeks, twisted the flesh with her fingers and said, *Don't you DARE fuck this up, Michael Jonathan Wilson. Promise me, okay? PROMISE.* Real fuckin hairdryer treatment, pointing right at me and shaking. Like I'd already done something wrong! Mum never usually let rip, and *never* talked about football. Usually it was all *Listen to your teachers* and *Revise for your exams* and *You'll never get anywhere in life if you don't do your geography homework.* Then there she was, almost crying. Begging me to be a footballer. So I told her what she wanted to hear. *I'll be the BEST EVER,* I said. I gave her a big wet kiss on the forehead and told her, *Don't you worry about NOTHING any more, Mum. You're gonna live like the QUEEN from now on.* The main thing was to get her to let me leave school before exams I was gonna fail anyway, but when I said that – *Don't you worry about nothing, Mum, I'm gonna look after you* – I really meant it, you know?

It was already eat-your-dinner-off-it clean, but she redid the kitchen again anyway. Then she started dusting in the lounge. Then the Hoover came out. I just sat for a bit, back on that couch of ours, staring at the TV, this zoned-out half-grin on my face like I was hypnotized. I wasn't even watching what was on. I didn't know what was on. I just knew that somewhere in the corner of my vision there were colours moving, people moving, in the screen. The hum of the Hoover stopped. Mum pointed towards the box and said, *So, you'll be on there soon then, eh?* I smiled. *Yeah. Yeah. I suppose.* Then I said, *I wish Dad was here. He would have laughed his fuckin head off. Fergie. In our house like that. It's mad.* Mum gave me another clap across the head for swearing, but it was a soft one this time. Then she unplugged the Hoover, sat down next to me and said, with a relaxed smile, *It's okay, Mikey. It's best your father wasn't at home this afternoon. We can tell him all about it when he gets home.*

THE REAL BEGINNING

Imagine: it starts off small. You're three years old. The sun's out. It's the summer of 1978 and you start kicking a red ball around the back garden with your dad. You're not really that interested at first but he's noticed you, so when he rolls the round shape your way, you do it – you stick out your foot, it hits the plastic, it feels all right. The ball bobbles a few yards, then Dad claps, and he smiles a natural smile. You chase and stick out your foot again.

At your fourth birthday party the back garden is full of other kids and their parents, but instead of playing with them or joining in the games you spend most of the afternoon with Dad, Uncle Si and your big brother Guy, kicking and sliding around on the grass, lost in the game. Like you've never done anything else and don't ever want to stop. Like you've totally forgotten it's your birthday and it's not supposed to be a day like any other, which is mostly spent doing EXACTLY THIS. A few months pass. Uncle Si builds you a mini net for the back garden, two fat little posts and crossbar made out of wood carved from a tree in his garden. He knows his stuff all right, he's made that thing with care, but by the end of the summer the net looks tired and worn out. Then, in September 1979, you get sent to a big grey building called a *school* where you have your first knockabout in a decent playground. It's better than sitting on your backside looking at numbers or words. It's better than anything that happens in a classroom. Big news.

Time passes slow, and it feels like for ever until finally you turn six and then seven years old. You see that some kids are good at this magical game called football you're learning, others are not, and you – it's amazing – are one of the best. Unlike the boring old real world there's pure justice in this new world of sport coz the more you practise the better you get, and after that practice comes love, from family, friends and teammates who want to pick you out of the line-up first now, instead of ignoring you or pulling your trousers down in front of girls. You join the school under-nines team. You start off as a defender. You're a natural: composed, solid, always in control. A steady future beckons. But after a few weeks you ask the teacher if you can play up front. Why? Coz you're pretty fast compared to the others, and even though you're only eight you can see there's not much glory in being a fuckin right-back.

Soon you're playing real matches, on actual pitches, against other schools. And in your first one, after just a few minutes, this is how it begins. The ball comes to you on the edge of the box, you run with it, you thump it as hard as you can towards the goal up ahead, and even though the keeper's the size of a hamster and the netting's the size of an elephant and you secretly know you scuffed the shot, you score your first ever goal. You forget yourself. You feel like the Master of the Universe. You see your dad on the sidelines cheering. That day in 1984 he buys you a Manchester United replica kit – the first present you've ever got that wasn't obviously bought by your mum. And there's more to come, an extra special treat. He's gonna take you to a match for the first time, at a *proper stadium and everything*.

You know what United is already. You *know* you're a United fan, you always have, it's what all good people in the world *just are* and always have been. You know you're a Red just like you know you're a human and not an alien from outer space, a boy not a girl, a Manc not a smelly Scouser (you've never met one of those and hope you never do) – but even though you've sat in your front room and watched the scores coming in every Saturday afternoon, though you've seen United matches on TV and had a United calendar up on your wall for the last three years, the team haven't actually existed, have they? On the short walk from your home to the ground, surrounded by thousands of other fans, Dad puts his arm around your shoulder and he makes United, the idea of United, multicoloured and possible and real. He doesn't usually talk much, so you pay attention when he tells you about this big stage where *you're gonna see the greatest bastard show on earth*. At a set of traffic lights, waiting for green, you shut your eyes tight and try to imagine it. You can't.

Dad says this place you're getting closer to with every step is not just called Old Trafford – it's known by right-thinking Reds all over the world as the Theatre of Dreams, and he and Uncle Si have been going there all their lives. Not only that, but their dad did the same thing for most of his life too. *That's Granddad Peter, who died before you were born,* he says, eyes like cotton clouds, all soft and misty. *Granddad got these tickets when the league started again after the war. Worth a bloody fortune now. And cost a bloody fortune too.* You don't know which war he means, but you don't ask coz something strange is going on with your dad's eyes. They look almost too big for his face. Still, you don't wanna do anything to change them so you just hold his hand, tight, tighter. *Always the same seats*, says your dad. *Right on the halfway line. You'll see soon enough.* Maybe he says something else after that, but it's lost in the growing noise of the crowd.

When you get to the stadium, this *Theatre of Dreams*, you can't speak. The whole thing *feels* like a dream. The noise. The smell. The swearing and the screaming. It's like a different game; it has nothing in common with your crappy school games where hardly anyone watches or cares about anyone except their own kids and nobody takes it seriously except YOU. You separate as Dad goes through the turnstile first with the tickets, then you follow behind him, then the two of you lock hands again. You pass a man selling programmes (*bloody rip-off*, says Dad, handing over the cash), go up the steps, through the mass of supporters, out into the open, looking down onto the vast green below. And then you shuffle over to those seats your family's been sitting in since what sounds like the beginning of time. The seats are red plastic and feel cold against your arse, but they're a part of history. You sit down and wait. You ask, *Why is it just me and you today?* Dad sees you looking at the two empty seats to your left and has a sneaky look of his own. *Well*, he says, *coz your Uncle Si's being stubborn about, um, a financial matter to do with the family business. Fuckin Wilson Electrics, Mikey, it's all he thinks about. And Guy? Well, he's at drama class, or ballet, or whatever the hell your mother sends him to*. The referee blows his whistle, and the action begins. Dad says, *Mikey, let's just say that some Reds are more equal than others.*

After the game ends you can remember hardly any of what happened in between. No action, no chances, no nothing. Your brain is empty of memories, except for one. The feeling of being right there with Dad as the first goal goes in, when he jumps up, throws a fist into the air and shouts out, *Come oooon, yoo fuckin Reeeeds!* You've never seen him like this before. You don't recognize him at all. Years from now you'll still remember that strange groaning sound, from the centre of him, and the even stranger thing that happens next: his glasses falling off his nose, crashing to the ground a couple of rows ahead, down below. They might be broken, you think. They might be lost. You shout out, *Dad! Dad!* But he doesn't answer. The glasses might be gone for ever, or have to be repaired. That could cost half a week's wages. He might never be able to *see* again – but he doesn't care at all. He's in another dimension. Free.

On the way home you tell Dad you want to play for Manchester United one day. You'd give anything to play for that team, even just once. You'd saw your own arm off for just a couple of minutes on the pitch, just one kick, while he watched from the family seats, waving and cheering and shouting your name. Dad thinks about this, then in this strange faraway voice says, *I could have been a pro, you know, Mikey. Even had a few trials back when I was a teenager. With Preston North End. With Blackpool. With Crewe*. He tells you he got injured and had to give it up. Bad luck, that's all. He knows what's required. *Well, short arse, you're probably not good enough to make it*, says Dad as you walk away from the ground. *But if you are, I hear it's a pretty good life*. His voice changes. Goes quieter, higher. Lighter too. *Never mind that all that shite*, he says. *Do you wanna go bowling tonight? How about it, eh? At the alley?* He says, *If we're lucky, maybe your big brother will grace us with his presence.* Then he flicks his fag onto the concrete in front of your toes. What's left of the little stick burns and flickers, the smoke spiralling upwards. You step on it. Look up. Grin.

A few days after your one-on-one at Old Trafford, you ask Dad if you can join a Sunday team as well as the school one. He says YES. And

– surprise, surprise – you do well in it. You're smaller than most, but you're the best in the squad by a mile. By so much it's embarrassing. On your debut, you score. After a few games they make you captain, even though you're new and more than a year younger than anyone else. You find it easy to give orders during the games, shifting players up, down, forward, back, like snakes and ladders sliding about a board. On the pitch, you don't even have to think. Good things just happen. And you love being team cheerleader, keeping everyone up up up, always clapping, shouting, COME ON LADS WE'RE STILL IN THIS even when you're losing 5–0, or worse. Which is most weeks. One game, Dad and Uncle Si stand on the touchline together, talking about something in low voices like they're at a business meeting, not a footie match. Even though it's a Sunday, Uncle Si's got a suit and tie on. Running past them, running for the ball, you think how he's younger than Dad by five years, so why does it always seem the other way round?

Just as you're getting used to your new team, making a few friends, having fun, Dad moves you to a bigger, better team miles away coz he says *It's all Pakis and niggers in the first lot you played for anyway.* But you know it's coz the team was shit, he's seen you might actually be decent and he's had his bloody eureka moment. He's imagining spending the rest of his days showing off, arms folded, big grin on his ugly mug, saying *That's my kid, you know!* to everyone he meets. As if *he's* actually *done* something. Coz he made you, you're part him, and he's part you. You hear this in his voice when he talks about the future, like it's a bright, open field he owns. Like it's a jackpot on the pools. He's probably imagining how good it'd feel to quit his job, tell his boss what to do with himself. Every night, fat and snoring, dreaming about riding off into the sunset on a horse called Freedom from the Man and flicking the Vs as he goes.

You don't exactly know when this started but one evening, lying in bed, trying to get to sleep, not sleeping (you can NEVER get to sleep), you realize that football's changed for you, maybe for ever. Now, when Dad drives you to and from games and practices, he's giving instructions most of the way. Poking his finger, giving orders and replaying mistakes. Saying you've made a lot of them. These days, when he hovers on the touchline, all itchy, hopping from foot to foot, kicking every ball in his mind, sucking hard on a cigarette like he's taking revenge on it, you recognize the tight, tense look on his face from when he bets on the horses. He still does that, though Mum thinks he gave it up ages ago, when she told him it was *me or the bloody bookmakers* and didn't let him in the house for three days. Dad pops in there on the way to your team practice sometimes, and sometimes on the way back as well. It's your little secret, you and him.

SUNDAY 12 AUGUST 2007
PREMIER LEAGUE

UNITED 0–0 READING

ATTENDANCE: 75,655

GIGGSY WATCH* – MadRed4Eva666 says: Know all you haterz out there R gonna diss me for speaking da truth, and yeah he hit da beans on toast, but Giggsy let us down today. Crosses NOT GOOD ENOUGH! It's a big season 4 him and he's in trouble. Got 2 prove he's not past it or else OUT THE DOOR. Like the Gaffer says, No one is bigger than the club!

Average Fan Rating: 6/10

The first game of the 2007/08 season was the most boring Mike Wilson had ever seen. Nil–nil against Reading – hardly an advert for 'the best league in the world' as they kept telling him every time he turned on the television. 'The envy of the rest of Europe,' the commentators called it. 'The dizzying height of the beautiful game.' But the real problem was that the vast crowd, bigger than ever, was so quiet that Mike swore he could hear the sound of Alex Ferguson's chewing gum chattering about inside his mouth. The sound of prawn sandwiches being chomped in corporate boxes. The sound of life dying. Manchester United were supposed to be the reigning League Champions, but it felt as if the crowd wasn't at the Theatre of Dreams at all – in their minds they were really down the road at Edgeley Park with Guy, watching eleven Stockport County donkeys hoofing it up and down a mud-soup pitch, wondering how they could be having more fun on their precious weekend afternoons. This was Mike's

* All reports taken from randomly generated comments left at AllThingsGiggs, 'The Blogosphere's Premier and Only Site dedicated entirely to the exploits of the Premiership's Greatest Ever Player'

first home game without his brother in years. He sniffed. Looked around. Listened hard.

The United hush was scary sometimes. Grown men sitting on their hands, worrying about how it was all going to go wrong, moaning endlessly about imaginary demons. Mike never used to notice it when he was with friends or family, but now it was all he could think of. The older men in the polite stands got used to complaining years ago and, despite more success than they could have dreamed of in the relegation days of the seventies, they were in the habit of unhappiness and could not or would not change. As for the youth, they'd never known anything else. They'd never suffered like his generation had. All they'd ever known was gold so they didn't value it, or even recognize it. On Mike's left, in his brother's old seat, was a man in his thirties. Mike turned towards him.

'All that talent on the pitch!' he said. 'All that ability! And where's the passion, eh? Where is it?'

Mike didn't wait for an answer. Instead, he got up.

'SING YER AAARTS OUT FER THE LADS!' he screamed, standing in a sea of sitters, arms aloft, spread wide. 'COME OOOOON, OOOZ WITH ME?'

Two men down the front shouted out, 'We are, young man!', raised their plastic cups of coffee to the skies, then sat down. All around, there was silence. Mike was sure people were looking at him. Then Wes Brown miskicked the ball, high, wide and very, very ugly, out for another throw-in, and the crowd groaned as one. Mike tutted. It wasn't the same at Old Trafford since they banned alcohol in the seats.

Three of the groaners, who sat behind him at every home game, were, in his opinion, perfect examples of the type that had become all too common. The Three Unwise Men, Guy used to call them. All in their fifties, though they looked twice that. Obviously only let off the leash by their wives once a week, only allowed to travel to Old Trafford and back, then locked up in the doghouse again till the next home fixture. Filthy old duffel coats as miserable as their faces. Heavy creases under their eyes. Expressions that probably hadn't changed since the glory days of Best, Law and Charlton – and even then they wouldn't have been happy. Once, Mike had turned round just after United had scored to see the three of them, not cheering, not smiling, not even standing up. Just grumbling about how 'we should have been given a free kick before the goal'. Complaining the defender hadn't been sent off, saying the referee was 'obviously a bastard Arsenal supporter'. As Mike followed the zipping ball in today's match, focusing on the Ryan Giggs runs that almost but didn't quite work out, the crosses that were just too long, the occasional shots – off target – the Three Unwise Men let their tongues loose.

The first one, Dave, had a high, whiny voice. Mike imagined him working in insurance, a pariah in his office block. The second was Bill: the alpha male, the loudest, the angriest. Who responded to every opposition free kick like he'd just received news of the rape and murder of his only daughter, by a City fan. To Bill, everything was a disgrace. Everything was an affront to dignity. Everything was a conspiracy. And then there was the third Unwise Man. In a lifetime of matches Mike had never heard his name spoken. He was mostly quiet, in sulky agreement with the others, nodding and grunting at what they said, no matter the topic. As far as Mike Wilson was concerned, he was the worst of the lot.

Together these three made a kind of constant, discordant hum, spreading out like a toxic spill, several rows in all directions. Mike sniffed again. He zipped up his jacket and rubbed his hands together. He said nothing. Some people were only happy when they were unhappy – but not him. Mike Wilson gloried in the glory of the team. Their joy was his joy. Their success was his success.

'Bloody Giggs!' said one of the Three Unwise Men, Dave this time. 'Get him off the park. He's past it!'

Mike felt obliged to react.

'Er, Ryan Giggs, *O-B-E*, that is!' he shouted, without turning round.

Mike did his breathing exercises. He tried to ignore the blasphemy behind, to not let it all get to him. But there should have been more tension. More passion. Yes, the game was bad, but the atmosphere had been flat since kick off, except for the occasional 'Ooh' or 'For fuck's sake!' or 'Pass it, you useless bastard!' punctuating the silences. It was as if the crowd was waiting for Christmas, or even February before they were prepared to get excited about football again. The men in grey suits might have been keen to whip football fans into a round-the-calendar frenzy, but trophies were standard currency at Old Trafford these days, and no trophies were won in week one of the league season. So why bother wasting breath? Most of the time, the team were going to win anyway. The team were going to be just fine. That seemed to be the thinking. A few rows below, two regulars discussed how early they should leave in order to avoid the traffic.

No such trouble getting excited for the Reading fans. The several thousand packed into the corner of the stadium were still delirious from having earned a second season in the Holy Land of the Premier League. They sang constantly. Nothing was happening on the pitch. The Reading fans didn't care. They were high on good fortune, and success against the odds.

As full time approached, Mike's one pound bet on the first goal scorer – on *any* goal scorer – looked increasingly optimistic, and eventually he gave up, tearing his slip into quarters, eighths, sixteenths. Meanwhile, the Reading fans started making the noise he hated more than anything in the world. More than having to get up early on a Sunday. More than the thought of City actually *winning* something. That humiliating little sound.

'SSSSSSSSSHHHHHHHH.'

Again. Longer.

'SSSSSSSSSSSSSSSSSSSSSSSHHHHHHHHHHHHHHHHH.'

Then a weak chant in response.

'Yu-ni-ted, Yu-ni-ted, Yu-ni-ted . . .'

An ironic round of applause went up from the Reading contingent, thinking they'd won that particular battle. Which they had.

At that moment, Mike noticed something that made him forget the match, the Three Unwise Men, everything.

A man on the row in front was biting into a cheeseburger. Tomato ketchup leaked out of the sides. Grease oozed between the man's fingers. He chewed enthusiastically, then less so, then spat out a mangled chunk of browny yellow-red, dropping the rest of the burger onto the floor.

'Hey you,' said Mike. 'What's up?'

The man brushed bits of burger off his tongue with a gloved finger, retching. Then he smiled.

'Fuckin shite, mate . . . the scran here's a scandal. Pricey an all!'

Mike said, 'So what! You just chuck it? This is Old Trafford!'

The man looked at Mike. 'Did you want it or something?' He bent down, picked up the rest of the burger and held it out. 'You're bloody welcome to it.'

Mike shook his head. 'No, no,' he said, his voice weaker now. 'It's just. I dunno. Holy ground.'

The man gave a half-smile. 'Fine. Whatever, mate,' he said. 'Whatever you say.'

And, with that, he returned to talking to his friends. The full-time whistle blew. Both men had missed the end of the match.

For Mike Wilson, it was a long walk home after the game. It always would be now. They'd argued about it for weeks during pre-season, but Guy had stated his case a hundred times: from now on, he was taking his kids to see their new local team, Stockport County. Once again, on the way home from the Reading game, Mike phoned him and, once again, Guy was firm.

'Mikey, I'm bored with the billionaires' playground,' he said. 'I'd rather spend my pay on passionate half-talents fighting it out on a crappy pitch than stick it out with the bloated, predictable big league. The players are basically whores, bruv. Know what I mean?'

Mike did not know what his brother meant. He was starting to think something was wrong.

But, despite recent changes, some things stayed comfortingly the same, no matter what. When United won a match, Mike Wilson went out to celebrate. If the team lost, people knew better than to cross him before the next game. If it was a draw, like today, he spent the night at home. It always hurt, regardless of circumstances, but Mike understood that you couldn't let it beat you. As Giggsy always said, 'It's the disappointments that keep the desire going.' And at least United hadn't *lost* on opening day.

Hands deep in pockets, walking back from the ground, Mike headed for home by his usual route, sure he could sense people staring as he passed. He walked by the guys outside the ground selling the *Red*

Issue, up Sir Matt Busby Way, then round the corner at the shops, taking in the smell of salty chips and vinegar from the Legends Takeaway and stale beer and cigarettes from outside the bookies. That mix of aromas always made Mike think of his father, and the very first game he came to as a boy. Back then, before what he called 'the big P45', Gregory Wilson acted like anything exciting could happen, any time. And believed it probably would.

In among that crowd of fans full of the talk of another new season, Mike hummed some of his favourite United tunes and thought about his father, these people he knew, these streets of the Republik of Mancunia where he lived, and imagined a future where anything could happen. The season was waking up. After all those long, dead summer days, finally existence had a shape again. No matter today's score – as he reminded himself, you had to think big. Like the Gaffer did. You had to remember that life was not just about what happened on any one afternoon. Life was about the long game. And, as he'd proved over the years, that was a game Mike Wilson was pretty good at playing.

It's been said before, I know that. But here's the filthy little secret: sometimes things are repeated coz they're TRUE. Still, don't believe me, sunshine, check the history books! Go online! Phone a friend! Nearly every lazy, halfwit, armchair pundit in the Western world agrees. It was the most exciting time in the club's history for young talent – in ANY club's history – and, suddenly, I was in the middle of it. That's like getting odds of a hundred thousand to one and watching your horse romp home, the rest of the field little dots in the distance. It's like getting odds of a million to one. More. I felt pretty fuckin lucky, I can tell you that, but I was burning up too, you know? Coz United could have, and should have, won the league in my first year on the books. And while the Class of 92 were being born, lifting the FA Youth Cup to the heavens in celebration with yours truly making a tasty cameo, the big boys let it slip.

Leeds weren't even better than us. They were an average team of clunkers and thumpers in the dirty Yorkshire tradition. Most of that team have now been forgotten, except for one ex-United player on the slide (little Gordon Strachan) and one French *artiste* (big Eric Cantona), who was on the way to sweet redemption. He signed for them part way through the season and scored a handful of goals while we crumbled, losing three games in a row at the death. They called it the league title nobody appeared to want, which just goes to show how fuckin stupid the boys in the box really are. No clue about the real world, these fellers. Too comfy in their fuckin seats, warming themselves in TV studios and thinking about snapping the next cheque from above into their greedy beaks. Too busy filling airtime with guesswork to see the light right in front of their eyes. The point is: United wanted it more than ANYTHING. United wanted it TOO much. In 1991 and 1992 all the future legends were breaking through, knowing the club was close to something great but not quite there yet. In 1991 it was the Cup Winners' Cup – at the time, a massive breakthrough – but the big prizes were still in the distance. That whole time, everyone was getting war-ready. I joined the club at the start of all that, a long string of names everyone remembers. Well, *almost* at the start.

Ryan was the first. His senior debut was when he was just eighteen, in March 1991. That was a good few months before I joined, but as I'd wanted to tell the Gaffer that day at our house, I already knew who he was anyway. We were in our usual seats for his debut, Dad, Guy, Uncle Si and me. Dad said, *That'll be you soon, if you don't fuck things up*. There were plenty of reasons for me to be watching his progress. He'd even played for Salford Boys, like me, before getting signed. Giggsy had been known around Old Trafford since way back in 1987 when he got snaffled from the City youth set-up, where he didn't have a contract yet, but they assumed he'd stay on with them anyway. (Bet they sacked the guy who made THAT mistake.) 'New George Best' tags had been getting glued to every half-decent spotty kid in Red since the sixties, and that label ended up crushing plenty of good souls over the years. But rumour was, this boy was once-in-a-lifetime special. Right from the off, people talked in this strange way. Like he was an angel or something. He had this *sureness*. One of the coaches told the *Evening News* years later, *Know that rumble just before an earthquake hits? Everyone just* sensed *what was coming*. Ryan was faster than anyone I'd ever seen. That lightning pace. That touch. On someone else's team, a boy like that could ruin you. On your side, he's an oil well. A gold mine. A retirement home in the Bahamas. And, even after all these years, Alex Ferguson still says the best thing he's done at United was sign up young Ryan Wilson. (He changed his name later. Loyalty to his mum after his parents split up, apparently. But he'll always be a Wilson to me.)

It's mental how things are sometimes. In the early days I thought I could do anything, take on anyone, fear nothing and nobody. Just BEING a United player was being a God. But the first time I saw Ryan Giggs on the training ground, I couldn't move. I just pure couldn't believe he was there. That first training session together I hardly stopped looking the whole time, like I was waiting for him to do something, say something, slap me around the chops and tell me I wasn't making all this up. Me, a United trainee. Him, sharing the same space. The new reality – it didn't make sense. In the end of session kickabout I was so busy admiring the lining on his boots that I didn't notice he'd passed me the ball. It rolled out of play and I got fifty press-ups for daydreaming. *Not a great start, Wilson,* said one of the coaches. I tried to answer but, again, no fuckin dice. I opened my mouth to speak, and nothing. The coach stood over me and put his foot on my back as I was finishing the press-ups. *Forty-seven, forty-eight, forty-nine* – and then he pressed downwards with his studs.

So Ryan was older than everybody and he was the first to break through, coz he'd basically skipped the reserves and gone straight in with the first team. (Very rare.) He was a sensible lad, even then. Hard-working. Full of flair on the pitch, but not one of these party-all-night-long, dick-never-in-the-pants types. A real role model. Even then you could see he was gonna be around years later, a director of the club or something, you know? But not drawing attention to himself. Sitting among the real fans, in the cheap seats, instead of larging it with the suits, supping champagne and caviar. Anyone with half a brain knew he had no interest in money or women or poncing about in a sarong. Just in the beautiful game, played beautiful. So when one of the coaches called me 'Little Giggs' after a Ryanesque dribbling goal I scored once in training, passing five of the other team, taking it round the goalie and then tapping it in, I used it like a badge from then on. Even though I wasn't that little, and looked nothing like Ryan Giggs. Let's face it. I was an ugly fucker. You wouldn't get us confused.

After him, there was a rash of kids like me. It was almost like his breakthrough was the official okay for everyone else to push for the same. Gary Neville debuted in September 1992, against Torpedo Moscow in Europe, and David Beckham got his first appearance in the same month. Nicky Butt was another local kid, the best in those days, all the midfielders said so. Scholesy was a bit behind, not in the first wave of us who won the Cup. He didn't debut till September 1994, and neither did Phil, the younger of the two Neville sisters. (Everyone called them the Neville sisters, just not to their faces.) Ryan, David, Nicky, Gary and Phil – they were all playing in the academy or the reserves with me.

All the key people were around the club, somehow, by the autumn of 1992. On the fringes, yeah, but READY. And where did it come from? This burst? Well, like Mum says, *Most clean things are built out of dirt*, and though the suits running the league had been too busy chasing Murdoch's millions to notice it, the Gaffer had been carefully assembling us pawns for a long time. Christ, he'd been letting little David Beckham into the United dressing room since he was *eleven*, slowly seeping the Cockney out of him, hoping the boy would grow up to be worth the trouble. Then there were the Lee Sharpes of this world. He was a bit older, a smooth type who'd looked like he was gonna be a United great, then almost was, then wasn't. Cock first, brain second, that lad – which is why he's ended up doing reality telly and talking about the good old days. But that's football, right? Some focus on the game, some get laid and go home for an early bath.

Still, football's a fuckin lottery. Not all of us were lucky. Along with me and Giggs and Scholes and Beckham, there were lots of other kids you've never heard of who came through the ranks in the nineties. Michael Appleton (Salford lad, lifelong United fan, played twice for the first XI then got moved on). Ben Thornley (sued the player who injured him. Ended up at Salford City). Later, guys like Alex Notman (last seen playing for Wroxham FC in the Eastern Counties League). Might as well have been called Mickey Mouse or Donald Fuck-a-Duck though, coz you don't know who any of these guys are, do you? And there were hundreds of others. During my time, whenever a lad got dropped, injured or moved on to a smaller club, I held a breath in my chest. Coz every time the knife sank into someone else, I took one step closer to the first XI. The fact that I was still there meant I was still wanted. Someone was watching me and liked what they saw. Lucky, lucky me.

And do I feel like I've been lucky in my life? Well, I've been fuckin BLESSED. Wouldn't you say so? Born with talent like that?

A PLACE TO PLAN FUTURES

You're growing up fast, Mikey Wilson!

You turn ten years old, your head all football stickers and football magazines and football posters going up on your walls. You sleep think talk United. Jab at the patience of adults with your ball-by-ball description of how Norman Whiteside scored that curler to win United the 1985 FA Cup final, which you saw on the big telly in Uncle Si's lounge and WILL NEVER FORGET. You tell anyone who'll listen that Whiteside's only a few years older than you really and that YOU'LL be doing that soon. You talk about this for MONTHS. Other kids get tired of you going on, but who cares? Coz if you're gonna get to play in that Theatre of Dreams then you have to be, like Dad says, *Dedicated, focused, and prepared to leave ordinary mortals behind.*

So you shed friends like old skin. They're gone and forgotten. You're making the sacrifices, readying yourself for tougher battles ahead. *You have to want it more than anyone else, Mikey,* says Dad. *Want that ball. Make like it's the end of the world, everyone's starving, and the ball's the last pig on earth.* You prove you're worth investing in. You listen hard to Dad's speeches. *The best players,* he says, sparking up another fag, eyes alight, *the immortals – the Bests and Pelés and Maradonas of this world – they're* consumed *by the game. They* live *it, every second. It's all they* see. *It's all they* think *about.* When Dad's talking it's like he's talking to himself. Sometimes he doesn't even look at you. And most of the time when you say something, he doesn't answer back. Why not? Sometimes you get your drills wrong, and notice his temper is getting worse.

You're expanding by the day. You can almost feel your muscles strengthening, tightening, your legs stretching and neck thickening with every passing second. And in games, you see that not everyone acts like you do on a football pitch. The world's full of kids who don't mind giving eighty, fifty, thirty per cent. Kids who aren't *consumed*: kids who, though their bodies are on the pitch, have minds that are thinking about school, about computer games, about the legs of the girls at the desk in front. But Dad says you're BLESSED BY THE BIG KIND HANDS OF GOD coz you don't even SEE the girls' legs. You only know one way, which is to give everything, all the time, no matter what. In matches, in training, in the playground or the street. Always committed, always consumed. Blinkers on, ready for the next test. This sets you apart. Everyone knows it.

Fast action needs to be taken to rescue Mikey Wilson from *an ordinary existence*. So when you leave your local primary school, age eleven, you get a place at a secondary miles away with a good sports record and a rubbish everything else record – it was ALWAYS GONNA HAPPEN, but Mum and Dad fight about it at the top of the stairs while you hover at the bottom, clutching the banister, wondering how you're gonna get into your room. Her saying, *You're taking away his education!* Him saying, *This IS his education!* and *You wouldn't understand!* and *I hate you!* Like *Dad* is the kid, kicking and screaming till the tantrum pays off. Nobody admits it's weird. Not even Guy, who's a pro when it comes to saying stuff you're not supposed to. He's just turned sixteen, he's five whole years older and knows everything about everything, but Dad spends most of his time concentrating on you. Coz he knows that if Guy was gonna be a jackpot on the pools, it'd be obvious by now. He'd already be on his way, and Dad would be halfway to that beach house he talks about like it's a real thing, in a real place, in the actual real world.

Another year and you're not a short arse any more. Nice one! You've shot up towards the sky, you need a whole new wardrobe (Mum not happy – clothes are pricey), and your feet now creep over the end of the bunk bed you and Guy have always shared, you on the bottom, him on the top, always together. United posters are on *all* the walls of the bedroom now, every white space covered in goal celebrations and action shots and team photos. All except for the bit by Guy's pillow where there's something else. It's a magazine centrefold of the top half of a naked blonde, close up, ever-so-lightly pressing in her huge breasts with two fingers of each hand, covering just the nipples, looking into the camera and licking her lips as if she's very, very thirsty.

Something about that picture bothers you.

Over the next few months hair sprouts from under arms and between legs, you start to stink, you grow even taller, you wake up every morning with an aching hard-on and believe you can run past any defender, beat any goalkeeper in the world. School is just a place to play at break, lunchtime, after hours, and a place to plan futures. You're chasing real life while the other robot kids follow orders and programme themselves for test after test. These come round all the time and everyone's always pretending the next ones are *even more crucial than the last* when they can't be, can they? Not EVERYTHING can be more important than everything else, can it? You ignore your school reports. They say things like *Lots of ability, no application* and *What a shame Michael doesn't appear to want to learn* and *An intelligent boy who seems determined to fail.*

Even though you want to make Mum happy, you CAN'T work hard at school, coz your time is needed for another, more precious learning experience. Even visits to the headmaster don't touch you. Nothing he says matters, though God knows the old guy tries to turn you around. He even calls you and Dad into his office together, to shame you, jointly. But father and son giggle like girls when he talks about being *desperate to penetrate your consciousness*, and he sends you away. At home, Mum's standing at the front door. She says, *Tell me! Tell me! What happened?* She looks like someone's died, but there's no way you're playing that game. The two of you shrug shoulders and say, *Nothing*. Sometimes, you and your old man are unbreakable.

SUNDAY 19 AUGUST 2007
PREMIER LEAGUE

SHITTY 1–0 UNITED

GEOVANNI 32

ATTENDANCE: 44,955

GIGGSY WATCH – CityMustDie_3 says: Difficult day for the boys, no doubt, and RG didn't act like a captain out there. Chelsea lookin good 4 league. These are dark days, people, but you've gotta KEEP THE FAITH! RED ARMY FOREVEEEEEER!!! PS Enjoy it while it lasts, City LOSERZ. You can all SUCK IT.

Average Fan Rating: 5/10

The United end at the City of Manchester Stadium cleared out fast. A large family contingent sitting in front of Mike Wilson had left about five minutes before full time, predicting relegation. The rest of the ground steadily emptied, until nearly everyone had gone home except for the stewards and people employed to pick up the litter. Mike remained in his seat, singing softly.

Will never die, will never die,
Will never die, will never die,
We'll keep the red flag flyin high,
Coz Man United will never die . . .

A steward approached. 'Is something wrong, sir?' he asked.

Mike shrugged. 'Only the fuckin score.'

The steward smiled. 'Well, we get a lot of complaints like that round here. Funny, I suppose, but the VIPs are the worst. Tend to get pretty rowdy when things don't go well.'

'Are you accusing me of something, sunshine? I sit with the ordinary fans, you know. I think of myself as an ambassador for the club wherever I go. I do charity work.'

'No, sir . . . sorry. I didn't mean to . . .'

Mike sighed. The anger was gone already. 'It's okay,' he said. 'It's just . . . us ex-players get a bad rep sometimes, you know? It's tough. You're always on duty.'

The steward stood back so Mike could pass. 'I understand entirely, sir. I apologize. Have a pleasant day.'

Mike put on his jacket, whistling quietly as he walked past the steward and towards the exit. The City of Manchester Stadium, he thought, was a dead place.

The old United tune still circling in his head, Mike made his way back home, taking a diversion through the city centre and wandering the streets a while. His head was full of maths. He was calculating games played, goal difference, odds. Mike couldn't think, talk, he could hardly put one foot in front of the other. After this result, City were top of the Premiership table while the current league champions, Manchester United, lay in sixteenth, their worst start to a season since Year Zero, 1992. That year, a young striker called Mike Wilson made his debut and United went on to win the inaugural Premiership title. But Mike was retired now, his service to the cause was of a different kind, and he couldn't see the Red Army rising again. Mourinho's multi-millionaires were already top of the league, which meant Mike was going to be forced to support Liverpool in the late kick-off against Chelsea. He felt queasy. The season had only just started and already it felt like it was nearly over. Today, even Ryan had been booed by a small but noisy section of fans who thought he should do the dignified thing and retire. Mike hoped he'd soon wake up in a cold sweat, thankful for a harmless bad dream. But at least he didn't have any TV or radio duties to take care of, unlike some of the ex-United media types he'd come through the ranks with. Mike imagined having to tell co-commentators, through a painful half-smile, that the Premiership was *a marathon not a sprint*. He pictured himself sitting there, awkward in his seat, in a brightly lit studio, trying not to say *fuck*.

Mike had to find a sensible way of wasting the rest of the day. So, on the walk home, he phoned Guy to see if he wanted to come over and play *Football Manager*, but Guy was on Florence Nightingale duty – his wife Sally was ill again. It seemed like Sally was ill for half of every season. Weak blood. Weak joints. Headaches, coughs, colds. Since having kids, the woman was a walking virus. Mike phoned a couple of friends next, ex-players like himself, but phones rang out or went straight to voicemail. He left messages, waited for replies, then gave up. Mike sat on a bench in Piccadilly Gardens, watching the buses go in and out of the station, wondering whether to go home or stop in a pub to take in Liverpool versus Chelsea. What if he was recognized again? He wasn't in the mood for it today. Mike didn't want to go anywhere. And he couldn't face more football. He couldn't face anything at all. So he decided to walk all the way home.

Later that evening, Mike trudged up the hill leading towards his road, imagining stamping a foot hard into the face of Geovanni Deiberson Mauricio Gomez, City's scorer. Then Mike replaced Geovanni's face in his mind with each and every player on the City team. Micah Richards had a good game, so he was first. Kasper Schmeichel, son of United legend Peter (and therefore a traitor guilty of high treason), was next. This helped pass some time and very slightly improved his mood, while harming no actual people, who were probably all nice decent blokes who were nice to their mums and had lovely wives and children and didn't deserve to be kicked. Once inside, Mike collapsed into the softness of his favourite chair, thinking about his home, this place he woke up in every morning. He intended not to leave it for the rest of the night. Maybe he'd get up for a couple of toilet breaks, but that was all. Actually, he didn't even need to do that. He could always piss in a bottle.

Mike lifted himself and reached under his backside, searching for the remote. On nights like this, MUTV was always a good option. Most likely they'd be showing something from the team's glorious past, to soothe the pain. This was a channel that knew its audience.

Perhaps they'd go for a documentary about George Best and the swinging sixties. A cheerful interview with Fergie about his finest achievements or a cosy fireside chat between him and Denis Law, in someone's mansion. Maybe they'd be replaying an old game in full – a victory – perhaps against a certain set of local rivals.

As he was thinking this, the home phone rang. It couldn't be Guy because they'd spoken already today. It couldn't be his mum because they'd spoken yesterday, before her yoga class. And nobody else had the home number – you had to keep some things private. So Mike picked up the phone, knowing exactly who was on the other end of the line.

'Hi, Dad, how you doin?' he asked.

The voice sounded far away when the reply came through. The line crackled and buzzed. In the background, a splash. 'Great! The sun's shining and I'm gonna dance all night. How the fuck are YOU?'

Mike crunched on a crisp. 'Spectacular,' he answered, idly flicking channels between the news and sport, which were both reporting on the United versus City result. 'What is it you want?'

'Well, that's a fine way to talk to your father.'

'Okay okay. Did you see the game then or what?'

'Damn right I saw the game,' said Gregory. 'A fuckin travesty it was! They should have gone down to ten men – bunch of thieving bastards, that's what they are. Blue scum. And we should have had at *least* one penalty. I tell you, those fuckers at the FA, there's a bloody conspiracy! Anti-United, every last one of them. That's why they always give us these shit referees, these London-centric cunts who don't want to see the North prosper. What can you do though, eh? You're fighting hundreds of years of prejudice, that's what you're doing!'

The tone was playful.

'We were pretty shit though, weren't we?' said Mike.

Gregory exhaled slowly. A gap. 'Yeah. Shit as shit could be. You know, sometimes I wonder, son . . . is it time for Fergie to go?'

Mike began to laugh, then the laugh took him over. When he finally regained his composure, his father had hung up.

People are idiots.

They think that coz you're good at sport, you're gonna be Mr Popular – but a football team is like an army. Every team has a chain of command, and in any chain of command only a few links really matter. Besides, pitch performance guarantees no fuckin party invites, know what I mean? That's all about the usual: who shouts the loudest and who's first in the queue to call everyone else a poof.

At my school, the kid at the front of that queue was usually a boy called Jay Gibbons, the big centre-back in the school team. If not him, it was someone like him. Todd Drinkwater. Davey Fairweather. These boys with steady English names, alcoholic dads and big fat mouths, they're usually the ones with small cocks, the ones who piss about in the showers and lie about how many girls they've shagged and how dirty they were, telling the stories right down to the filthy details. Which girl they fucked up the arse. How they had three sisters at once. How they went all night. All this crap, all this bullshit, showing off while they're pretending to do it to all the other guys in the showers. Acting out the whole performance, like we couldn't have guessed for ourselves what doggy style looks like. I never got that shit. I mean, why do you have to act like a bender to avoid getting beaten up for being a bender?

Back then, around 1989 or 1990, we were being left on our own a bit more. Dad had started to go away on work trips to the north-east with his new council job. Mum was in St Helens some nights, looking after her cousin, at church on others, maybe at confession. (For a woman who never did anything wrong she spent a lot of fuckin time saying sorry.) Meanwhile, I was top scorer in both the school under-sixteens (even though I was the youngest in the team) and my Sunday league one as well. But even when we were celebrating my latest goal it was like no one wanted to come near in case I gave them a disease (or in case Jay said something about it). All right, I was pretty intense. I wasn't much of a looker. I didn't go out or crack jokes. But why was everyone always taking the piss? *They're probably just jealous*, said Guy. *Ignore it.* But I pushed him to explain. My big brother answered in a whisper, like Jay might be listening in. *It's good to be different to everyone else, Mikey. You know, to see the world differently. Be interested in different things. Come on, I'll get us something from the chippy.* There was about a year when that was Guy's answer to every question: *I'll get us something from the chippy*. It was easier than going home and taking the chance of maybe or maybe not finding Dad on the couch, settling in for another night there.

It was around then, when I was fourteen, that my hair started falling out. Like Bobby Charlton after Munich, going bald too early, but this wasn't a crazy comedy-comb-over kind of baldness, but hair falling out in thick clumps, suddenly leaving big holes in my head going right through to my skull. One morning in spring 1990 I woke up and saw some hairs on my pillow. Thought nothing of it. Forgot about it. But a week later it had kicked in, big style. I sat in my room one night after practice, staring in the mirror, picking at the hair that was left, amazed at how easy each strand was to pull out. How it didn't hurt at all. Just a soft tug behind my ear brought out half a handful of dark, thick lines, each one withering, wet, gloopy, and stuck to my hand. I looked like I was dying of cancer or something. After a few days of this, not going into school, making Mum bring dinner up to my room on a tray, I thought: fuck it. Sometimes you've just got to man up. So I got out Dad's electric shaver, plugged it in and set to work, washing what was left down the sink. The little hairs kept popping back up out of the plughole, like they didn't wanna be flushed away, but they didn't have any choice. Going skinhead changed the whole shape of my face, you know? And when I went back to school, others noticed.

At the end of lessons us kids walked down to the station, and usually we had to wait for a bus. Half an hour a day, that place was chaos. There was this shop where we hung around, and every day we mobbed the place, this tiny little open-box square next to a greasy spoon caff. Something about the place, or there just being no teachers or parents, turned even the quietest kids into buzzing rebels, on a mission for a sugar rush. Kids of thirteen, fourteen, grabbing at hundreds of types of chocolate, sweets, crisps, bubble gum. The younger ones screaming over each other, trying to get the attention of the counter assistants, who both looked like somebody's mum – so that's how we treated them. Once, I saw a kid *chuck* his money and leg it coz he didn't wanna miss his bus. That station was a battlefield, only with flirting as well as fighting, all the fit girls standing in groups, gossiping, trying to get boyfriends or dump them while the boys made out they weren't fussed either way. This one Friday there were even more kids hanging around than normal. Some were in the shop coz there were no buses yet and it was pissing it down outside. I was at the back of the queue when I got the idea that maybe I didn't need to queue at all. My two pockets lay open, waiting. I went red hot, looked up and saw Jay, right there, nodding.

Jay had reached inside my brain and seen what was going on inside, before I'd even worked it out myself. He smiled this dark little smile and nodded his head again, all slow this time, all sure. I couldn't look away. I dropped the chocolate from my hand to my pocket while staring at him, felt it hit, then turned around and ran down the high street, not looking back until I was three whole bus stops closer to home. When the bus finally caught me up and I got on, dripping wet, the other kids gave me a round of applause. Jay laughed and said I was a natural. Said he reckoned you could take whatever you wanted from that place. You could go in wearing black and white stripes and carrying a bag with SWAG on the side. He said we could make a lot of money by selling on to other kids at school, at half retail price. That afternoon he let me sit on the back of the bus, and at the next school team match he passed me the ball, three times. Set up a goal for me as well. Which we celebrated together. And that day in the showers, when all the stories and lies and adventures were being told, nobody called me a poof.

I went back to the shop the next week for more, but cool this time. Why not? I hung around at the back of the queue, inspecting the goods, like I was looking oh-so-carefully for something that – surprise, surprise – wasn't there. I felt like a pro already. Slick. Clever. In total control. I slipped one chocolate bar in my pocket, then another, then another, another, then left the shop, all casual, with pockets bulging, pilfering extras I didn't even want on my way out. All the time making sure I was covered by other kids standing between me and the counter. Checking the dirty old camera in the back corner couldn't make me out. I didn't start running till I got out of sight. I thought I was going to faint. I kept running, though I didn't need to. I ran and ran, my newly shaven scalp cold and unprotected from the rain.

I ran for five stops this time, and the bus gave me a proper hero's welcome – clap clap, cheer cheer from all directions. While the noise echoed round the bus, adrenaline zipped through me. It popped and fizzed. It crackled in my bones. Then, without thinking, I called out, *Hey, everyone, who's hungry?* I felt like fuckin Jesus or something, feeding the five thousand. Like Santa Claus. Throwing around presents to good little children like it was Christmas morning. Kids held their arms out and begged, crowding me with reasons for being first in the queue. One didn't have any pocket money left so hadn't had any sweets all day. One said he *never* got pocket money so *never* had any sweets. One said she'd had hers stolen by an older girl. I did what I could and sat down at the back of the bus like that was where I belonged.

But Jay wasn't feeling so generous. He stood up, pushed me off my seat and asked what I was doing. Said we had a deal. Said I shouldn't be *giving away good stock for free* – he could *fuckin HAVE* me if he wanted to. And I figured he probably could. At that second I was so afraid of getting hit that I had to make sure it couldn't happen. So I punched him, hard as I could, on the right cheek, my fist a tight white ball. The sound it made on his skin was a dull *crack*, which made me sure he was gonna get up and kill me unless I did something about it. So I hit him again, this time on his nose, which began to bleed all over his shirt and blazer, turning both a beautiful bright red. All that colour. I looked at Jay's punctured face, his bloody expression. I thought, I made that happen. It was my victory. And that's what I kept thinking.

So I hit him again. And again. And Jay didn't hit back. And the crowd cheered. And they screamed. And they told me to *TEAR IZ ED OFF!* And *CRUSH IZ BALLS!* And *RIP IZ AART OUT AN EAT IT!* They told me to *FUCKIN KILL IM!* All these kids, who never talked to me, drooling, smelling blood.

When he fell to the floor, I kicked.

WHAT THE TEAM NEEDS

Over the next couple of years you go to every United home game. Mostly the family line-up is you, Guy, Dad and Uncle Si, usually in the same seats. (Or at least until United lose and Uncle Si decides what's happening on the pitch is directly affected by the Wilson family formation. Then he changes everyone around.) For Dad, every match is a life-lesson opportunity. He unravels the games, telling you what you'll need to know when you're a pro – *when* – pulling the play apart and putting it back together in brand-new shapes. He's got so much to teach that it's hurting him. He can't get it all out of his mouth quick enough. He's explaining how beautiful the beautiful game really is while Guy's got his head in the programme, reading up on stats, or talking to Uncle Si about his business, about how he wants to grow up to be like him, a lion with a healthy bank balance and a glorious future at Wilson Electrics. Half-time in one game in mid-winter, Uncle Si puts an arm round Guy and says, *It's not complicated, lad. Work hard, reach high, and hope. Chances are, you'll do just fine.*

But Uncle Si's not always right coz on the pitch, even though they're working hard, things aren't going right for the Reds. United have been shit since that 1985 cup final, since Whiteside's winner, and Ron Atkinson's got the old heave-ho. It's November 1986 now and the new manager is some bloke from Scotland called *Ferguson*, who Dad says will be lucky to last six months. He fancies himself as a replacement-in-waiting, and says all the new man needs to do is kick out the team boozers and instil a bit of good old-fashioned kick-yer-arse discipline. But it's obvious what the team really needs. Once, when United are losing, Uncle Si picks you up out of your chair, lifts you up and shouts, *Fergie! Fergie! Sign him up!* Guy laughs at that, but you wonder whether he's laughing AT you. For having a bit of ambition.

On nights you're not playing for the school or Sunday league team, you spend most of your time kicking a ball round the back garden with Guy – even when he wants to read or play inside you MAKE him practise coz you probably only get one life and it's IMPORTANT now. You narrate a running commentary out loud which always ends with AND WILSON SCORES AGAIN! Guy gets tired pretty fast. He still plays for the school, in centre-midfield, but tells you one night when the lights are out that he's kind of bored, and is just putting off telling Dad he's gonna give up the game coz he thinks he'll go apeshit. You don't mention that Dad couldn't care less what Guy does any more. Coz he's not blessed like you are. (Remember, though, your talent is not yours: *it belongs to Jesus*, as Mum keeps reminding you.) Besides, Dad doesn't notice much of anything these days unless it's in a pint glass. He grinds his teeth. In the mornings. At nights. Sometimes, you think you can hear that grinding sound leaking through the walls.

Guy's been saying he's gonna take over Uncle Si's empire since he was twelve. He's a teenager who *actually likes maths* and talks about learning how to do accounts like it's actually something fun. So it's odd when one night he tells you he really wants to be astronaut. See the earth from above. Look down on all the countries of the world at once. Float way up there in the dark, weightless, gazing down on humanity. You can't think of anything more wet, and tell him to stick to doing sums and licking Uncle Si's arse. You tell him he's too old for that sort of talk. He laughs, punches you on the arm and says, *You're a real fuckin idiot, Mikey.* Later the same night, after lights out, facing the ceiling, you end up telling Guy you wish *he* was your dad, not your brother. You do mean it, but say it coz you think it'll make him happy. You think he'll say, *Thanks, son.* Ruffle your hair. Then laugh. Like Uncle Si does to him sometimes. But Guy makes you promise to never to say that again, telling you *our dad's in a very difficult financial situation, and he's doing his best. Just you remember that.* He seems pretty angry. And so are you actually, because if nobody tells you what *a very difficult financial situation* actually means, then how are you supposed to know?

The winter of 1986 comes and goes and always, every day, there's football. On the telly, in the papers (reading the sports pages every morning, spilling bits of cereal on the print), on the radio, going to or coming back from a game. Monday after school: school team practice. Wednesday after school: school team games. Thursday after school: Sunday league team practice. Sunday morning: Sunday league team games. And then there's United. So you don't really see Mum much except at dinner or breakfast or when you need money, and if you do she gives you this sad-eyed look as if she's thinking that really, truly, if she's honest, she would have been happier if this God she talks about so much (but who never DOES anything!) had given her two pretty pink girls, not noisy, sulky, smelly boys who never want to sit still for a second, stay inside, hold her hand, say anything about anything, ever. Except *you-know-what. THAT BLOODY GAME*. Girls she would have known how to love. Girls she could have shaped and taught things to and wouldn't have had to give away to the world so soon. You guess all this one hot sunny spring afternoon as she stands at the back door watching you do keepie-uppies – thirty-three, thirty-four, thirty-five, head, left shoulder, right foot . . . But kids aren't mail order. You don't know if you're gonna give birth to Lex Luther or Superman. Peter Davenport or Denis Law. You just roll the dice, cross your fingers and pray.

That day, when Mum calls you over from the window, you see what's really going on. But you can't admit you know what she's thinking, even though her eyes so obviously say, *What did I do to deserve this?* Her eyes look at you and say, *You're gonna be just like your father*. They say, *I've lost you already*. So you remind her that you're gonna make a load of money and buy her a big house when you're a rich, famous United player – a place hundreds of times bigger than the semi you live in now – and she smiles sad-sad-sadly again and goes back inside. You love her but it'd be *really* wet to say that, even *wetter* than wanting to be an astronaut, and anyway it's NOT YOUR FAULT SHE'S SO FUCKIN MISERABLE, IS

IT? So you just turn around and go back to your game. Guy's waiting in goal, and it's penalties. United versus City. The FA Cup final. Always the same ending. Mikey Wilson, the local boy born to play at the Theatre of Dreams, scores the winning goal. He skids over towards the crowd (the hedge between the garden and the railway line) and cups his hands round his ears.

The applause rings out.

He grins.

SUNDAY 23 SEPTEMBER 2007
PREMIER LEAGUE

UNITED 2-0 CHELSKI

TÉVEZ 45
SAHA 89 (PEN)

ATTENDANCE: 75,663

GIGGSY WATCH – JohnTerry'sMumIsMyBitch says: Ryan BACK TO HIS BEST! All you knobs slagging him shouldn't even BE on this site. Who says the legs have gone? Played the full 90, made the Tévez goal and volleyed a chance just over the bar too. Like Goldfinger used to say, 'Ryan makes you believe there is a football God.' Well, hallelujah, people. Praise the Lord!

Average Fan Rating: 8/10

It was the eighty-ninth minute of the game. Manchester United, Champions of England, were about to take a penalty to make it 2–0, they couldn't lose the match now, and for the first time in weeks they'd played with attitude. A big roar went up round Old Trafford as Louis Saha stepped up and hammered the ball down the centre of the goal.

At the second it hit the netting, Mike Wilson was hugging the man on his left. While doing so, he was thinking about how lucky he was to be living in this place and time. He could have been born anywhere in the world, in any century. He could have been born before football was invented, or in somewhere they didn't have professional leagues, somewhere the game was banned, or where people plain didn't like it. He could have been born on the other side of the Atlantic, deep in baseball country. He could have been one of the famous Mumbai

Reds, condemned to watch every match from thousands of miles away, late at night or early in the morning, wrapped in Red flags and fantasizing about one day making a pilgrimage to Football Mecca. Or one of the infamous London Reds, filling the pubs and bars of Camden and cheering, in fake-Manc accents, pretending they were born on Northern terraces. But he was lucky. He was born within walking distance of the Theatre of Dreams. Still gripping his new friend's shoulders, he thought, People in China *dream* of living in Salford. It could have been *much* worse. Finally breaking off the hug, Mike realized, with a shudder, that he could have been born a *City* supporter.

And he nearly was. Years ago, Uncle Si explained that when he was a boy he used to go with his dad and granddad to watch United one week, then City the next. Granddad Peter even had two scarves, one blue, one red, tied to each of his bedposts. He had a home game to go to every week.

'You wouldn't get that nowadays,' Uncle Si told Mike, with a smirk. 'That was a different world.'

Mike was just a boy then. At the time, he'd laughed. 'It was worse!' he'd said. 'I'd rather be dead than be Blue!'

Then it was Uncle Si's turn to laugh. 'You sure about that, young man?' he'd said. 'You absolutely sure?'

Mike remembered the old back-and-forth with Uncle Si as he returned to watching this match, in the same seats where they'd had that conversation, back in the days when there was a full Wilson complement at Old Trafford. He still couldn't believe that his family had supported both teams at once. Something about not being City made United more United and, as the game against Chelsea finished, Mike stood and started up a chant, arms outstretched.

My old man said be a City fan,
I said BOLLOCKS you're a CUNT.
I'd rather shag a BUCKET with a BIG HOLE IN IT,
That be a City fan for JUST ONE MINUTE . . .

The song made every part of him tingle. He never tired of it. But he hadn't enjoyed the whole day.

It had been scoreless after half an hour and goals had been rare recently, so the Three Unwise Men were content enough, wallowing in their own very particular kind of misery. Mike said nothing. Even though Chelsea were down to ten men they still thought the referee was on their side; 'a fully paid-up member of the Abramovich Yid Mafia,' as one of them called it. Then, after United scored, they went back to what they always did when there was nothing else to complain about, breaking out every time one of Chelsea's international contingent touched the ball.

'Cheating bloody foreigners!' shouted Dave.

'Fuck off back to where you came from!' shouted Bill.

Seething silently, Mike couldn't enjoy the game. Not while the Three Unwise Men were acting as if it was the thirties and all the players were supposed to be honest, working-class kids raised locally who worked in factories when they weren't playing, wore flat caps, got the bus to the ground and then headed down to the local pub with the fans for a couple of pints and a round of bastard dominoes after the game. There were a few in the United team today who didn't exactly have British passports – Cristiano, Nemanja, Patrice – not traditional English names, were they? – even Paul Scholes was from Oldham. Poor old unloved Wesley Brown, the only proper local boy in the team these days, wasn't exactly pasty-skinned either, and even Ryan, the original adopted Manc, had a black father. The game belonged to the world now. But the Three Unwise Men didn't register anything they didn't want to, and the more he tried to ignore them, the more they were all Mike could think about. Nearly the end of the first half, and they were having fun now.

'Some tan you've got on you there, Bill,' said Dave. 'From your holidays, is it?'

Bill said, 'Me and the wife got a week in Marbella on the cheap. They say you can freeze your bollocks off this time of year if you're not lucky, but it was baking, I tell you. Thirty degrees! I spent the whole time on my arse, under the sun. Another few days sitting in that deckchair and I would have come back a nigger!'

Dave started to chuckle. 'Well then, you wouldn't have to pay taxes any more, would you? And you'd be able to get all the bleedin benefits in the world.'

Every part of Mike wanted to turn around and get involved, tell the Three Unwise Men to *shut the fuck up or I'll fuckin . . .* – to *watch the game,* to *have a little respect* – but just then the first goal went in, the cheers went up and all was forgotten. It was a classy outside-of-the-boot cross from Ryan Giggs, the ultimate evergreen winger, and a first United goal for yet another new star in that long line of United stars, this one named Carlos Alberto Tévez, a man Mike was now certain he would love, unconditionally, for ever.

During half-time, Mike queued at the toilets, bought a coffee and bag of crisps and returned to his seat. Then he turned to his new friend.

'Giggsy's on top form just now, eh?' he said. 'That cross reminds me of one he planted on my head in training back in 1991.'

'No way!' said the man. 'You played for United?'

Mike shrugged his shoulders. 'Ryan was the best in those days too.'

The man looked at Mike as if doing so for the first time, tried to assess whether he was joking, then put out his hand to shake. 'Terry Masterson,' he said. 'Civil engineer. And BIG United nut. A pleasure to meet you.'

Mike shook Terry's hand and smiled. 'Mike Wilson,' he said, smiling. 'Also a United nut. Much obliged, I'm sure.'

'Wow,' said Terry. 'I don't think I've ever met a real United player before. When were you in the set-up?'

'Well, I got signed as a trainee when I was pretty young, and played for the first team in the nineties. Came up with Ryan, David Beckham, the Nevilles. The Class of 92, you know?'

Terry snapped his fingers. 'Hey, I know you! I do! You were a striker, right?'

Mike nodded modestly. He knew not to show off in these situations. Fans didn't appreciate showing off.

'So, do you keep in contact with any of the old team?' asked Terry.

'Of course,' said Mike. 'Live through something like that and it binds you. But I'm working with a non-league team these days. Getting my badges. I wouldn't want the boys to think I was after favours.'

Terry nodded. 'Of course,' he said. 'You're a man of honour.'

'Still, I am in contact with some of them. Red once, Red for ever, you know? And I saw Ryan a few weeks ago, in Salford. Having a quiet drink.'

'What was he like?'

'Just the same. A perfect gent.'

'Hey, you ever sit together?'

Mike shrugged, grinned. 'What can I say? I prefer the cheap seats.'

Just then, there was a rush of applause from the crowd.

After the result was certain, even the Three Unwise Men couldn't put Mike in a bad mood. The last couple of minutes were the best of the season yet. The whole world, as he told Terry, was opening up into a 'José-Mourinho-free heaven'. After this, the media would start talking about United as contenders again. After the final whistle, Terry and Mike shook hands once more.

'Right then,' said Terry. 'See you next time?'

'Absolutely.'

'Just wait till I tell my old mates that I'm sitting next to a real United star!'

Mike laughed. 'Hey, that was a long time ago. I'm just an ordinary guy.'

That night, Mike went out, as tradition dictated. But not for as long as usual. He had to be up early the next day – every day was full of new challenges – so he was home in time for *Match of the Day 2*, a simple pleasure that never became any less pleasurable. The assessment of the presenters was that the referee may have made a few mistakes, the penalty being one of them, but as far as Mike Wilson was concerned, everyone knew they were anti-United on *Match of the Day*, Sunday edition included. The couch was full of ex-Liverpool and Arsenal players. He still enjoyed the programme, though; a highlight of what had been an unusually quiet week. Until today, all he'd done was work and sleep. Curry on knee, Coke in hand, in an old T-shirt and jeans, Mike raised his can to the skies at the league table. United climbing to second, Chelsea down in sixth.

After the programme finished, Mike studied a more detailed version of the league table on the computer in his United room. There was hardly any space in there – it was cluttered with trophies, framed pictures and old programmes. There was a bed in the room, but you couldn't sleep in it. Then again, Mike didn't need to. It was needed for more important things.

Guy was giving me his old comics from when I was six or seven. Footie comics mostly, old *Roy of the Rovers* and all that. You know: last-minute goals, amazing comebacks, players magically returning from retirement or injury, hobbling onto the pitch, straight out of hospital and onto the park for one last moment of glory. The whole lot. But not just football comics – plenty of commando stuff too, mostly hero stories based on the Second World War, where the goodies were goodies and the baddies were dead. There were heaps of them. Sometimes I read the comics, sometimes I didn't. They filled time between football, that's all.

Once I started secondary school, Guy started giving me real books – but nothing that looked like work. Nothing that like looked like it came from a teacher, or had even been *read* by a teacher. Nothing too thick, or with that tiny writing jammed into all corners of the page. He started me off on serial killers. Stories about men who'd escaped the law for years, gone on the run, or built up these big cults about what hard bastards they were, then cashed in by writing about it. Lots of tough guy pictures on the front. Tattoos. Fat rings. Fat jewellery. The whole kit. The books usually had long titles. I still know some of them coz they were so stupid, you know? There was this one called *I'll Rip Your Face Off*. No joke! I'll rip your bloody face off! Another one was called *Eye-Gauger: How I Carried Out My Crimes*. I'll never forget that one if I live for a hundred years. I mean, how do you write a book like that and not get caught? Don't the pigs read?

About six months later Guy had moved onto some pretty hardcore Mafia stories, some well serious ninja shit, and a few violent rapists too. More hardcore, yeah, but no big deal. They were all about big muscly loners breaking all the rules, shooting loads of folks dead and running off with the girl. Whether the girl wanted to be run off with or not. But Guy said these books were different. We had to hide them from Mum and Dad, for a start. Even from Uncle Si, who was famous for his who-cares, hippy-shit, anything-goes attitude to the big bad outside world. These books had picture sections in the middle, showing crime scenes and dead bodies – fuck knows where Guy got this stuff from. Hey, I don't mind saying, it was mainly about the blood and guts for me. All that red spattered over floors, walls, cars, beds. I remember one over a pool table. A few of the balls still waiting to be potted. And who doesn't want to see what a rotting body looks like? As long as you don't have to smell it.

Guy never spoiled things by talking too much about them. He'd be sitting there, having a joint out the window (none for me, Dad said the wacky baccy was a *guaranteed one-way ticket to a contract with Stockport County*), and he'd chuck something my way he'd just finished. Maybe he'd say, *You want this? The feller chops this girl's hands off and stuffs them in her mouth.* Or he'd say, *Have a look at this. The bloke gets put in a bin bag and rolled off a cliff.* And I took whatever he gave me. At lights out, bored, knackered, or both, I got out my torch and read *Bronx Hard Bastards* or *100 Most Gruesome Unsolved Murders* or *True-Life Horror* till I fell asleep on the pages. In the mornings, red-eyed from staying up too late, I'd tell Guy everything he knew already. It all came pouring out while we were brushing our teeth, getting dressed, like about this lad from Melbourne who cut a cross into the forehead of his victims with a Swiss Army knife, then killed them, then videoed himself having sex with them. The most fucked up things, like it was a game. Both of us acting hard, pretending it wasn't giving us nightmares. Me sometimes adding a bit to the story to make it sound better. Usually Guy would leave it, but sometimes he'd say, *You sure you got that detail right, Mikey? Don't go changing history now.*

Then, another change. Guy turned seventeen, I turned twelve, and the Mafia and the serial killer books disappeared. On Guy's half of the wall, down came the United posters and the blonde, and up went Che Guevara and lots of old commies with beards. Not a great trade really, but at least everything was still red. Around that time, everything seemed to be changing. Guy stopped going out at night and gave up getting drunk on cider or cheap cans of lager down at the roundabout. He said to me one day, all serious, *I'm nearly a grown-up now, bruv, it's about time I started acting like it.* He worked hard at school, starting talking about *the revolution, man* and watched loads of war films, always talking about conspiracies, plots and takeovers. Guy said the books he used to give me were a waste of time and he moved, quick smart, from murders to massacres. *Hey, don't be a dumb fuck all your life*, he'd say, tossing me a copy of some weirdo thing about the Russian Revolution or the Nazis. *Look at THIS.*

He went through this whole phase of being crazy about the Nazis. Where before there was one dead body at a time, now there were hundreds, sometimes *thousands*. Piles of bodies. Naked bodies in heaps, in ditches. Bodies being shovelled up by these big tankers and forklifts. Then there was all this stuff about prisoner experiments, on the dead and the living. I couldn't look away, you know? I had to know what people could do to each other. Guy was always telling me about mass killings, bomb plots, about people who disappeared in the middle of the night and wars you never heard talked about on the news. (The wars the little grey men didn't want us to know about. The things that got beat to the headline slot by celeb hatches, matches and dispatches. By the sports headlines.) Sometimes I wouldn't believe him. I thought he was making it up. I mean – *Palestine*, the *Congo* – they don't sound like real places, do they? So I wasn't your average thirteen-year-old. I *knew* something about the world, you know? I already knew it was big, and fucked up, and full of liars and cheats worse than the kids I played with and against every week. At least Guy was interested for long enough to teach me about the world outside football. Which meant I wasn't the usual idiot stumbling into the game.

Your average trainee teenager thinks the whole world's just a fuckin football pitch, and his only job is to have fun on it then go get laid (which is easy coz he's a footballer). He's never known anything except people telling him he's great. He's gonna be a star. These kids, these idiots. The whole street knows what's happening to them and they talk about it all the time, coz there's bugger all else to talk about. Neighbours, friends, his parents and their mates, every fucker he bumps into in the corner shop – *How's the football going, superstar? You rich yet? Buy us a pint eh, champ? How about a house? Hey, dickhead, why won't you buy me a house?* Everyone he talks to telling him he's gonna be Ryan fuckin Giggs. And he believes it. They all do, these chancers. They think it's real, when it's got nothing to do with real. Guy made me realize football was a way OUT of the real world.

ARRIVAL AT THE THEATRE OF DREAMS

You tell your mates this is *supposed* to happen to you. You're *supposed* to be lifted out of school, away from homework, exams and choosing which shit job you hate least, then training for it, then doing it for fifty years, then dying. You're *born* for this existence. That's what Dad says. That's what everyone says. Other kids ask if you're nervous, most saying it like they want you to be. You bluff it, and when Guy asks if he can help, you snap. *I'm okay*, you tell him. *Only mard arses panic. You're just jealous coz they didn't pick you.* Guy's about the only one who's really, totally, no-fake happy for you, but you can't let him be, can you? In the final hours before you have to report for the first day of duty, you feel like a tourist. A liar. A loser. That swagger drains away and you wonder if you'll ever get it back. (Dad says you need to toughen up.) Yeah, you're gonna be in the dressing room, on the ground, you're gonna see your heroes in the corridors, sometimes you'll even share the same pitch – but this doesn't feel like your life any more, does it? Why not?

You've been sleeping in that same bedroom your whole life, and those walls are full of life-size posters that are about to turn into people. Sparky is on the bedroom door above a sign you carved in wood years ago saying MIKE AND GUY'S ROOM – NO BIG PEOPLE ALLOWED; a sticker of Lee Sharpe is on the mirror near the window, and Brian McClair is above your bed. Shiny, two-dimensional, paused in mid-kick, every night he looks over you sleeping. (You're a bit old for that now, but you've never got round to taking him down.) You can't get used to the fact that these posters are gonna be real, breathing things who talk and speak and move and make United life *happen*. Affect people all over the world. Reach into families and living rooms and filter through into pubs and car radios. It isn't just the players either. The belly of the stadium, it's so big, you reckon you'll probably get lost in it. (And you did once, when you were eleven, trying to find the toilets at half-time.) From what you saw on this TV programme, *The Life of Man United's Superstars*, the first team all have massive cars. But you can't imagine a time when you'll be able to *drive*, never mind afford a car like Bryan Robson's.

When you were little, you thought walking through the players' entrance would feel natural. Right. Like arriving home for the first time. But when it finally happens, when you turn up bang on time and they let you in the door, you imagine someone putting their hand on your shoulder and saying, *Sorry, son, no kids allowed*. Or those dreaded words, *Mikey, I'm afraid there's been a terrible mistake*. But it doesn't happen. And once they lock that gate with you inside, you never let anyone know what you're thinking. From the very first hour, you keep your head down. Graft. Do as you're told. Every night Dad's right there in your ear. It's you and him *against the bastard world*. Which is why you need him. Why you need each other.

Through all this, Dad sees you're getting closer and closer to the dream, and he acts like it's obvious. *It was always gonna happen*, he tells anyone who asks. But he never smiles or laughs. Sometimes it's like he's annoyed at you for getting signed up. Isn't this what he wanted? Maybe he's still angry he didn't get to meet Fergie. You tell him, *I'm sorry, we were just worried you were gonna ask him for a loan or something.* You say, *I'm okay, Dad. You don't have to do all this stuff for me any more.* But you reckon he's not tuned in. Some nights he doesn't come home. Some nights he turns up late, slurring his words and talking about his trials. How he could have been the greatest player Manchester had ever seen. How you don't deserve to be as good as your old man, and how, if you ever score for United, he'll probably shatter into a thousand pieces. Each piece of him drifting, splitting, drifting some more, up into the sky above Old Trafford. Mum just says, *This one again, Gregory?*, shakes her head and sends him away. Once, you ask him where he goes when that happens, but you get no answer. If Dad doesn't like the sound of a question, he just makes out it was never even asked.

But like good old Uncle Si says, in Unitedworld, working hard does actually help. You join in the July of 1991, just sixteen years old, but soon you're playing in the academy team. You do well. (Always do.) You're scoring. (Always do.) You're climbing, climbing. (No matter what's happening off the pitch, you always leave that shit on the other side of the white line.) Not much contact with the Gaffer, but you're told to expect that. Not much contact with big players, but you're told to expect that too. Sometimes one or two names play with the newbies, usually when coming back from injury. One night you run all the way home from the ground. *Mum! Mum!* you shout up the stairs. *Mark Hughes played with us today!* A voice calls back. *Mark who's . . .? Mark who's what?* You can't believe what you're hearing. You wish you were born into a different family, one that's not full of idiots. *No – MARK HHHUGHES played with us. I passed him the ball! He passed it back!* Mum appears on the staircase, hands on hips. *Son, you should say your aitches properly. You'll never get anywhere in life unless you say your aitches properly.* You think you're an adult now. Soon you'll be earning good money, and then, what will you need parents for?

Meanwhile, Dad borrows a fiver, just once, to bet on a sure thing – probably coz Uncle Si won't lend him money any more. When the sure thing loses, and you ask for the fiver back, he reminds you that *certain other people have a debt to pay*, that *some of these debts can't be measured in pounds and pence*, and that *they're gonna take a long old while to pay back*. You grunt. You laugh a dry laugh. *So I'm not getting my fiver then?* you ask, squaring up. You and your dad. You're the same size now.

Most of the time you're in the youth team, but early 1992 you get your first game for the rezzies. (They call it the rezzies instead of the reserves, so it sounds like a club you wanna be part of, not a home for new kids and rejects.) That's the same week the first team beat Sheffield United and fly past Leeds to the top of the First Division. The atmosphere is super-charged inside Old Trafford, and outside it too. In the papers and on the box. When you see them about, the kids you used to go to school with, Jay and Davey, ask if United are really as good as people are saying. The best United team ever. *Oh yeah*, you tell them, shrugging shoulders. *Course. We're gonna win the league!* As if it's a daft question. Like success is something you can be sure of. But that's how it feels, isn't it? After twenty-five years of false starts, people are starting to believe.

Belief is infectious, and with belief comes opportunity. When you're off duty, girls are everywhere – like they've been hiding in trees and behind lampposts, just waiting for the right time to shimmy into view and make their pitch. They come up and ask you out now, even though you've still got those squashed up ears that used to put them off. They offer things you don't understand. There's a whole bunch that hang out in the park, and one of them is shagging Guy for a bit – she tells friends she's only going out with him to meet you. This one called Fiona offers you *the best blowie you ever had* if you can get her into the game against Everton. But Dad keeps you focused. *Plenty of time for dipping your wick when you retire*, he says. *It's a short career, this.* You answer with a smile. *I know, I know,* you say, doing an impression of Dad's voice, low and thick with the sound of home. *The history of football is littered with talented young men ruined by chasing fanny.* He hits the side of your skull with his hand, then rubs a knuckle on it, trapping your whole head under his arm. *Surrender! Surrender!* you call out. *Who am I? Who am I?* he asks, still rubbing. You scream, *My lord and master! MY LORD AND BLOODY MASTER!* Dad lets you go, kisses the spot he's been hurting then says, *And don't you forget it, sunshine.*

Back in the United dressing room, the team sing songs taking the piss out of Leeds coz they're doing well just now. They've just paid a million pounds for some frog called *Can-to-na*. Rumour is, he's been smuggled into England and tricked into signing for the wrong United. *Sure, Mon-syaw Eric, sign ere please. Just write yer name on the dotted line. That's it. Nice and clear. We've got yer now.* Sometimes when you're singing, laughing and joking in the dressing room, you feel you could die and you really wouldn't mind. Even though you're covered in bruises and so stiff you can hardly move, even though Guy says he'll give Mum and Dad six months, max. (Guy reckons that if she doesn't kick him out then he'll end up in the clink or next on some loan shark's list of victims.) These times in the dressing room, all the team together, are the only times you forget who you are. Feel like you have comrades. Fellow soldiers in the battle for the Holy Grail. Boys who'll give their lives for you, just like you will for them, the second the call comes from on high. These times, you feel a hundred feet tall.

The rest of the time, you're shitting yourself.

There's a tough regime already – hey, this is *United* you're talking about – but it's an obsession. You can never do enough. You want to squeeze every ounce out of yourself. So not long after the real beginning you start setting your alarm for super early every day. You do fifty press-ups, fifty pull-ups, fifty sit-ups before breakfast which, on days you're at home, Mum serves up with this big fuss like you have to be looked after extra special. (Guy tells Mum she's treating you like you're the *fuckin Dalai Lama or something*.) You start watching what you're eating. Measuring everything. Getting early nights. Doing extra runs in the morning and free kicks after training. (Want to be seen, but never say so.) Going further, harder, hoping to get noticed. You're always knackered, always nervous. If the Gaffer comes to talk to the team, if he comes *anywhere near*, your legs become sponges. It's tough to get to sleep and tougher to get up in the morning. But you say fuck all about it. One day the physio asks if you're coping okay with the training and you reply, *Course I am. Why? You want me to give you a few tips?*

Before joining United you thought all you wanted was a chance to prove yourself, but no. You wanted someone to put an arm round your shoulder and say, *Don't worry, Mike. You'll always be here. Just relax.* And no fucker does that, do they? Even when you're with the other lads, you're really on your own. You learn that fast. Guy says everyone gets stick at the beginning. (And you get a lot.) Everyone feels like they don't belong. (And you really don't feel like you belong.) Everyone gets called a poof and wonders why everyone else seems so far away. But you don't want to let it go. It's one thing being ignored in a kids' team, where it's all part-time. Where it's all about who's hard, who can afford the most useless crap, whose girlfriend's got big tits and a tight arse. But you always thought it'd be different in the grown-up world. Isn't it supposed to be all for one and one for all now? Isn't it?

SATURDAY 8 DECEMBER 2007
PREMIER LEAGUE

UNITED	**4–1**	**DERBY COUNTY**
GIGGS 40		**HOWARD 76**
TÉVEZ 45, 60		
RONALDO (PEN) 90		

ATTENDANCE: 75,725

GIGGSY WATCH – MarryMeRyan?: Major love for Giggsy out there today. Captained the team. 100th league goal. Special. But lots of U part timers sayin U always believed in the Legend when half U lot were slagging him last week! @ MadRed4Eva666 U NO WHO U R! Peace out.

Average Fan Rating: 8/10

They still loved him. And why not? There was no reason to fall out of love.

All around Old Trafford, families with small children, couples, everyone from groups of young men to old ladies wrapped up in United scarves and gloves, sipping coffee out of their flasks and listening to the radio commentary – everyone stood to clap when Ryan Giggs was substituted after sixty-five minutes. Mike Wilson was listening with one earpiece in, the other one dangling, allowing him to enjoy the radio and the noise of the ground at the same time. The commentator listed Ryan's achievements. The list took a long time to read out.

'And there he goes,' said the commentator. 'The last of the gentleman footballers.'

Then the commentator actually applauded.

As far as Mike was concerned, this kind of thing had been going on for a lifetime already, and it felt like these days a new record was broken every time Ryan stepped onto a pitch. Each time he lasted one more game, ran one more mile, survived one more day, a new burst of editorials was spawned, filling the pages of the newspapers, the infinite scrolling space on internet blogs, airtime on TV and radio stations, all of it salivating over yet more talk of the Premiership's Greatest Ever Player. And tomorrow there would be more. Started off by Ryan's hundredth league goal for the team, United had coasted to victory against relegation favourites Derby County – so there had been plenty of time for contemplation. Plenty of opportunity for reminiscing, putting his achievements into perspective, comparing him to all others who had graced the same stage at the Theatre of Dreams and Nightmares in the last century and more. Even a Derby goal had barely registered with the home fans, who were in the mood to pay tribute. When Sir Alex Ferguson waved his player off the field, it seemed like an act of tribute. It gave both sets of fans, and neutrals everywhere, a chance to love.

Two minutes to go in this game, and the noise around the ground was dense, all-consuming. Thousands of fans were singing Ryan's name while he sat in the dugout, a study in calm contemplation, apparently untouched by the adoration of thousands. Mike watched Ryan pull off his left boot and peel down his sock, inspecting something on his foot. Mike wondered: Would he ever give up? Would he quietly, steadily, play less and less, retiring at just the right time before being pushed? Would he move onwards and downwards, perhaps spending a final season or two in the lower divisions, or cash in with a short, alien spell in Japan, or the United States, or Dubai? Would he manage the Welsh national team – would he fail in that job, as all others had done before, or sprinkle his magic there too? Would he become the world's dullest pundit? Plough the lecture circuit? Set up a charity? Abandon football and become a Buddhist monk? As Ryan made himself comfortable among the other squad players and substitutes on the bench, some born after his United debut, some who had never known anything but a United team with him in it, it seemed as if he was going to go on – as a player – for ever. And, to the tune of 'Love Will Tear Us Apart' by Manchester's own Joy

Division, the crowd sang, noisy and proud and out of key, as the game spilled over into tensionless injury time. Mike closed his eyes, put his hands in his pockets, concentrating on the sound. All he could see, hear, feel, was that song. So loud, everywhere. In his ears and in his gut. As if it was the only song in the world. Which for a while, for Mike, it was.

Giggs . . . Giggs will tear you apart again . . .
Giggs . . . Giggs will tear you apart again . . .
Giggs . . . Giggs will tear you apart again . . .
Giggs . . . Giggs will tear you apart again . . .
Giggs . . . Giggs will tear you apart again . . .
Giggs . . . Giggs will tear you apart again . . .
Giggs . . . Giggs will tear you apart again . . .
Giggs . . . Giggs will tear you apart again . . .

I hadn't slept the night before. I hadn't slept in days. The room was just a big empty space I didn't understand what to do with any more.

Those long years in the bunks with Guy, all I wanted was a quiet room of my own. Christ, the amount of times I'd yelled at him to *shut the fuck up* when he was snoring so loud he might have woken himself as well as me. But now I was alone in the silence, thinking about sound. I knew how Guy moved when he was having one of his nightmares, the exact way the bed squeaked when he was having yet *another* wank, the way he'd talk to me for hours about the future and how you had to *grab it by the balls, Mikey, and not let go!* – then fall asleep in the middle of a sentence. Now he was gone. For the last five nights I'd been lying awake thinking, Could I have stopped him? Thinking, This Sally he was moving in with. I'd never even met her. Thinking, It's too fuckin quiet for me to get to sleep. Then the phone rang and I picked up before anyone else could get to it. *Hello?* said a voice. *You clear?* I got dressed, and left. Well, I wasn't gonna get any fuckin kip, was I?

Jay's parents had gone away for the week, so we had the big old house to ourselves. When I got there, the front door was open, the stereo loud. There were spliff ends on the pavement out front and empty cans of Boddies by the doorstep. About eight or nine fellers were listening to music in the lounge, tanking beers and arguing about bands. Todd and Davey were playing cards. I sat down and picked up a can, splitting it open, listening to the chat, then Jay offered me some weed. I did remember what Dad said – and, as I reached my hand out, I did wonder whether I was signing myself up to a career at County, or a non-league outfit, you know? Ruining myself. But for as long as I could remember I'd been focusing on my game, my game, my game, and for a second or two, that didn't seem enough to fill up a whole life. Guy was gone. To live with a *girl*. And, rumour was, scouts were coming to see us play next weekend. How was I gonna survive till then without losing my mind? I inhaled, deep, and exhaled. Jay smiled. He said, *You're all right, Mikey*. And I felt like I knew what he meant. That night, we got pissed, fighting and throwing things around in the back garden, singing 'I Wanna Be Adored'. *I don't have to sell my soul, he's already in me*, we sang. Then Jay said, *Who's up for a bit of poker? Let's make it interesting, eh?* It felt like Manchester was the centre of the fuckin universe. The coolest place on the planet. And it always would be. I got home a couple of hours before I had to get up.

Which was why I was late the next morning, running down the hill for the bus, school tie in one hand, bag swinging from the other, realizing too late that I'd forgotten my kit and the PE teacher was gonna murder me. I reckon that was Guy's fault, coz if he'd been home he wouldn't have let me go to Jay's in the first place. Or it was Dad's fault. If he wasn't working away he would have locked me in my room. Coz of the timing, you know? Coz this was the week I was gonna open the door to that big bright field for all the family. (Hold on: if it was so important, then where the fuck was everyone anyway?) As I ran for that bus, gaining speed, gaining, gaining, I thought of the thrill last night when the cards landed right and I pulled the chips towards me. The sensation that could only mean someone was watching over me. And I was gonna be just fine.

Twenty minutes later, sweaty and hot, my mouth dry and sour, I wasn't in the mood to be dicked about. Mr Cobb always stood with his back straight when he gave instructions. Sometimes he forgot to do any teaching and just talked about how he was cheated out of the GB Olympics team in 1984. When I said I'd forgotten my kit he reacted like I'd just committed a murder and, no joke, looked like he was gonna have a heart attack. I started to laugh. Couldn't stop myself from telling him, *Do your worst, knobhead*. And why not? This time next week I could be free of this nowhere place, these nothing people – but Cobb fuckin lost it, spitting as he shouted. I was actually worried. Maybe his big brother had moved out as well. Maybe his dad was working in Newcastle all week too. *Are you okay, sir?* I asked. Cobb grabbed a chair and made me stand on it. Held me by the arm and threw me up there. He came up close. Face even redder now. Purple. He was about to explode.

Repeat after me, Wilson. Say: I must learn some respect.

(You say it – this isn't funny any more.)

Say: I am a raving poofter and I have an arse for a face.

(You wait, see he's serious, then say it. Stifled giggles from the class.)

But I am an arseface poofter who will never forget his kit again.

(You say it.)

Or else I will have to do PE naked and everyone will see my tiny cock.

(Very quiet, you say it. So he makes you say it again. Louder.)

OR ELSE I WILL HAVE TO DO PE NAKED AND EVERYONE WILL SEE MY TINY COCK.

(Face burning up. Head cold.)

He walked round me as I spoke, circling, then lead the class in a big round of applause in my honour, celebrating how I'd finally admitted the ugly truth. Then he dismissed everyone, explaining that today was athletics, and an extra two laps of the course as *a thank you to Mr Do Your Worst here*. It all happened very very slowly, this talk, with me not crying (don't cry don't cry don't cry), with some of the other kids moaning about the extra run (Jay, bags under his eyes and way down after last night's poker game, was one of them), but most of the class was just laughing, even though it seemed like they were laughing at Cobb as much as they were laughing at me. (He knew that, didn't he?) Jay laughed harder. Like he didn't really find it that funny at all. Which reminded me of someone. And I couldn't let that go, could I? Not any more. Kids should have known not to take the piss, whatever happened. Even Jay. Especially Jay, who'd crossed me before. So when he waited till Cobb had gone, and hissed *tiny cock* right in my ear, smiling, I couldn't let it go.

This, in so many words, is what I told the pigs when they asked why I'd broken that kid's arm and cheekbone. Why I'd kicked his head in, in front of twenty witnesses. Bust his nose and dislodged three teeth, the ones front and centre, with my fist. I was calm by then, and made it sound reasonable. Turns out, lying is pretty easy. Sitting behind one of those small, wooden desks in the police station, a grin creeping across my face, I suggested to the pigs that the whole thing was provoked by *an uncalled-for public humiliation by someone in a position of responsibility*. I suggested that maybe someone like that shouldn't be teaching any more. *Isn't that child abuse?* I asked. The pigs shuffled in their chairs. Snorted a bit. Said they'd pursue the matter with the school, put me on a warning, and let me go.

LIFE AHEAD

At the end of March 1992 you score your first goal for the rezzies, and it's your BEST EVER. You take it from halfway, right on the touchline, and head straight for goal, homing in, skipping past two, three, four tackles. It's so smooth, so easy, you can't believe it's you doing it. Past another defender, another, thinking the ball is gonna slip away, amazed it's still at your feet when you get to the penalty spot. There's one more defender, maybe twice your age, twice your size as well. The man's a giant. You hold him off, spin round, take a swing and kick it hard into the top left corner as the keeper lunges, stretching out his fingertips to reach it but knowing he won't. The net bulges, the ball hits the ground and you celebrate like you've won gold at the fuckin Olympics. You kiss the badge. You kiss half the team. You drop to your knees and cry out, your voice high and out of control. You do all the things you think are only for dickheads until you find yourself wondering where this other person has come from, this full-up-to-bursting-with-emotion stranger who acts like the whole world is watching when actually it's just the coaches and about four others singing, *There's only one Mikey Wilson and he's okay. The boy born on Sir Matt Busby Way!* And there *is* only one Wilson. *You*. As you kneel in the penalty box, smothered by all those new best mates diving on top of you, looking out through the pile of legs and shorts, you see your whole future.

You see yourself being called into the Gaffer's office to be told you're gonna be given a senior contract. You see yourself signing it. BIG FAT LETTERS, BOLD AND BRIGHT. You see your first senior game, coming on as a sub for Robbo, see him slapping the side of your face and saying, *You'll be fine. You were born to play for United*. You see the solo goal you score on your first team debut, the headlines hailing the sixteen-year-old 'Little Giggs' born just yards from Old Trafford who's bound to bring the good times back. You see the smile on Mum's face as you pull her brand-new Merc (just like Fergie's) into the drive on Christmas Day. (Actually, you know now that Fergie's got loads of cars. Might have to buy her more than one. No problem.) You see the league title. The European Cup. An improved contract. Front cover photo shoots in magazines and newspapers, and not just the sports pages either. The *Sun*. The *Mirror*. The *News of the Screws*. Even though you're a loyal citizen of the Republik of Mancunia so don't really care (real United fans hate the England team – it's full of Cockneys and Scousers), you see your national debut. (That's the breakthrough that finally stops Mum talking about *when you go back to school . . .*) You see the World Cup final. The winning goal scored in the last minute, ball hitting net as the telly commentator says those lines he'd scribbled in his notebook years ago and has been dying to say ever since – *And* finally *the ghost of sixty-six is LAID TO REST!* You see your testimonial. A stylish, adoring wife dripping from your arm. (Every fucker has one of those.) A girlfriend in the stands, keeping a jealous lookout. (Everyone has one of those too.) You see yourself carrying your son on your shoulders as you do a tour of the pitch on your final match. The chants. The cheers. The adoration. You see your CBE, then OBE, then knighthood, and your mind's *really* racing now. You see your emotional retirement speech, explaining your success is really all down to the Gaffer (though he lets you call him plain old Alex these days), who came to your house, got down on his knees and begged you to sign for United when you were just fifteen. Proudly telling a friendly media scrum that he only did that twice, and the other player was this lad called Giggs. Does anyone remember him? (That gets a big laugh.) You see the sign being unveiled on the new Wilson Stand selling Wilson Bitter, Wilson Cola and Wilson Burgers with Wobbly Wilson Fries and even see, way off in the future, someone on the telly asking a one-hundred-year-old Sir Bobby Charlton, *Where's the next Mike Wilson going to come from?* You see Sir Bobby smiling and saying:

Well, Tim, you only get one Mike Wilson in a lifetime. And that's if you're lucky. I'm just grateful I watched the great man in action. (Bobby shakes his head and smiles.) *What a player! Really, I thought I'd never see a greater artist than George Best but this lad . . . well! What can you say? I'm glad I lived to see it.* (Tears well up in Bobby's eyes as he struggles to keep his composure.) *I . . . I can die now.*

You get up off the floor, beaming, and the coach shouts, *Hey Pelé! Ready to retire, are you?* You shake your head, still grinning. *Well then*, he screams. *Get on with the bloody game!* The team loses and you hardly get a kick the rest of the match. But you don't care. Coz you know what's coming. And what's coming is good.

Let's say I'm ninety, I'm talking to the journo guy writing my biography (it won't be the first book written about me – Giggsy's had fourteen so far), and the guy asks, *What single event, more than any other, led to you being a Manchester United footballer?* In that situation I'd say, *Mum writing to* Jim'll Fix It. The programme will be long forgotten by the time I'm ninety, but fuck it, whose story is this anyway? Google might still exist. The leeches can look it up.

So it was the winter of the 1988/89 season – a poor one for United – and I'd already been in bed for a week, locked away in the spare room like the family freak. Dad was threatening to dump me at the tip or the orphanage unless I shut up moaning. Guy was sleeping on the couch coz I was making so much noise. What can I say? I'm not a great patient. Guy reckons I'm shit at having to sit still coz I've made a living out of moving around. Dad says it's coz I've got a low pain threshold: or in his words, *Coz you're a bleedin poof.* But, whatever the reason, this thing was murdering me. I was sick for days. I had a fever. My throat was so sore it wasn't worth the effort to speak and I looked like I'd been shot in the head, chest and back by a tiny gun. Two hundred times. How many matches did I miss? Too many, that's all I know. Still, there's nothing you can do about chicken pox. You just have to wait it out, in a cold room, hoping you're not one of the fatalities.

One night, the sweats were worse than usual and by three a.m. I still wasn't asleep. Mum heard me and got up. A few minutes later she came into the room holding a glass of whisky and a sponge, opened the window to let some air in, sat down beside me, put the whisky down and said, *Purely medicinal.* Then she dabbed my head, making it cooler. *Aah,* I said. *That's good. Don't go.* We sat for a while before she told me to drink the whisky, and I did as I was told, knocking it back fast, hoping it wouldn't burn. Course, my throat lit up like a firework. But as the hot burning turned to gentle warmth inside my chest I closed my eyes and let my shoulders go, wondering how long they'd been tight for. I hadn't even known they were tight at all. Just then Mum asked me to imagine the place I wanted to be most. She asked me to imagine I was there, then tell her where I was thinking of. *I wanna go backstage at OT*, I said. She wrote a letter to *Jim'll Fix It* that night, pretending to be me, and posted it before the eight o'clock collection the next morning.

A week later Mum came into the room with a piece of paper in her hand, a polite No from the show's producers. *Perhaps we'd have had a better chance if you were dying*, said Mum, fiddling with the letter. *Bunch of bastards. But let's not give up, eh?* And she didn't. You've gotta remember that back then, the idea of me signing for United seemed as likely as Mum getting signed up for Salford Ladies by Jesus Himself. Yeah, we'd been working towards it for years already. Me and Dad telling ourselves and each other it could be done. But there was no sign yet that we weren't just insane dreamers. In 1988/89 I was thirteen, still playing for my school and an average Sunday league team, and a dream was exactly what it was. Seeing the dressing rooms, the corridors. Standing by the side of pitch. Those things were impossible. There was no way we could afford to pay. So when she sat there on my bed making a list of everyone who might be able to help get me a private tour round Old Trafford, as far as Mum knew, that was as close as I was ever gonna get to playing for United. That night, she stayed up writing to everyone on the list. By hand. For each suggestion, there was at least one question or complication.

1. ALEX FERGUSON, MANAGER (ask secretary politely for address?)
2. ASSISTANT MANAGER (name? does anyone hold this post?)
3. DONNIE, works in the Manchester United Superstore (does he have access backstage?)
4. RAB, the man who sells Dad the *Red Issue* on match day and says he's 'best mates with the manager of the youth team'

5. GEORGE BEST (still alive? If so, still got connections to the club? If so, in fit state to help?)
6. MAKE A WISH FOUNDATION, ETC. (are these charities just for kids with terminal illnesses?)
7. MANCHESTER UNITED OFFICIAL SUPPORTERS CLUBS (directory for this?)
8. MANCHESTER UNITED PLAYERS (approx. twenty-five players – check for those holding charitable posts)
9. MANCHESTER UNITED YOUTH PLAYERS (perhaps youngsters more likely to help?)
10. MANCHESTER UNITED FAN GROUPS (perhaps someone in a position of responsibility has had a private tour before or knows who might organize this without charge?)
11. JIM'LL FIX IT (write again to find out how they call in favours for the show?)

Mum looked up addresses for three whole days. I laughed and told her to take off half the names on the list. There was no fuckin way this was happening. But telling her that made her worse.

Every morning and night I got a bedside update on Mum's progress. She went on field trips, searching people out. She trailed around outside the ground on match days, asking questions. She went to the library for research and kept a folder of replies, rejections, advice, and new ideas she had as she went along. It was another three weeks before the breakthrough – it turned out Rab the *Red Issue* guy wasn't full of shit after all. And you can guess how we felt when we got a letter back saying a recently signed youth player had permission from the manager to do a private tour, free of charge, as a favour to Rab. Another two weeks later I was back to full strength and back at school, and Mum had to write another letter to tell the teachers I had to go to my nana's funeral in London. *Little white lie*, said Mum, licking the envelope, giving me a cheeky wink. *Just this once, eh?* And once was all it needed.

The day of the big tour I was up at six, gobbling breakfast with my legs bobbing under the table. Mum made sure I was smart. Clapped me on the side of the head and told me to behave, or else. I headed out early, my cassette Walkman playing 'Twenty Red Terrace Anthems' as I paced along that route to the ground I knew so well. I sang out loud as I walked. It was gonna be the BEST. The best the best the best. But when I got to the ground, there was a delay. They hadn't opened up for the day yet. I had to wait twenty minutes before anyone pulled up the shutters and opened the door. And once they let me in, the receptionist said I'd made a mistake – there was no booking for this morning. Only one tour this afternoon for someone with a different name. I begged her to help me. Explained how ill I'd been and how this was a favour. I checked her badge, used her name. *Claire*, I said. *Please*. Claire said she'd have to speak to her boss, went away (FOR AGES), came back and said, *You'd better sit down. You could be lucky. But maybe not*. Then she went back to her post.

I had to wait another hour, Claire looking over at me from time to time, shaking her head then checking her watch like it was DOING SOMETHING WRONG, or like the watch had the answer to why I'd been forgotten. When I was sat there, legs still bob bob bobbing like mad, giving Claire the big brown sympathy eyes in the hope that it'd make a difference, I thought about just getting up and leaving. But then I'd have to go home and tell Mum. Could I do that? Really? Fuck United, I thought. I didn't need them, did I? Just as I was wondering about the answer to that question, a door opened, a figure standing there with bright white light bleeding out from behind him. He was wearing a United tracksuit. He seemed like a grown-up. A smiling, handsome grown-up. One who wasn't going to make me go back home to break bad news, or ever send me away from this beautiful place. *I'm Ryan*, said the figure, putting his hand out for me to shake. *Claire over here tells me you've been at death's door. Well, if this doesn't make you feel better then nothing will. Come on, let's have a look around. And after, if we're lucky, they might let us on the pitch*.

I'm not an idiot, I know I was a lucky kid. And for people on the outside, it might look like that luck was all about my dad, but in a way his job was easy. All he had to do was push, you know? Push me to do things I already wanted to do. The thing I'd say to my biographer is: we all know who made the real difference. And once I'd seen the belly of United HQ, once I'd had a kickabout with Ryan on the hallowed turf, there was no way I was gonna miss out.

SUNDAY 16 DECEMBER 2007
PREMIER LEAGUE

BIN DIPPERS 0–1 UNITED
TÉVEZ 43

ATTENDANCE: 44,459

GIGGSY WATCH – IH8Scousers: Well done the boys, and respect to the old master 4 setting up the winner. We're gonna shit on the Liverpool tonight! I'm gettin my load ready as we speak, ladies and gents, and it's a full on stinker . . . RED ARMY!

Average Fan Rating: 7/10

The Anfield trip would be Mike Wilson's first United away game outside of Manchester in too long. Guy had been the last of the Wilson clan left, and when he pulled out there was no point Mike going on his own. It was enough being alone at the home fixtures, which he'd been doing for four months now. Every fortnight he walked alone down Sir Matt Busby Way, and ate alone at the Legends Takeaway, where he and Guy used to guess the team together, predict the score and shovel down fish and chips, talking tactics. (They'd eat on the street, standing, watching fans troop past.) He'd been alone getting his programme and *Red Issue*, alone putting a bet on at the bookies inside the ground, alone getting coffee and crisps in the crush at half-time, and alone trying not to spill his drink on the way to his seat. Four months was long enough for anyone. It was time to make some changes. And at least now the team were gathering momentum, that poor early-season form looking more and more like a blip. He booked a seat on an unofficial fan bus, paid his money and counted down the days.

But Mike knew that, out of town, fans turned into different animals. Alcohol was all on these trips, and people looked at him dumbly when he refused beer as if they didn't even understand the concept of a man who didn't live to get drunk. Some reckoned it was an ex-player habit and said nothing, some wouldn't let it go. But now Mike was sure he could cope with the looks and the jokes of these men who lived their life for a sport they weren't fit enough to play for more than ten minutes at a time. As he reminded Guy on the phone that morning, United were 'taking the good fight deep into Scouse territory' and no one was going to 'stop Mike Wilson from witnessing victory first hand!'

Then he began to sing.

Just like on the terraces, it was the songs that mattered. They started up as soon as the United boys boarded the bus, and Mike bellowed as loud as anyone. Leading the 'Ji-Sung Park' tune as the bus turned onto the motorway, he felt like he'd already arrived somewhere special. He could no longer remember why he'd stayed away from these trips for so long.

PAAARK, PAAARK, wherever you may BEEE,
You eat DOGS in yer OME COUNTRY,
It could be WORSE, you could be a SCOUSE,
Eating RATS in yer COUNCIL HOUSE!

He liked to shout the end of every line.

Mike sang along with his new friends. One was an older, much larger man called Ledley, and the others were Ledley's pals, some from a five-a-side team they invited Mike to join almost as soon as they met. (He'd accepted the offer without thinking, and was due to play his first match next week. Even though he was injured.) The five men were spread across the back seats of the coach, laughing and joking like children on their first day trip out from school. Ledley had seemed quiet at first, but not after three cans of lager. He stood on his seat, bald head sweating, stomach poking out, and started up the next song, proudly out of tune. The rest of the coach sang along.

GAAAARRY Neeeville is a Red, is a Red, is a RED,
GAAAARRY Neeeville is a RED, HE! HATES! SCOUSERS!

Mike wondered which songs Liverpool supporters were singing at that exact moment. The idea that anyone could hate Gary Neville, it was a mystery. And then he began to think about how, before Gary got injured at the beginning of the year, he always seemed angry at something during matches. Raging against getting older, perhaps. Against not being able to guarantee a place in the team any more. Either that or he'd forgotten he was playing a game, and really, truly, genuinely thought he was at war. Mike wondered which was worse. Having a career suddenly end, or just very slowly fading. Knowing you were getting weaker with every passing day. The whole coach was really swinging now, and as the Gary Neville song finished someone at the front started up Mike's favourite. To the tune of 'You Are My Sunshine', it was purely for the hardcore.

You are a SCOUSER, an ugly SCOUSER,
Yer only HAAAPPY on GIRO DAY.
Yer mum's out THIEVING, yer dad's DRUG-DEALING,
So please don't take my hubcaps aWAAAAY! . . .

Mike sang louder, louder, up and out.

. . . You look in the DUSTBIN for something to EAT,
You find a dead RAT and you think it's a TREAT,
In yer Liverpool slums, in yer Liverpool slums,
You SHIT on the CARPET, you PISS in the BATH,
You finger yer GRANDMA and think it's a LAUGH,
In yer Liverpool slums, in yer Liverpool slums . . .

As the words rang out, Ledley and one of the others, a middle-aged man called Gaz, pulled down their trousers and started waving their backsides out of the back window of the coach at the cars behind. Two sleepy little penises hung out and flopped around. Mike laughed, looked away and said to no one, 'Crazy bastards.' Then he sang louder.

. . . You speak in an ACCENT exceedingly RAAARE,
You wear a PINK TRACKSUIT and have curly HAAAIR,
In yer Liverpool slums, in yer Liverpool slums.
Your mum's on the GAME and your dad's in the NICK,
You can't get a job coz you're TOO FUCKIN THICK,
In yer Liverpool slums.
He's only a poor little SCOUSER, his face is all BATTERED and TORN,
He made me feel SICK, so I HIT HIM with a BRICK,
And now he don't SING anyMOOOOORE!

'All the best tunes come out on days like this!' said Ledley, pulling up his trousers.

A man Mike didn't know spoke next.

'Hey, mate,' he called over to Ledley. 'There are only a couple of *actual* Scousers in the Liverpool team these days.'

Ledley's eyebrows slid down his forehead. His mouth crumpled. The man tried again.

'I mean, they're all bleedin dagoes these days, aren't they?'

There was a moment of silence before Ledley replied. 'Well yeah. But a couple of Scousers is a couple too many if you ask me!' he said, with a grin.

The other man laughed, the tension swam out of the window, the two clinked cans and the bus cheered like a goal had already been scored. When the bus pulled up outside Anfield, the men booed, and Mike thought of how Uncle Si always used to say that United was the most loved, and most hated club on earth. Close by, at that moment, he was certain of it: someone was disrespecting Sir Alex Ferguson. Making jokes about Rooney's taste in prostitutes. Ronaldo's taste in himself. Astonishing as it was to consider it, somebody somewhere was probably even criticizing Ryan Giggs. Mike could almost smell the wickedness. He shook his head and took in the view.

Half an hour later, three thousand Manchester United fans were packed into the away section at Anfield: the game was a sell-out, and from a few rows below Mike could hear Guy's favourite chant being sung by a group of four middle-aged men in Santa suits.

FEEEED the SCOOOUSEEERS,
Let them know it's CHRISTMAS TIIIIME . . .

The United fans were ten times louder than they ever were at home. He'd forgotten how loud crowd noise could be – the opposite of the Three Unwise Men and their muffled moaning. As the game kicked off he thought about Guy and his brother-in-law Danny at County, part of a small crowd, probably freezing, cheering on men no fitter than him, so close that when he shouted at them to shoot, the players could shout back, or chase them out of the ground.

'Sometimes you've got to take a stand, bruv,' Guy had said, last night. 'You can't let those fleecing bastards control you for ever. Sometimes I think that if Osama Bin bloody Laden bought United tomorrow you'd find a way to back him. But not me. You're on your own.'

Mike had felt exhausted. 'You know who you sound like?' he'd answered, his voice breaking. 'Fuckin *Dad*.'

Guy was quick in reply. 'Yeah? And you sound like a kid.'

Both men slammed down the phone.

But by the following day the argument was forgotten. Mike phoned Guy from the ground just as the game kicked off.

'All right, our kid! It's *kicking off* here,' he said when Guy picked up. Then, trying not to sound too interested in the answer, Mike asked a question. 'Hey, what's it like over there?'

'Good, thanks,' Guy replied. 'These boys are real fans.'

'Wish you were here?'

'Not much. I'm just talking about Rooney and Ronaldo to Danny here. They've got nothing in common with you and me, Mike. Rooney's an Everton supporter, a *Scouser*. And Ronaldo's a Madrid fan. They're just hired help. These boys . . . I dunno. We own this club. The supporters. Know what I mean?'

In the background, 'This is the One' by the Stone Roses started playing on Ledley's mobile as the teams came out of the tunnel. A familiar warm shiver went through Mike.

'Nah, mate,' he told his brother. 'I don't know what you mean. Anyway, have a good time. If you can, *loser*!' He flipped his phone closed to prevent reply.

Mike tried not to think about Guy during the game, but it was tough. Since Sally had finally agreed to marry him, something had changed. Since they moved to south Manchester to get their children into posh schools. It seemed like Guy really believed that getting married and having children made him a better man. As if these were difficult things to do. And *everyone* was doing those things now. Falling into line. Even the rebels had become nine to five-ers, and out of all the boys he knew at school Mike was the only one left single now. That is, except for a few of those who married young, like Jay, who were already getting divorced.

Mike stood to cheer the players coming out of the tunnel.

Mike thought the game against Liverpool was a modern classic. Set up by Ryan, Carlos Tévez popped out a toe in front of the Kop just before half-time and the travelling support celebrated. The chants got bigger, darker.

'Bye bye there, Scousers!'

'You bunch of Hillsborough bastards!'

'Ninety-six was NOT *ENOUGH*!'

(Mike booed after that last one. Some lads had no brains.)

The game went by fast, especially after the goal. Even though it was only 1–0, the lead felt safe to the fans in the away end. The last few minutes of the game played out as if everyone had accepted the result, even the Liverpool players. It was almost embarrassing. In among the rowdy United end, Mike prayed for drama. He wished Gary Neville wasn't injured. His mind loose now, he wondered whether Neville would ever play for United again. If he didn't, that left only two from his era: Paul Scholes, and Ryan. Over the years, all others had left the good ship MUFC. Some had jumped. Most were forced to walk the plank.

The coach was rocking on the way back to Manchester. The driver stopped twice to beg people to behave, but with no success. Again, the backsides came out. Again, the songs were sung. Louder. Harder. Every word was a national anthem all of its own. Grown men wept and clung onto one another in a frenzy, celebrating the team's big win. Mike arrived home smelling of sweat and dirt. He decided not to have a shower straight away. Not to lose the stink.

As he fell onto his couch, he picked up the remote and began to flick through the sports channels searching for a clip of the Tévez goal. Mike felt high on the game. He thought about the things he might do in the week to come. He might go and see Mum. He might visit his niece Millie and nephew Robbie, maybe take them out to the cinema, give Guy and Sally a few hours to themselves. He might speak to Dad about the Liverpool game. Then there was the coming working week, which he was hopeful for. He closed his eyes on the couch, still in his clothes, and fell into a deep sleep for the first time in weeks.

In Mike's dreams, Ryan took a corner kick again and again, and Tévez's foot got on the end of it, the stocky little player stretching out that toe, stretching out that toe, stretching out that toe. United fans erupted in joy each time. Then, in the dream, Ryan ran over to the camera, grabbed it by the sides, and kissed it.

A MESSAGE FOR ALL

Imagine: it's sudden.

One Tuesday morning, when everyone wakes up, it's finally just *happened*.

And it's not how you imagined. You didn't think you'd be half asleep, wandering from your bed to the fridge at two in the morning, about to reach in to get some milk when you noticed it attached to the door. You didn't think that once you'd seen it, you'd stand still for a few seconds, listening to the strange echoing silence, aware of the coldness of the kitchen floor beneath your bare feet. Didn't think you'd laugh out loud, in shock. And you didn't think that when Mum came down the stairs and asked what was happening, you wouldn't have an answer. When she notices you standing there, refusing to move, she guesses right away. As if somehow the fridge itself is a clue. At the very second Mum starts to cry, you speak. The first noise that comes out of your mouth is, *I'm sorry! It's not my fault!* She answers, *Oh God, Mikey, what have you done?*

Half an hour later, Uncle Si arrives in T-shirt, pyjama bottoms and slippers, holding up a bag. *Twenty-four-hour Chinese*, he calls out, smiling. *Anyone hungry?* Mum hugs him hard, them both standing in the doorway, you standing right behind her. Uncle Si holds Mum in his big tattooed arms, winking at you sadly over her shoulder, and for a few seconds you hope he'll never leave. You think that maybe his suitcase will arrive in a minute and he'll unpack and move into the spare room. Uncle Si pats Mum's back then strokes her head, like she's a child, saying, *Shh, it's okay now. Debbie Debbie Debbie, it's all gonna be okay.* Then he holds out the bag towards you and tells you, *If we're not careful, sunshine, there'll be egg fried rice everywhere.*

Uncle Si stays for over an hour. He takes the food out of the bags, serves up at the dinner table and insists you and Mum sit at it. *Just like normal*, he says. Then he sits with you both, keeping conversation flowing. You get a pass coz of your special football diet (you have a few forkfuls, to be polite), but he makes sure Mum eats plenty and, as ever, he has a big appetite of his own. Uncle Si talks about the business, how Guy is doing, and how he thinks Guy will be able to take over from him one day. Apparently, Guy's a natural. He tells Mum that both her sons are good boys and that's coz they were raised well and Mum nods her head silently, trying not to explode. Uncle Si doesn't leave any gaps in his chat. He never stops talking. He's too kind to make you do any of the work yourselves. Then he clears up after dinner, does the washing-up, gives Mum another hug, and goes. At the door he says, *You'll be fine*, and he kisses your forehead.

The timing is interesting, but maybe that's on purpose. Anyway, doesn't matter, does it? You have to carry on. You don't tell anyone at United. Don't want them to pity you. Or worse, tell you to take time off. So, the next morning, you do exactly what you'd planned to do. Rise early, do your exercises, measure out then eat breakfast, as normal, and kiss Mum on the cheek before you leave. You hug her tight just like Uncle Si did, stroke her head and whisper, *Wish me luck. I'm off to make us rich!*

Under-elevens football league report
Salford Advertiser
November 1986

SEVENTH HEAVEN FOR WILSON IN 8-2 THRILLER

Barry Hill Diamonds 8 Foxton Juniors 2

SHOCK TRANSFER

Before this game hardly anyone in the City of Salford Junior Football League knew the name Mikey Wilson. After it, everyone will. Wilson joined top of the table Barry Hill Diamonds just three weeks ago from strugglers Park Dean Juniors, where he had put in some good performances in recent weeks – but surely no one could have predicted the instant impact he'd have on his new club's fortunes. This crucial game between first and second in the league promised to be a thriller right from the first minute, when Adam Brown scored for Foxton almost right from the kick-off. His distraught manager, Eddie Roberts, said after the game: 'I thought this was gonna be easy!' But Eddie could not have been more wrong.

GOALS GALORE!

Two minutes later, Barry Hill winger Jamie Foulkes had to come off with a sprained ankle, and was replaced by unknown new boy Wilson, who showed why he could be the difference between the two teams come the end of the season. Over the next ten minutes he scored two solo goals and a fine header direct from a corner – rare at this level of the beautiful game. Foxton did score a second in the twenty-third minute but they immediately gave away a penalty when Sammy Thamesworth was elbowed by Daniel Stanton. Barry Hill captain and manager's son Johnny Bryant Jnr converted the spot kick and at half-time it was 4–2. Then, crucially, Foxton heads went down.

WHERE THERE'S A WILSON THERE'S A WAY

In the second half Barry Hall went all out attack, and the team seemed to pass the ball to Wilson every time they got over the halfway line. A few minutes after the restart he scored a twenty-yard screamer, and after a tap-in a couple of minutes later it looked like the game was over. But there was more to come! In the last ten minutes Wilson struck twice more taking his tally to seven, instantly making him top scorer in the league. Also, setting a new record for goals scored in a single game by one player in the City of Salford Junior League. As one spectator said: 'It's like the lad's got magic feet.' His manager, Johnny Bryant Snr, agreed. He said: 'Players like Mikey Wilson are what this club is all about. He's a real prospect.' The opposition manager was gracious in defeat. 'That boy is something special and they earned their win,' he said, 'but I'm still proud of my lads. We defended well today.' Well, Eddie Roberts was certainly right about Mike Wilson, but obviously nobody had told him the final scoreline.

BRIAN HARGRAVE,
SPORTS REPORTER

SECOND HALF

THE WORLD BEGAN IN 1992

'You have to want to get up and go and train. Once that goes you should pack it in.'

Ryan Giggs

HELLO! HELLO!

It's the twenty-first of November 1992 and at this precise second in history all in the world of Mikey Wilson feels good, well, happy. You're an up-and-coming United SUPERSTAR in the making, about to make your first dramatic impact on the field of play. In the film of your life this is the beginning of that crucial second act: the mood of the piece is dark and mean, it's a typical, rainy, miserable English day, and the action starts – bam! – right in the middle of a league game. First there's a close-up of you sitting on the bench, waiting. Then a close-up of the Gaffer's face. He's chewing gum, fast. So fast he looks like he might just chew his jaw right off. Then there's another close-up, this time of Ryan Giggs, the team's fresh young inspiration, winner of last year's Young Player of the Year award and already favourite to retain it. (But not if you've got anything to do with it, right?) Ryan's running down the wing like his survival depends on reaching the touchline and putting in the perfect cross. The camera cuts from his face to his feet – nimble, quick, and so speedy his legs are just a blur, scissoring back and forward like a ballerina on a grassy green stage.

Here's the set-up as the camera zooms out from Ryan's boots to the action on the pitch: Manchester United, fallen giants, titleless for twenty-five years, struggling in mid-table mediocrity and already out of Europe, need a win (or perhaps some inspiration from a certain local lad?). You're in the match-day squad for the first time. So far, you've been sitting there all quiet, hands deep in oversized jacket pockets. Brain buzzing. Hands shaking. Toes numb. Things must be happening – you've heard cheers go up behind you, big guttural roars of excitement, encouragement or insult – but you're not really following the game. All that matters is whether you're gonna be part of it. If, after seventeen years five months and twenty-eight days of being a man-in-waiting, a pretend human being, if after all those years of pointless meaningless NOTHING existence, you're FINALLY gonna GET ON THAT FUCKIN PITCH AND PLAY.

And then it happens. The REAL beginning of your life.

With a twitch of his head and a wave in the direction of the battlefield, the Gaffer tells you to warm up. *O fuck,* you think, *O fuck O fuck O fuck fuck fuck.* You're a jelly baby. You can hardly run straight. You feel drunk. Maybe you are. You focus on the white paint down below and try to block everything else out but it's shit-your-pants time, this moment. Life-flashing-before-your-eyes stuff: your tiny, football-obsessed mind pulses with memories, in burst after dizzying burst, of everything that's ever meant anything: *first kick in the garden – in the playground – first goal for the school team – first time watching United – moving to a better team – moving to an even BETTER team – getting noticed by the scouts – Fergie at the front door – the world changing and twisting – through the gates at Old Trafford – work work work – hope – more work – more hope – wait wait wait wait wait and now READY.*

Your new best mate Nicky Butt is ready too, looking up at you each time you cross as you warm up, stretch, sprint. That bright look in his eyes meaning *Hey, it'll be us soon! Fuckin hell! We're gonna be real United players!* And he's right: nobody's gonna take it from you. You take every bad thought you've ever had and imagine yourself screwing it up into a tight ball and kicking it into the stands. Way up into row Z. Out of sight. You try not to think about the last week at all. The note on the fridge: DEAR WORLD: I'M LEAVING YOU BECAUSE I'M BORED. The police round till all hours the night before last, asking endless questions with no answers as Mum paced the kitchen, offering to make more tea for the pigs every five minutes, then forgetting she'd done it, then asking again. Uncle Si right there with you as you were asked, *What do you think it means? Do you think this might be a suicide note? Son, do you think your dad might have done something daft?* You won't let yourself think about all that. Why would you? On today of all fuckin days! You clench your fists tight, then unclench them. Up in the stand, you imagine Guy putting an arm around Mum and whispering in her ear, *Aren't you proud of our Mikey?*

Butty gets his debut first (with a cheeky look your way and a wink as he goes on – you're basically blood brothers now), then a few minutes later, it comes. You get the call to go over the top. Saddle up and ride. Put on your armour, strap on those shin pads and come join the war *against the mighty Oldham Athletic*: not historically a *major* foe, but not one you're about to underestimate either. Not after all this time. You're shaking, standing there waiting for the board to go up with your number on it. (Ha! Your *number*!) Right there you want to just say SCREW IT ALL and KISS THE GAFFER RIGHT ON HIS RUBY RED LIPS to say THANK YOU for picking you up out of the Salford dustbin, taking you far from the sad fucked up madness at home and making you a real person, in PARADISE. From now on, you'll be away mostly. On the move, with the team. This is the start of it all. The banter. The practical jokes and nicknames. Buddying up in bunks. Hotels, planes, buses, press conferences and interviews. Sitting in comfy chairs in front of all those cameras saying things like, *We're just taking one game at a time . . . the three points was all that mattered today.* And the best thing is, it'll all happen far from home. But your debut isn't a big moment for Alex Ferguson. It isn't the big speech you've been imagining. There's no great inspirational touchline talk. No real instruction or Churchillian call to arms. He just says, *That's you, son. Five minutes left, up front. See what ye can do.* Then you're nearly, very nearly, ON. A Manchester United player at last. Like Bobby Charlton. Like Bryan Robson. Like Ryan bloody Giggs. As your mouth is saying, *Yes, boss,* your brain is thinking, *If I piss myself in these shorts, will it be obvious on* Match of the Day?

It's mental, the way the mind works: you remember everything about that moment, the complete scene, right down to the details, like you're Mum's all-seeing, all-dancing God looking down on the pitch from his great seat in the sky, not a scared kid shivering on the touchline.

- Weather: light rain, slight easterly wind
- Temperature: bloody freezing
- State of pitch: muddy as fuck
- Footwear: brand-new boots, not yet broken in
- Underwear: lucky boxer shorts (happy Red Devils holding pitchforks), and
- Overwear: a shirt that's too big for you. Number 14. Tucked in.

(That morning you looked at yourself in the bathroom mirror, and even though you felt like a twat doing it, you actually said out loud: *You won't be a sub for long, Mikey Wilson!*)

You know the whole United team for the day, off by heart. You know the names of the opposition. A statto's always a statto, on the pitch or on the couch, right? You'll never forget any of these things you notice as you step over that white line onto sacred ground. They're gonna be the first notes in the scrapbook, after all. The *senior* one. (So far there's one from school and three packed youth books, which Mum keeps by the trophy cabinet in the front room, easy access for whenever she wants to show you off to visitors.) United have already won this particular battle by the time you put toe to turf – that's why they've brought you on. Coz it's 3–0, the game's nearly over, and nothing's at stake. One of your old poster heroes, Choccy McClair (who's already scored twice and is being rested) jogs off the pitch and slaps your hand, without speaking. The Gaffer barks an order, moving Ryan in behind. You think to yourself, *Good time to make a cameo*. You think to yourself, *Where the fuck is Dad?* And then you start running like hell.

For the first minute you're on the pitch Oldham are looking for a consolation. They have a corner, and you try to impress the Gaffer by defending instead of hanging around up field. So you hover at the edge of the area, wishing the ball towards you, wishing, wishing, then watching as it fizzes past your ears. Everything's happening. Everything's happening. You can't clear your head and THINK. The ball flashes into the box then right out again, getting punched away for a corner on the other side. Then, the opposite: everything's in slow-motion now.

They seem to take for ever to put it back into play, these Oldham lads.

What are they waiting for?

Don't they know how important this is?

When the ball finally gets flighted in, you hover and wish again, for just a touch.

For the first time in your life, you talk to God (Sir Matt Busby).

You ask him for a favour.

He answers instantly.

This time the keeper catches it, rolls it out of the United box and after a few passes side to side in defence the ball gets threaded through to Ryan out on the left side of the pitch. Along with thousands in the stands you shout out his name, then your own, then leg it as fast as you can. All the time shouting your names. *Ryan! Mikey's ball! Ryan! Mikey's ball! Pass it! Pass it! Over the top!* You're behind the chasing defender, but put your head down and pump your legs, so hard and high that you pass him, easy. Everyone in the crowd can see how much it means to the new local lad, and they're bound to remember you for the next game. Halo glowing, boots sparkling, Saint Ryan attempts a lob – it should be beautiful, exquisite, gorgeous, just right – but he's only a human being so even he makes mistakes, and he gets the pace of the pass all wrong. People in the stands groan, yell, roar advice. The ball bounces once, twice, three, four times. Bobbling nowhere, slow. About to go out for a goal kick at the other end of the field. But you know that whatever happens you're gonna get to that fuckin piece of air and leather before the centre-back shepherds it out of touch.

And you do. You sneak in and steal the ball from between his legs, turn and trap it, ready to look up and head for goal. Just like you did for the rezzies. (You're already seeing the screamer you're gonna score and considering celebration options. A tribute to the Gaffer? A novelty dance? A serious pout, hands on hips, to show YOU HAVE ARRIVED?) At that split second, the eyes of thousands of people are watching you. Cameras record, and if something happens they'll magic you into the homes of millions more on *Match of the Day* tonight. This is your chance. And what if you don't get another? So when the defender, Danny

Tredwell, whips the ball away from you and turns to take it away, you chase. You chase because you don't want everyone to see what you are: a boy among men. In your head the challenge is perfect – you slide in and take it back from him, safely, skilfully, as the crowd start up into wild applause.

But it isn't perfect at all. It's the opposite of perfect. You break the defender's right leg with a clumsy, flying, two-footed challenge from behind, and break one of your own too. The heavy bastard crashes down on top of your left knee and lets out a quiet cry, like a child, as the high-pitched SNAP of your bone sounds like a twig coming apart. As you hear that sound, Sir Matt hits the pause button on time, and that sound reminds you of one autumn day, years back, maybe ten years, when Dad took you and Guy out to the park on a Sunday morning. A rare thing. A one-off. The three of you, racing each other through the forest, seeing who could make it to the gate first, hearing lots of little snap sounds going off like fireworks beneath your feet, deep inside clusters of crackling leaves. You wonder if, wherever he is, Dad has heard that SNAP and thought of the same thing.

Back on the pitch, in the match, even the referee is stunned.

Seconds pass.

More seconds.

And more.

Still dazed, he looks down at you for what seems like for ever before he reaches into his pocket, draws out a red card and holds it up. You look away to avoid seeing it and ball up in agony, next to the defender, who does the same. The stretcher comes to take you both off. No applause. Not even any boos. The ref's face seems to say, *I'm sorry, mate, my hands are tied*. The crowd are in shock, people checking with each other: *What happened? He did WHAT? Who IS that kid anyway?*

Your debut lasts exactly one hundred and thirty-three seconds, from the moment you see Guy and your mum clapping and crying in the old family seats and tag with Brian McClair, to the moment you're back off the pitch asking the physio what's happened and wailing about how you can't feel your foot.

Later on, a doctor asks if that's a record. If it is, you don't want it. You're hoping that somewhere in a land far away, an alternate universe maybe, there's another match going on against Oldham Athletic, at that exact time. Maybe some *other* dickhead is making his Man United debut, lasting a hundred and thirty-*two* seconds before making his poor, long-suffering, kind, supportive, good soft sensitive Mum WHO DESERVES NO MORE PAIN IN THIS LIFE OR THE NEXT leak tears and tears and tears onto her cheeks, that will probably carry on for all time and spread, flooding the pitch, the whole stadium, all Manchester. Maybe if it was all happening to someone else as well, the sensation of sharing would make all this feel that little bit better. Maybe not.

And your big moment? On *Match of the Day* they run a feature about the worst debuts ever. Meanwhile, the Gaffer shocks the entire world of sport (and probably a few in other worlds too) by admitting that one of his own players has ACTUALLY MADE A MISTAKE. He says to the interviewer, *It's not like the lad. Madness, it was pure madness. I'll be speaking to him, there's no question aboot that, but for now our thoughts should be with the boy Tredwell and his family. I know I speak for everyone at this club when I say we all hope he gets better soon. Awful, so it is. Just awful.* The boys in the box can't get enough of it. They smell blood, drool, ATTACK. But if there's one thing worse than that lot, it's the press – so you know what's coming. Loads of stories about famous nightmare debuts in the history of the game (own goals, gaffes, goalkeeping errors), every last one with pictures of Muggins Wilson right there in the centre of it all, being carried off next to the man he nearly murdered.

YOU nearly murdered.

When Mum comes to visit, she's carrying her usual paper under her arm. And yes, the back page is a close-up of the guilty party. You're staring out at yourself in horror (at the pain or at something else?). The first thing Mum says is, *I wish your father was here. Gregory was always good in a crisis.* Talking like the fat bastard is dead already. As it happens, you're pretty sure your dad would be useless in this situation. Forcing yourself to sit up in bed, you feel your leg throbbing, making you dizzy, like maybe that delicate head of yours is gonna fall right off your shoulders. You wonder if Danny Tredwell's mum reads the same paper as yours. Then you consider sending flowers to Mrs Tredwell, with a note. You reject that idea. Then you remember who passed you the ball.

A month later everyone else on planet earth has forgotten that pass – according to the boys in the box there's *no stopping the Welsh boy wonder* after he scores a screamer against City in December 1992, the year the brave new world begins. Year One of the Premiership.

But you aren't going to forget that easy.

Are you?

SUNDAY 23 DECEMBER 2007
PREMIER LEAGUE

UNITED 2-1 EVERTON

RONALDO 22, 88 (PEN) **CAHILL 26**

ATTENDANCE: 75,749

GIGGSYWATCH – RonnyIsGod says: Typical – shite all game, misses shed load of chances, then gets an iffy pen at the death and United are rescued by Ronaldo – AGAIN. You gaylords are too busy bumming Giggs to notice but he's the luckiest United player EVER. Ronny rules.

Average Fan Rating: 8/10

Finally Mike Wilson began to feel festive, remembering all at once why he loved this club and also this game. Yet another match that looked like a draw, yet another that wasn't. Yet another late penalty, this time won by you-know-who and delivered sweet and straight into the top right corner by Cristiano Ronaldo. The United title challenge was building and, for the crowd, that early-season sluggishness was now just the memory of a mirage. It was never there. Most people can't believe they ever thought it was real. After eighty-eight minutes Ronaldo scored his second of the day and, yet again, Mike was hugging Terry. The Stretford End sang loud.

He plays on the LEEEEEEFT,
He plays on the RIIIIIGHT,
That boy Ronaldo makes Beckham look SHITE!

Terry glanced at Mike. 'They're saying Madrid might make an offer soon,' he said. 'But look around. Why would you leave?'

Ronaldo had been playing well. Mike gave a stiff little nod.

'He looks like he could live for a century, that boy,' said Terry. 'Play till he's fifty. He could even play more times than Giggsy, eventually.'

'Whoa there, soldier!' said Mike. 'Watch your mouth!'

Terry grinned. He listened to the explanation.

'Ronaldo's too smarmy, cocky, too self-obsessed. He'll never inspire love. Adoration, yes. Respect, maybe. But not love.'

'You get all lyrical when we score,' said Terry. 'You should hear yourself.'

Nothing gave Mike a rush like a United goal in the dying minutes. Nothing felt as good as being in that crowd, in that place. After United took the lead, Mike didn't even look round at the Three Unwise Men because absolutely nothing was going to spoil his mood. Nothing was going to take his happiness away. Even though he had reason to be annoyed, whatever the result of this game. Even though he'd been messed around, yet again. Even though nobody took him seriously and, really, that just wasn't good enough. He'd been turning it over in his mind before the game, and every so often the thought bubbled to the surface of his consciousness again. Some people (who would remain nameless) never believed he'd succeed. Some people (who would remain nameless) seemed to *want* him to fail. Now he was doing all the right things, being all green vegetables and early nights and clean boxers, they didn't know how to react. As United players dived on top of each other in celebration, Mike thought about how he might go away over Christmas. It wasn't too late. And really, who would care? The more he thought the bigger the thought became, until he forgot a goal had been scored and that he was supposed to be celebrating a last-minute winner. He was sick of people's excuses. He didn't do this to himself, did he?

'And they still love him,' said Mike, on the phone that night. 'It's amazing.'

'Amazing,' came the reply.

'After all these years,' said Mike.

'After all these years.'

'You've got to respect it,' said Mike.

'That's right,' said his father. 'You have.'

Both men stopped speaking.

In the silence, Mike got up, pressed the speakerphone button and walked over to the fridge, opening it and looking at what was inside.

'You still there, Mike?' asked his father.

'Do you think I should eat?' said Mike. 'I think I should eat.'

'I'm going surfing this weekend. The surf is great down here this time of year. The sea, Mikey. The blue of the sea, it's so light it's almost white. I wish you could see it.'

'You have to know where you're going before you can book your ticket. So where's my destination?'

Gregory coughed. 'Son, come on now. I have reasons for the things I do.'

Mike kept his tone light. It almost sounded like he was joking.

'Okay, do what you want – just stop telling me I've got to see things then. Either shut the fuck up about it or spill the big secret. Where are you – the Seychelles? The Cayman Islands? How about Jamaica – I hear the women are easy in Jamaica.'

Another silence on the line.

Mike closed the fridge. 'Can't be arsed cooking,' he said. 'Besides, there's nothing in. Fuck it. I'll get a takeaway instead. You want me to order you anything?'

'All right all right,' said Gregory. 'Fair point . . . But I tell you, Mikey, the surf out here . . . And the weather! Hey, do you think Ronaldo will go to Madrid?'

Mike didn't answer. Gregory continued. 'I reckon Fergie'll never let those bastards lure him away. Not even if they offer fifty million.'

Eventually, Mike replied. 'I don't know, Dad,' he said. 'I'm really not sure what'll happen in the future. And you know what? Sometimes I wonder whether there's any point thinking about it at all.'

THE KING OF CITIES

It's the summer of 1993, you're just about fit again after eight long months of hurt and hard graft, and you pick that casino coz you've heard a couple of the lads in the dressing room talking about the club hangouts. You don't get invited on the nights out yet; you're still pretty new, and the injury hasn't helped, but there'll be plenty of chances to make friends. And anyway, you might not-quite-accidentally bump into a few of the boys down there – maybe strike up a bit of chat. As you tell Guy on the phone the night before, when you're making plans: *Players need places where they're not gonna get snapped by photographers. Classy places, away from hangers-on. From scum prepared to suck anyone's cock to get their fifteen minutes, know what I mean?* Guy makes you promise not to take too much money along, but you laugh and tell him you couldn't take much if you wanted to. You're still getting paid in sweeties and the promise of things to come.

You go down there for eight – early but not too early, that's what you reckon. The best chance of blending into the background, slipping in among the crowds while the bouncers are distracted by all the big names and big wallets on their way in. But there's no queue when you arrive and the guys on the door see you coming. Your ID is shit. Obviously fake. Even with a few days of stubble and wearing one of Guy's suits the bouncers tell you to *fuck off back to school*. Your reaction only makes it worse. And even though Guy (who's forgotten to bring his ID, the idiot) is twenty-two today, he looks pretty young for his age. Which doesn't help. But just as you're giving up, some luck: *Bryan bloody Robson* crosses the car park on the way to his motor. You can't believe it. *I – I'm eighteen and a half!* you stutter, pointing at him. *Ask the team captain!*

The bigger bouncer looks at you carefully. Brings his face down to meet yours. *Oh yeah?* he says. *You play for United? What, the under-elevens?* It's a weak joke but the guy's made himself laugh, and the other one has an idea. *Hey, Robbo!* he shouts into the night. *This boy says he plays for United. Is he telling porkies?* The world slows to a stop. You pray to Sir Matt. Then Captain Marvel turns round, stands still for a second, looks over at you, you wave, and he makes a decision. *Plays for the reserves,* he says. *Nice lad.* There's no way he could have recognized you from so far away, but who cares? The team's gonna win the league. Robbo feels all right. And now he's done his good deed for the year. *All right, kid,* says the bigger one. *But no trouble, or else you'll be out on your arse.* He lets Guy in as well. Guy grins, gives the thumbs-up, pats you on the back and says, *Nice one*. You want that to happen every night.

First you have a couple of drinks at the bar, where they don't seem worried about your age at all. If you're in, you're in, that's how it seems. The first drink goes down fast. So does the second. Most of the time you're sitting there going over the scene in your mind. YOU CAN'T BELIEVE YOU'RE HERE. Thinking about what to do with yourself while you're waiting to get found out and dragged away from this big glitzy palace of gold and red and velvet and dapper suits and split-up-the-side dresses and green card tables, and back out onto the street where you belong. But soon you relax and forget you were ever anywhere else. You're knocking them back, toasting the future. Toasting every damn thing you can think of. *To birthdays every day!* says the birthday boy. *To world domination!* says you. *To getting filthy rich!* says him. *To five girlfriends at once!* says you. Then the two brothers discuss your great career. How many times you've spoken to the Gaffer, what he's said to you, what the man behind the headlines is really like. You don't say anything about how you're getting on with the other lads, but you don't need to. Guy guesses without even being given a hint. Which, if you think about it, is enough to make you bawl.

No other players have turned up yet, but really, family is all that matters, and Guy's the only family you need. (Mum's at home where it's sulks all round, boxes of tissues and crying at the soaps.) You chat away with your big brother, living the life. You even mention what you think Dad would make of all this, and decide the old bastard would be into it (it's the first time you've referred to him in months, and even now you can't say his actual name). The world seems like a heaven. One with a funk soundtrack – snare drums a-clacking; bass guitars a-slapping. While the soundtrack plays, barmaids smile and make sure you have enough to drink. They all make like you're rich and famous, especially after you say you're down for the night with a few first teamers. You drop a few names, but not too many. Say you're waiting for Ryan (which always gets people going). You play it pretty cool. Like it's no big deal. *Is there anything else I can get for you gentlemen?* asks a blonde one. *Are you here for the night, gentlemen?* asks a brunette. *Are you feeling lucky, gentlemen?* says a redhead. *Well, gentlemen, have fun at the table tonight. I hope lady luck is with you.* The redhead is all smiles. Everyone is. The smiles say, *This is a happy place, gentlemen. A happy place. A place of dreams come true.* The redhead lets a finger or two linger just too long at the base of the drink as Guy puts his hand round to pick it up. Or is that just you imagining it?

Every time the redhead says that word – 'gentlemen' – Guy smiles. *I could get addicted to that*, he says, laughing. *Do you think she'll go out with me?* You could just agree; it's obvious he's not being serious, but he's still with Sally, he's *always* got somebody, and the sound of his voice makes you want to attack. So you laugh, all cold. *Yeah right*, you say. *Course she will. Coz she's not told to flirt and get us drunk and stupid, is she? She's just being nice because she likes us. She wants to meet us for a drink after her shift finishes, tell us her troubles. Maybe fuck one of us. Maybe both of us. Maybe at the same time, if we let her. One at each end.* You act like you hate Guy sometimes.

Okay, Mikey, he says. *She's probably not interested. But maybe she is! Whatever, you don't have to be a dick about it.* There's a moment where you stare at each other, neither wanting to be the first to give in. Then you both crack up laughing and Guy orders another round. *Two pints of Boddies*, he tells the same barmaid, totally straight face. *Shaken, not stirred; okay baby?* That big brother of yours, he's so funny you think you might actually wet yourself. For a second, you think you have.

Guy's always been a bit of a lightweight, so after a few pints he's already letting his tongue loose. You're trying to talk about training, about the goal you scored (a one-two with this other kid who's just joined, which makes you feel kind of old), but he keeps interrupting, saying how you only ever talk about one thing. You're full of shit these days, says your brother, and do you ever think about *him*? Actually, what do you even *know* about him? Do you even know what he does in a working day? That hurts, coz you do know, but you take the insult like a proper man. You don't need a fight in here. You wanna come back – make friends, become a regular, slap the arses of the barmaids and have a laugh with them later on this season, the next, and the next after that. Book it out when you win the treble. Buy drinks for everyone. You wanna come back and buy the place.

So you keep everything friendly. *Well, that kind of talk's no good for a night out*, you say, all upbeat. *Come on. We're here to have FUN*. Guy's still stony-faced, but you're not gonna let him spoil your big night. Your first night out in months, for Chrissakes. Your leg back to full strength and a whole career ahead of you. Guy's on the edge of his high stool, at the bar. Making to leave? Why? You might have missed something. Fuck it. *Hey, gorgeous*, you say, smooth and sultry. *I'm sorry. You're the best brother in the world. Lemme give you a kiss.* Then you lean in, slow. As if you might actually slip the tongue in. That always cracks him up. *All right!* he screams. *Leave it out! Leave it out!* And – phew! – you're back in the game. Still, a couple of near-disasters tonight already.

A little later Guy takes off his tie and pulls open the top button of his shirt. Another couple of drinks get drunk. Then you suddenly get an idea and you HAVE to act on it. Your brother's feeding you some lame story about a customer who wanted to pay him *in kind*, which is *obviously* a lie. (Everyone knows those I've-got-a-faulty-boiler-and-just-wish-some-big-strong-man-would-come-and-fix-me women don't really exist.) So you cut him off mid-sentence and drag him away from the bar. You push him right over to the counter and tell him to empty out his wallet. You say, *Hey, do you ever think about just risking* EVERYTHING? Before he can answer or complain you've grabbed the money out of his hand and have half a week's wages turned into chips. Then you head to the roulette table and place them all on red.

The wheel spins round. The ball bobbles up and down between the numbers, rattling around. As the crackling noise slows down it's like people from all around the casino are leaning in, getting sucked into your table. These people, they can smell action. Everyone's trying to get a good look, not knowing whether they want you to win or lose. Guy looks like he's gonna have a heart attack. If you lose, he's gonna *batter* you. The bill hasn't been paid yet, it's all been going *on the tab, darlin*, and you need Guy to settle it. So you hold your drink tight to your chest and, for the second time in one night, you make a wish. (To Sir Matt again, obviously.) And for the second time in one night, your wishes are answered.

The little ball settles on red.

Sound as a pound! Drinks all round!

You shout it out, glass to the skies, then notice the rhyme.

Ha!

You gather up the chips and shove them all back on the table.

Then you win again.

It falls on red.

And again. And again.

On magic, magic red.

Guy's been frozen still right by you, like he doesn't even *understand* what's been going on. It's all been so fast. Seconds, that's all. No more. But then he gets it, this situation, and he takes charge. He says, *Mikey, this is a fuckin . . . no shit . . . stone cold MIRACLE going on here! A* MIRACLE*! But we've gotta STOP.* He holds his arms out at his sides, hands outstretched, fingers splayed – like he's trying to stop the world spinning. Finally he says, *Come on, let's fuckin DO ONE!* So the winnings are grabbed and cashed in, then Guy pays the bill, a dazed look in both your eyes. You're dizzy with it all. How much have you won? You don't even know. You just know it's more than you can carry, more than you can ever spend, you're sure of that. You're gonna be rich, for ever! (Mum's gonna get that Merc. And Audi. And Jag.) Next thing you know, you're stumbling out of the casino, trying to be all polite, but laughing and tripping over your words, hearing the bouncers call you *a pair of dickheads* and saying you'll never get back in. But who cares? You're outside, free, where it's all dancing and howling at the moon and singing *This is the* *oooone, this is the ooone, this is the oooooone* while doing the Stone Roses monkey dance. The night is clear and cool, Manchester looks good. It's the king of cities. *You should have asked that barmaid out*, you say, with a smirk. *I think she would've shagged you.*

It's a bit of a walk to the bus stop, and after a while you calm it, the two of you. Adrenaline seeps out into the darkness. Lactic acid leaks round your bodies, making arms and legs shaky. There's silence. It's becoming real, what's happened. You've not been so happy in . . . in . . . you don't even know. And you want to share it. As you walk on in the direction of home you reach out to your brother. *That feeling, Guy, you know . . . when the ball falls in the right place on the roulette wheel . . . that feeling . . . it's just like the one you get when you've scored a goal. Hey, Guy! Hey! Now you know what it's like to be me!* Guy staggers on, a bit ahead. *Fuck off*, he says. *Fuckin idiot. Just leave me alone, okay? You're hammered.* You're losing him, so you try another one of your greatest hits. *That's not true!* you say. *I haven't had a cunt all night drinkstable! I mean, er, I'm not as thunk as you drink I am!* This time, he doesn't laugh. Doesn't even smile. *Goodnight, knobhead*, he says. *See you later*. And he leaves. Guy goes back to Sally's place. You return to the old room and, as you're walking back, you wonder what life would be like if Guy just kept walking and never turned around.

The next day, all the talk is of your great night out, how much you won, what you're gonna spend it on, and when you're going back to the casino. You've had more good times, together, in the last month than in the whole of the last year, which has mostly been spent trying to drag yourself back to fitness. But life's opening up again now. The good times are on their way back.

For me it's like, where were you when Diana died? When Kennedy was shot? Where were you on the twenty-fifth of January 1995, United versus Crystal Palace, when Cantona kicked out in London? Well, I was on a rare day off from football duties – so I was in the pub.

Back then, when I was still in what Uncle Si called *the prime of my glorious career*, I hired out my season ticket for a tidy profit. When I was still a player, why would I need my seats in the granny stand? They'd only be going to waste every week. (At this time, Guy took Sally's brother Danny for a while. Even though he was one of those I-don't-really-support-anyone-I-just-hope-*sport*-wins types and didn't deserve to go.) Besides, if you weren't *playing* for United, why would you want to make the hurt worse by being so close to it all? But sometimes, just sometimes, I liked to watch matches on a big screen, with real fans, the ones that can't afford season tickets or don't get the chance to buy one. Among ordinary people, like I used to be. I wanted to hear the gossip. See who they rated and who they didn't. Players pretend not to care about these things – we say we don't read the press, don't listen to the phone-ins, don't follow every word said about us, everywhere, all the time. But we're liars, every last one. Actually, some of us? Lying's the only thing we really know how to do.

Back in the mid-nineties the evening games were shown on a dodgy foreign channel the landlord at this pub near Old Trafford linked up on match days. (The pigs knew about it. Half of them came in to watch the games, never once having to dip into their pockets.) I went to the pub to get a taste of that United atmosphere, but kept my profile low, did nothing to draw attention. Wore a cap and sunglasses. Stayed quiet. Course, the team was doing great, even though I was out injured – once we broke the twenty-six-year duck in the league, all of a sudden it seemed like we could win everything. In 1994 it was the double. The last great hurrah of the United Old Guard, who won the league at a canter and smashed Chelsea in the cup 4–0, with just a hint of youthful promise still waiting, mostly, in the wings. Then the Gaffer sold three big names and bought nobody, and all the talk on the radio, the box and the terraces was of the United tradition of putting faith in young players. The last quarter-decade of failure and mistakes was forgotten fast. Everyone wanted that time gone from their minds.

While I was healing, building my fitness back up, every United goal scored was pain as well as joy. Every extra cap, every prize or trophy won by one of the boys I'd come up with killed me a little bit. They'd even given the group a name. They called us (or them) 'Fergie's Fledglings', an oh-so-clever nineties take on Frank O'Farrell's 'Fledglings' of the dirty seventies (who have been forgotten). Now, nobody pays attention so nobody knows, but *that* one was an oh-so-clever take on the Busby Babes. And, for now anyway, I wasn't one of them. I had nightmares. Fantasies I can't even describe. I prayed for crippling injuries to ruin the careers of anyone who was at United when I was. Becks, Butty, Scholesy. Ryan Giggs. Eric Cantona.

Cantona: the footballer philosopher, the rebel, the cult hero who proved that not all players are thick pieces of shit good for just one thing. That collar up, scoring all those goals and then opening his arms and welcoming in his boys for a hug and kiss. He should have been my hero. Guy said to me once, *I don't get it. Why don't you worship this feller?* I almost told him, but how could Guy understand? He'd just taken on another three employees – the expansion of the Wilson Empire, he called it – and him and Sally were talking about kids. How many. What they were gonna be called and how they were gonna *give their child the best womb experience*. Meanwhile, I was a hundred years from all that. I couldn't worship anyone. As I settled on my lucky stool to watch United vs Palace on that winter night, unknown, hunched in the corner, hoping no one would recognize me, I remembered speaking to Cantona on the training ground. He smiled and just said, *It's okay, Mike*. I asked, *What? Is there a problem?* Then he smiled again. They say there was anger in him, even in those early days. That's why he'd left France. And once something's inside you, it's inside you for life.

People have forgotten this now, but first he got sent off. That was plenty for a set of bad headlines the following day, and probably a fine as well as a ban. At the second it happened I was packed in with a couple of hundred drunken Mancs shouting *the reeeefereeeee's a WANKER*. Eric headed towards the touchline, proud, unbowed. I struck up a bit of talk with some regulars, and they reckoned it was gonna be okay. Even though we were down to ten men. Actually, maybe COZ we were down to ten men, and in hard times good men pull together, right? I tried to convince myself that this, here, now, watching on the screen with everyone else in this battered old building with beer-damp seats and piss-wet toilet floors, was better than being on the pitch. As Cantona stepped off the green grass, heading for that tunnel, I turned on my bar stool and ordered a pint, and another one, for luck. Sometimes, I thought, I could *make* bad things happen.

By the time I turned back to the screen the pub had gone silent, in shock, as they watched the grainy pictures of Eric Cantona flying into a fan, in a rage. Over and over again. First in real time. Then in slow-motion. Then in super-slow-mo, the victim's face screwing up tight as all the ones around him opened wide. The commentators from Greece or Turkey or fuck-knows-where were so surprised that they forgot to talk, and when they remembered again they had no words to explain what was happening. No one had ever seen anything like it. Meanwhile Paul Ince raced over, fists first, brain second, and then the stewards and police piled in. Cantona was lost under the scrum of officials and fans. The temperature in the pub dropped. One or two called him a hero but most thought he'd been an idiot. He'd thrown away the title for nothing. Who was gonna be the great team leader now? One feller said he'd never watch United again, he was so ashamed, though nobody believed him. I finished my drinks in silence as around me noisy fights kicked off, and conspiracy theories were born about what really happened. Why had he done it? What made him so angry? Some folks claimed they could lip-read, and a lot of crazy shit was going around.

The man told Eric to *fuck off back to France*

or the man told Eric he'd had his mum last night and she *was good at sucking my cock*

or the man told Eric he was *fat*

or Eric had a history of being messed up in the head, the suits at United had been covering it up for years, and this was his public mental breakdown

or Eric recognized the lad, who was actually French, the two of them had a full-on scrap in a bar in 1989, and he was just going back in to finish off the job

or (and God knows where this one came from) Eric was taking his revenge on the supporters of Crystal Palace coz his granddad was murdered by three skinheads from the area in 1929 and he'd promised the old guy on his death bed that *the Cantona family will have their revenge*.

The rumours hung in the air, then spilled out the door and spread through the city.

I left the pub thinking maybe it was time I gave up drinking for good. It wasn't good for a footballer. It had finished the careers of plenty of United boys in the eighties, and you have to learn from mistakes of others or risk making them yourself, right? I wanted to be playing for years. Decades. For ever. Unlike Cantona, who retired suddenly at thirty as if it was an easy thing to do, muttering about how the game had gone corporate (didn't stop him doing Nike adverts later), I NEVER wanted to abandon the club. (In the end even Cantona compared giving up United to giving up heroin.) Right then, it felt like an easy decision, one I was sure I'd stick to. No more drinking: that was it. And DEFINITELY no more pissing my money away in casinos and betting shops. Passing the Legends Takeaway, hands in pockets, waiting for the riots to start, I was a better man already.

I spent the next couple of days on my own, doing training exercises.

That whole time, I was sure. Focused. Determined not to fuck it all up like United's latest hero had done, on a cold night in London. And why? For what? A whole lifetime, ruined in a few seconds. How could anyone do it? When Eric pulled up a chair at the press conference and spoke to the media in that slow, deliberate French drawl, talking like a madman, I just *knew* he'd never play again – I watched the video I'd recorded until I could recite the script by heart. *When ze seagulls . . . follow ze trawler . . . eet eez because . . . zey sink sardines will be srown into ze sea.* I nearly laughed myself to death, my mind already on my own glorious return, and how I'd fill the hole he left in the team, if only I could get another chance. Ha fuckin ha. How wrong can you be?

Fans followed Eric to his court appearance in glamorous Croyden, supporting him like he was a political prisoner fighting for fuckin freedom or something. Eric Mandela. Eric Ghandi. Eric bloody Luther King. You don't know this already? They chanted his name every game he was gone, they begged him to stay at the club, so did Fergie, and eventually he got his second chance. On the day he came back from the ban there was a billboard outside Old Trafford which became famous. (In those days, two teams played at Selhurst Park. Crystal Palace and Wimbledon.) The poster read: *We'll never forget that night at Selhurst... when you scored that thirty-yard screamer*, talking about Cantona's other, more successful appearance at the same place that season. What a lark, eh? Crowds gathered round and took photographs of it. Adults laughed like children. Inside the ground, on his first game back, he set up one goal and scored a penalty, strutting around the pitch in celebration like he'd just been on a long holiday and finally decided to grace the commoners with his presence again. The game was against the Bin Dippers, too, so he got total, instant redemption. The kids in the stands painted GOD IS BACK on their faces and cheered his name. Fergie's Fledglings - with Ryan right in the middle - gathered round when the goal went in and he hugged them tight tight tight. It was the beginning of a beautiful new chapter.

The night of his great return I blacked out, hit my head and woke up in hospital shouting about seagulls and trawlers till the nurses shut me up and put me to sleep. When I woke up I saw a doctor passing my bed and called out, *Hey, fuckface! I'm dying here.* I picked up a biography of George Best and hit my bedside table with it. (Where did the book come from? Had someone been to visit?) My brain was marshmallow. *Hey, don't go away!* I shouted at the doctor. *Hey you! You! I play for United you know!*

SUNDAY 10 FEBRUARY 2008
PREMIER LEAGUE

UNITED	**1-2**	**SHITTY**
CARRICK 90		**VASSELL 25** **BENJANI 45**

ATTENDANCE: 75,790

GIGGSY WATCH – SpiritofMunich_58 says: I just wanna be clear. Don't anyone DARE slag off the boys today. Nuff love to the whole United family. Busby Babes RIP. Never forget.

Average Fan Rating: 5/10

Mike Wilson was feeling thoughtful. He arrived at Old Trafford and took in the scene.

Some people said all clubs were the same these days. Some said they were all about money. That the heart had gone out of the game – too many millionaires, too many lost children from faraway lands hopping between clubs every time the transfer window opened, trying to learn English and get used to the cold. It was a business now, a slave trade in millionaires, a twenty-four-hour, non-stop sporting cabaret puppeted by the men in grey suits – Mike's Granddad Peter wouldn't recognize it. Some people said clubs like United weren't what they used to be. Especially since the Americans came to Old Trafford to suck out the profits and turn plus signs to minuses. The Glazers, United's new royal family, the pantomime villains, all *franchise* this and *crucial Asian markets* that, and trying to remember not to say *soccer* to the media. Loading the club with debt, siphoning millions for themselves while claiming to care. Some people said it made United the same as Liverpool, and Chelsea, and everyone else. It made them just a company. But Mike was sure that today the doubters would all be proved wrong. So far, contrary to the scare stories he'd read that made the opposition sound like animals, supporters on both sides of the divide were doing themselves and their city proud.

'Just you wait,' Guy had said. 'When the moment of truth comes, Manchester will stand together.'

Mike wished his father could have been there to see it. Even if he'd just flown in and right out again afterwards, not telling anyone else he'd come home, it would have been worth it. The old man would have been able to tell his friends in the middle of God-knows-where that yes, he was there on that great day. Mike imagined Gregory leaning lazily over a margarita at the end of a Caribbean bar.

'I went to see the Munich anniversary game,' he'd tell the barman on his return, 'and I remembered why Manchester is the best place on earth. Went with my youngest son, Mikey. He played for United, you know. And he's doing really good these days. Made a good life for himself.'

A tear would creep out of the corner of Gregory's eye. 'Fuck it,' he'd say. 'I'm proud.'

This and other daydreams zipped through Mike's brain, bleeding into each other, mixing, reforming stronger. Sometimes they were so powerful that they took Mike far from wherever he was, whatever he was doing. In his mind, the imagery was clear. And, though he was far from any coastline, as he breathed in and looked up at the famous gates, he was sure he could smell the sea.

Around the outside of Old Trafford, before the game, red, white and black flags read: BUSBY BABES PLAY ON IN HEAVEN, MAN UNITED 1958 RIP, with all the names of the dead players listed below. Mike knew every one of them. He knew how they felt when they put on that jersey. A sickening, shooting pain rushed through his leg. He leaned forward to read the homemade sign a fan had attached to the club gates.

THE LOST LADS OF MUNICH

GEOFF BENT, 25

left-back, understudy to Roger Byrne and Bill Foulkes

ROGER BYRNE, 28

left-back, Club Captain, England international, born in Manchester

EDDIE COLMAN, 21

right-half, born in Salford

DUNCAN EDWARDS, 21

centre-forward, England international, one of the finest footballers of all time

MARK JONES, 24

centre-half, England schoolboy international

DAVID PEGG, 22

outside-left, made United debut at seventeen. England international

TOMMY TAYLOR, 26

centre-forward, England's main striker, 112 goals in 166 United appearances

LIAM 'BILLY' WHELAN, 22

inside-right, Rep of Ireland international, 43 goals in 79 United appearances

All those names, which had not been forgotten. And all the others who also died that day also faithfully documented, typed out and placed in the centre of all the tributes. No one had been left out. The list of names was long, and he was keen to get inside the ground, but Mike made himself read every one. Take it in properly. Every life was worth the same, he thought. The pilot, the players. Even the media.

TOM CABLE, *cabin steward*
ALF CLARKE, *Manchester Evening Chronicle, journalist*
WALTER CRICKMER, *Manchester United club secretary*
TOM CURRY, *club trainer*
DANNY DAVIES, *Manchester Guardian, journalist*
GEORGE FELLOWS, *Daily Herald, journalist*
TOM JACKSON, *Manchester Evening News, journalist*
ARCHIE LEDBROOKE, *Daily Mirror, journalist*
BELA MIKLOS, *travel agent who arranged the trip (survived by his wife, also on the flight)*
CAPTAIN KEN RAYMENT, *co-pilot*
HENRY ROSE, *Daily Express, journalist*
WILLIE SATINOFF, *United fan, friend of Matt Busby*
FRANK SWIFT, *News of the World, journalist (also former Manchester City and England goalkeeper)*
ERIC THOMPSON, *Daily Mail, journalist*
BERT WHALLEY, *chief coach*

So, thought Mike. There was a City player on that plane too. He breathed out hard. Underneath that old clock, eternally stuck in time on the sixth of February 1958, he imagined describing the scene outside Old Trafford to his father, or Guy. He thought about what words he might use. If words could describe it at all.

By the club shop, a huge photograph was displayed of the Busby Babes team line-up, taken in the moments before kick-off in their final match, which they won against Red Star Belgrade. Fifty years later, the image had been transformed into colour and plastered above the sign: MANCHESTER UNITED. Mike hoped they would keep it there after the anniversary. Nearby, old black-and-white photos of the players were laid out on the pavement, crowds of children asking parents if they ever saw the Busby Babes play. Messages read: 'Hoping you rest, you were the best.' Mike thought of his father again, and his mother, and what she said when anyone asked what happened to her husband. 'We always remember. But we have to move on.'

As he passed through the turnstile, handed over his ticket, bought a programme and moved towards his seat, Mike wondered how it would go today. There had been so much speculation. A group of City supporters had begged in vain for a minute of applause instead of the planned silence, to cover the abuse that was surely going to come. Mike thought, Would anyone spoil it? Would some idiot shout out BOLLOCKS or imitate the swooping Munich airplane wings? But as the minute's silence went on, the matching blue and red scarves held high, he concentrated on those twenty-three lost lives of 1958, the team that fell out of the sky. Players born thousands of miles from Manchester, who'd played for three, four, five clubs all over the world, stood in silence, beginning to realize what it meant to be in that place. With those people. Remembering.

The crowd were in sombre, respectful mood. Even the Three Unwise Men's attitude was different for a while. Bill muttered approval.

'Proper fitting tribute, this,' he said.

His voice cracked as Sir Alex Ferguson and City's manager, Sven Göran Eriksson, laid memorial wreaths to mark the occasion. Around Bill, fans who had sat in the surrounding seats for years said 'hear hear' and forgot how they usually felt about him. It didn't seem like the match mattered at all, as a thirty-four-year record of no losses to City at Old Trafford blew away and nobody in the stadium seemed to mind.

During the game, the team themselves seemed strangely thoughtful too, as if the emotion of the occasion was too much, some wandering aimlessly about the pitch in the replica Busby Babes kit made especially for the day, as if they didn't know which decade they were playing in. The weight of responsibility. Mike could understand it. The Three Unwise Men (including Bill, who reverted to standard behaviour shortly after kick-off) said the team looked like they didn't care. How could a bunch of Portuguese, Brazilians, Argentines and Serbians even *understand* what was happening here? But Mike saw them, he was there too, and he was certain. They wanted to win – they *needed* to. United had fifteen shots to City's eight, but even Ryan's volley got turned over the bar. (Mike thought, How perfect would *that* have been?) After half-time, when most people expected an onslaught spurred on by a powerful blast from the Ferguson hairdryer, it didn't come. Some days it just wouldn't; Mike knew that better than most.

United's last-minute goal was just a consolation, coming after the Three Unwise Men, and others, had left to beat the crowds.

'We did those boys proud,' Mike said to Guy on the phone that night. 'The players and the crowd. We sang! We paid tribute! We didn't CARE about the title race. Some things are more important . . . I tell you, you should have been there.'

Mike could hear Guy's baby daughter, Millie, crying for Daddy. Mike kept talking, louder now, to be heard above the noise of the little girl.

'All right, so we lost,' he said. 'But when you're part of a family, nobody really wins or loses. Everyone's on the same side.'

Mike imagined his brother listening to this speech on the other end of the line, while Guy sat in his back garden, looking out onto his well-trimmed hedge, quiet street and sober village where he and Sally had recently settled. He imagined Guy listening hard. Mike thought his brother might notice how he'd never really talked like this before, about anything, except maybe in 1999 before the European Champions League final. He hoped his brother might pass Millie over to Sally so he could concentrate properly on the phone conversation. At that moment, Mike suddenly got the urge to mention their father. To tell Guy that he'd been in contact with him for years now, and to ask whether maybe he'd ever heard from the old man, too? To see whether he'd been keeping a similar secret all this time. To ask whether he thought that maybe this was the year he'd give it all up and come home. He decided to say nothing, but promised himself he'd mention it next time they spoke.

Later that night, Mike lay on his mattress. There was nothing like grief to bring a community together, he thought, as he drifted towards sleep, staring upward. And old Sir Bobby, he remembered, like the head of the family at a funeral, had been dignified as he headed into the ground with his wife. The crowd all clapped as he smiled, gave a sad wave, then disappeared inside. The crowd sang his name. Mike was so jealous he could hardly breathe. Of Sir Bobby, yes, of his record and history, which no one could take away. But of the dead players, too. What a wonderful thing, he thought. To die like that, in service, like a soldier, and to always be remembered. He wished he could climb back in time and make it to Munich. Sneak onto the plane and wait. It was something Guy and Sally, having emigrated out of Manchester proper, could never understand.

Mike considered putting the old United posters back up on his ceiling. Looking up at the dirty white colour above, stained and cut up and peppered with bits of Blu-Tack, he wondered if he'd been rash, taking them all down like that. Why shouldn't he be proud? Half awake, half asleep, he rolled over onto his side, curled up and drifted off into thinking the kind of thoughts that passed whole days of his life away, sometimes without him even noticing.

The phone rang three times that night. He didn't pick it up.

OUT ON LOAN
AT THE EDGE OF THE WORLD

The middle of November 1993, it finally comes. The hand on the shoulder. The sympathetic tone. The talk from one of the coaches you never even liked and expected to leave behind on your way to immortality. It's been nearly a year since your debut and in that time there's been a lot of sleepless nights and a real fight to get fit. A lot of time in the gym and precious little result, with no prospect of a breakthrough since you returned to the rezzies a few months back. Form hasn't exactly been sparkling. Maybe you just need more time to get back up to Premiership speed. But even if you'd been breaking records, would it have made any difference? Your injury came just as United finally reached the promised land, the first ever Premiership title. And timing, as Uncle Si used to say, is sometimes all that matters. The team's been doing just fine without you, the team is finally flying. So it's been on its way for a long time, this. But you still don't wanna see it coming.

You can admit it now: your behaviour has been textbook from day one. You've been predictable. You've made classic mistakes. You've kidded yourself it's all gonna be fine simply coz you want it to be. In November 1993 you really truly one hundred per cent believe you're on the way back. You think you're just days from the first goal of hundreds and the love of the Old Trafford crowd, who'll welcome back the talented local lad who looked like he'd never play again. Your debut will be forgotten, no more than a footnote in your twenty-four-carat career. A tricky, end-of-round thing on a TV sports quiz. One of those quirky, you'll-never-guess questions, which will stump everyone – then the quizmaster will laugh coz it's all so crazy and unbelievable that the great rough diamond Mikey Wilson (er . . . that's *Sir Mike* to you, dear commoners) nearly didn't make it in football.

After the talk from the coach, you tell yourself this is a new beginning, and that's what the other young United players tell you as well. The young kids, the other ones on the fringes. They sound like you used to, pleased to be rid of guys being shuffled onwards and downwards. *Just for a while, Mikey*, they say. *Just to get a bit of first team action, get yourself to full strength, then you'll be back, for sure.* And yeah, that does happen a lot. Christ, nearly *everyone* gets sent out on loan at some point. (Not Ryan though.) You can't just expect to walk into the first team. No one does that. (Except Ryan.) You're just heading south for a while, that's all. That hand on your shoulder: you pretend it doesn't bother you. You pretend you don't even care. *Where am I going?* you ask, all cocky, winking at the coach, whose name you keep forgetting. *Somewhere hot? Shall I pack my flip-flops?* The coach replies, *Keep talking like that, sunshine, and it'll be a long fuckin holiday.*

Before you know what's happening, you're flying down there, scraping through a medical, shaking some hands, getting whisked around a strange new stadium, whipping back north to Mum's to pack some things, telling her you'll be okay and not to worry (she cries, but then she cries at everything these days), and then you're booking a hotel room near Plymouth Argyle's ground. No point renting a flat or committing to anything major – you won't be there long. Better to spend a bit more, get a nice room, a place with a pool and gym. All the better for getting happy, fit, scoring some goals and getting back home fast. Besides, you've just had a big win at the casino. A BIG win. The biggest yet. So isn't it the sensible thing to spend it on a few luxuries? Isn't that the best thing for your career? The most economically sensible decision you can take? You're thinking about it when the phone in your room rings and it's Dad, the first contact since his disappearing act.

At first, you can't make sense of it. The sound of him. You feel like you're shrinking – what should you ask him first? What should you ask? But you don't get a chance to ask anything. Dad talks fast, making sure there's no space you can fill. (Which reminds you of something.) And he gives no explanation, no apology. He's drunk. He asks questions about your mum and your career and you forget to lie or ask where he is. You tell him about what's happened at United. You bawl. You tell him about Argyle. There's noise in the background, like he's talking to you from a bar. The line is distant. It crackles. *Listen, short* arse, he says, like he never left home. *After the last twelve months you're lucky anyone wants you, never mind a professional club. Snatch what you can and don't think twice!* All you can say is, *You fucking bastard, you're alive.*

What you mean by that is, he's alive and Uncle Si isn't. Just last week, ambushed by a heart attack while he was alone in the Wilson Electrics office, eight thirty at night, doing the accounts. A forty-seven-year-old man with no debts, no enemies, no skeletons waiting to burst out of the stationery cupboard.

At Uncle Si's funeral there were nearly too many people to fit in the church. People struggled to get in and had to stand at the back. One arm round Mum, Guy turned to you and whispered, *Some fan club, eh?* Christ, it wanted to make you bawl, it was the worst thing in the fucking world, but it was beautiful too. Still, you can't tell Dad that, can you? Whatever the old bastard's done, his big brother is gone for ever, and no one deserves to hear the news in that way. But who's gonna look out for you now? For Guy? For Mum? The world is full up with questions.

Dad is right about Argyle, though, so you decide to embrace this new thing. Not take any chances. Act right and hope. One of the other United lads tells you Plymouth is a nice place. He has mates down there, a cousin too. And he knows a defender who played for them for a season, then got snapped up by Everton. Or was it Colchester? He reckons you'll be all right. So, driving down the motorway, Dad and dead Uncle Si and Guy and Mum in your ears, you put the music up loud, singing along to the Super Manc Classix mix tape Guy made especially for you to listen to on this specific journey. He's doing a spot of DJing at this pub in town. The tunes on this tape morph into each other. Bit of the

Mondays. Bit of the Roses. You sing, *I AAAAM THE RESUREEEECTION AND I AAAAM THE LIIIIIIIIGHT!* When side one finishes you let out a roar. You shout at the top of your lungs, *Tuuuuune!* Then you flip the tape over. Your mind empties and is free free free as you belt out these songs, arse jiggling happily left and right in your seat. But after a few hours and a couple of times through the whole tape you realize just how far away this bloody place is, you start getting sweaty, your hands can't grip the wheel coz of the sweat and it doesn't feel like an adventure any more. You thought Plymouth was near London. It's pretty much Land's fuckin End, pretty much *France*.

As you tell Guy on the phone a few weeks later, it doesn't matter who the opposition is, the fans sing the same chant at every match. *Dirty northern bastards!* they belt out, pointing at the opposition fans. Coz everyone's northern to them, no matter where the other team is from. Manchester. Leeds. Birmingham. Cardiff. London. Southampton. Even Bristol and Exeter are dirty and northern from down there. *At least you aren't the only one,* says Guy on the phone, staying cheery. You answer, *Still, the dirtier and more northern you are, the worse it is.* Then Guy says he has to go. He's got things to do. Since Uncle Si's death, Guy's taken over the business. It's a small firm, but it's a hell of a big job for a man of twenty-three, especially given all the staff are older than him. Still, Guy says he's ready. And besides, as he tells anyone who asks, he feels it's his duty to uphold the family honour. You know he's gonna succeed. You even tell him that. But Guy seems to have less time for you these days, and even when he says he does, it's like you don't quite have his attention.

The strangest thing about the whole Argyle experience is it's actually all right being among people with different accents. If you weren't such a dick, crazy and homesick and always thinking about what's missing, you could make friends, get to know the places to go. The first few days you're there, you notice the weather is good, the people are friendly, and you walk down to the Barbican for a quiet pint, looking out onto the water and taking in the sea air. You think about how far it is to Europe. What it might be like over there. You look out onto the water and consider running away, just like Dad, to some far-flung place where drinks are cheap, the sun beats down and life is slow. (*Where the fuck is he? What made him go?*) Maybe you could swim to France, learn the language, call yourself *Jean-Pierre* and open the finest patisserie in Paris. You hear about that shit on the news all the time. People who just give it all up and go. Thinking about it, you get hot.

You've always been a footballer and always will be, but still, this thing rocks you. Everything in your life that used to be red is now green. Everything that was big and shiny and new and futuristic is now much smaller, and older, and it even *smells* different. At United the place smells of money that these boys don't even bother to dream about. Everyone's in the same scrappy position at Argyle. One-year, two-year contracts. Loan deals. Everyone trying for the same career kick-start that almost nobody gets. Older guys talk about dropping out, and other ways to live. Some are still thinking positive, but most don't reckon things are gonna get better. Argyle have been doing okay, but they've still got the likes of *York City* on the fixture list, for fuck's sake – when you think about turning out against York City you wonder how the hell you are gonna pretend that you actually give a shit whether the team wins or loses.

The manager at Argyle is Peter Shilton. He makes a real fuss of you, which gives you a tingle. Coz he's famous, that gives you something to tell the folks. *I'm working for the record holder for England caps,* you say, and Guy is pretty impressed by that. You even do a press call where you have to hold up the shirt with *Wilson – 11* on the back (your number!), shake the Gaffer's hand and tell local journalists how excited you are to be signing for such a big club. You aren't expecting all that – it's only a loan, after all; do they usually do that kind of thing? You don't know, but you're no idiot. You say to the press, *I hope to help the lads get Plymouth Argyle up where they belong. This club is a sleeping giant, but we're gonna wake it up.* Turns out, talking is easy. They ask you how it feels leaving your hometown club and you laugh and say, *Well, Home Park is my home now.*

That quote makes the papers the next day, which you buy three copies of, keeping one and sending one each to Mum and Guy, special delivery.

In the article in the *Herald* ('The Voice of Plymouth'), the manager hails your excellent youth and reserve team record, tells them how unlucky you've been with injuries, reminds everyone how very young you are (still only eighteen), and says he's sure you'll be a big success if you have some luck. He even hopes to make the move permanent if it goes well. *I hope so, Gaffer,* you said to him, forcing a grin. *Fingers crossed, eh?* All this time, through your own lies, you hear Dad's sandpaper voice. You're imagining him, belly out, in nothing but a pair of Bermuda shorts, right there, so close you can smell his breath. (Wherever he is, it's somewhere that serves bitter.) He's perched on a stool at his bar in the sun, one arm round some teenager, his other hand fondling a beer bottle. Shouting, *You're lucky anyone wants you!* Then diving into the pool, water rippling outwards as his feet scrape the bottom.

You're at Argyle seven or eight months. And in that time you go from being the exciting new signing to being simply ignored. First the manager thinks you just need to get up to match fitness so he gives you a run in the reserves, but performances don't improve. You score no goals in ten games and you're an unused substitute for the first team three times. Even when they're desperate they still don't use you. Then you injure your leg again in training – one day it just buckles, the same one – and you're out of action again. The doctor smiles sympathetically and explains that they might not have got to the root of the problem the first time. These things happen. (He says this as if it doesn't matter.) *Well, thank you very much*, you say, and limp out of the room.

So it's yet another training regime, another schedule, building the strength back up and watching everyone else run around while you can hardly walk. Even when you're finally healthy again, something isn't right. Sitting alone in your hotel room, or doing steady lengths up and down the swimming pool you know you can't afford to swim in any more, you try to work out what's wrong. Make sense of this problem, so you can solve it. But you're in another universe now, where the rules are different. There's no sense to anything. You're not as strong as you used to be. The pace is gone – it's like your limbs belong to someone else. Someone old, less talented, mortal. Sometimes you catch yourself dreaming of how things used to be. Or worse: dreaming of what might happen in the future.

One day, you hear a rumour going round the dressing room about who's gonna get the nod for a game. Your name comes up, you've had a good week in training, and the captain says he reckons you're gonna play. When the time comes, you check the team sheet. Scanning the paper for where they've hidden your name. You stand there for a long time before you can accept you've only made the bench. That night you skip watching from the dugout to go out on your own. (Which puts you on a warning from the manager.) By chance, later that night, some of the players come into the casino where you're drinking. They're celebrating a rare big win. Feeling like kings. Acting like twats. As if they're on their way to promotion when they'll probably get relegated instead.

You're on the slots when you see them, two quid still in there, money you don't wanna write off. But you sink your drink and leave before they recognize you. Sneak out of the place like a fuckin criminal or something. On the way home you almost phone Guy to tell him about Dad. Guy would know how to trace the old fucker, probably drag a few answers out of him too. But, you think, what if he calls the police instead? What if being found is the worst thing that could happen? What if Dad owes millions to some Manc gangster who'll chop off his fingers and feed them to him if he's ever found? Carve a swastika in his forehead and take him from behind? Leave him rotting on a pool table? You think of the consequences, then decide against calling Guy. It's not the last time you do this.

The next couple of weeks, you drift. And sometimes, sitting there in your stupid green tracksuit looking out at the other stupid players running up and down the stupid pitch who now ignore you or take the piss, you really do, genuinely, no-shit want to kill something. Coz until now you've kept believing the party line – that you're just coming back from injury, that's all, and you're still wanted at United. But you've not heard from anyone at the club in ages. Nobody tells you what's really going on, do they? If it's good news, every fucker wants to be first in the queue. If it's bad they just let you work it out for yourself, or else sit there like a dick not understanding why everything's sinking and you're sinking with it. One day, you finally fuckin realize you're not even wanted at Argyle. And meanwhile, the Ryan Giggs 1994 annual and calendar have both sold even better than expected, despite the fact that the subject barely does interviews or speaks in public. And when he does, it's in clichés and forward defensives. Ferguson is keeping him close, protected. Everyone knows it. The newspapers now call him 'Ryan's father figure' so often you can hardly bring yourself to read any more.

A few days later it's about halfway through some pointless midweek league game, and you're on the bench again. Argyle are losing – you don't care about that, but after this skinny local kid gets the nod to go on as a sub with ten minutes to go, you look around at the other boys in tracksuits and know you're not going to get on tonight. You think to yourself if you're not gonna play, then what are you doing there? Wasting your life, that's what! You need to get back home! So you stand, climb out of the dugout, take off your team jacket, leave it on the grass right there, walk through the corridors of the stadium, grab your stuff from the changing room, run to your car and put it roughly into gear, your insides hammering, hammering, hammering the walls of your chest. There are voices behind you – asking, *What the hell do you think you're doing, Wilson*? Asking where you're going, telling you to turn around or else not to bother coming back.

The voices get quieter, quieter, until you can't hear them any more. You stop at your hotel, throw everything into a suitcase, leave without settling the bill and drive overnight back to Manchester, stopping just once at a service station. You piss in the toilet's too-bright light and then sit dead-eyed in an empty café, eating a lukewarm burger before climbing back into the car. When you finally get to Mum's, you sneak in, quiet, careful not to wake her, crashing out asleep on your old bed just as the sun is coming up. Your last thoughts before falling asleep: *I'll go into Old Trafford in a few hours to explain that it didn't work out. I'll just tell them I need to be back at United. They'll take me. The Gaffer will understand.* But you sleep longer than you meant to, and the world has turned on its head by the time you wake up, groggy, mid-afternoon. You don't know it yet but Alex Ferguson's heard the news and already started the paperwork. He's officially gonna release you. You're already halfway out of the system and onto the streets, with no agent, no job, no nothing.

For the next twenty-four hours, no one will answer your calls.

So you go on the bender to end all benders, blowing every last penny in your wallet in the casino, throwing down bets you know have no chance of winning, to bring oblivion closer, fast. It can't come fast enough. You will it towards you with every bet. It's not fun. It's not supposed to be. The bouncers, the same ones who let you in when Robbo gave you the nod, who told you to behave or else, they aren't on shift when you arrive. But at the end of the night they have to pick you up from the floor to throw you out on your arse into the street. You're barred. You have to walk home coz you've literally got nothing left.

That whole time, the early nineties, they're just . . . not in my head. Being bought and sold like that, loaned out, not in control of anything. No wonder my mind turned to glue. But I do remember a few details from the Christmas of 1994.

Six months since walking out of the dugout and out of the game, walking back home from the third new job since September, in again tomorrow (new boys do the shifts no one else wants), I took a different route to the bus stop, cutting along Deansgate. Just to have a look. It only took a few more minutes than the other route. I promised myself I wouldn't get one, but in those days I even broke promises when it mattered. In the last couple of years I'd read every book written by or about a United player or ex-player, and there had been a lot of them. Every fucker got a book. The bit part boys. The wives. Even some of the *ex*-wives. You know the kind of thing . . . *My Life with Paul Parker*. I mean, who the fuck wants to read that? I pulled up outside. I forgot all about getting the bus.

There were stacks of copies in the front window of the bookshop, facing out onto Deansgate. A fresh-faced, pretty-boy picture, two big sad eyes making the subject look like the cute, babyish one out of some hot new boy band. Only twenty-one years old, and he was already an institution. A whole book laid out like a teenage magazine, right down to the bubble writing, love hearts, empty interviews (*what's your favourite cheese and why?*) and half-naked photos that didn't quite give the goods away but gave a pretty accurate idea of the contents. £12.99's worth of tasty present for girlies everywhere from your friendly Uncle Ryan, under the banner GET YOURSELF A FOOTBALLER FOR CHRISTMAS, and no one complained. No outcry from parents or the Church. No protests outside the shop. A young girl dragged her mother to the window, saying, *That's it! That's it, Mum! I want one!* I followed her inside and flipped through the pages.

It was amazing, what they were saying. What they were getting away with. The lies, you know. It *couldn't* have been him, this thing. It just couldn't. He'd done a few bad adverts (I couldn't even *look* at a vegetarian sausage any more), but I'd always reckoned that was the system, not the man. You're expected to do that shit. Agents and management *push* you. They whore you around and *use* you to get rich. They say everyone does it, that it's part of the job. They talk about *market opportunity* and *optimum revenue streams*. Poor Ryan didn't know what he was doing at first – how can you at that age? – but surely he knew better than this: he was supposed to be a United player, a professional, a *man*. And here he was, posing as the sixth member of Take bastard That. I stuffed a copy in my jacket and ran, as fast as my bad leg would let me, checking behind for shop assistants chasing lost stock. I do have some dignity. There was no fuckin way I was paying.

Once I was out of sight I sat down on a bench, my leg aching, and studied the evidence. They'd done a good job on him, I had to admit. They'd made him look like all things to everyone. Doing it over and over. Reminding everyone, with every headline and caption, what a success he was. The photos on the inside told the whole life story so far as his minders, press officer and sponsors wanted it to be: a shorthand whizz through the sanitized life and times of the golden boy wonder.

1. The innocent, thoughtful child, unruly curls brushed to one side.
2. The pure young boy playing for his nation. (Which was England back then.)
3. Laughing with an old friend in a bar. (But not drinking.)
4. Pulling on a United shirt, pretending not to know the camera is there. (But abso-fuckin-lutely knowing it is.)
5. Teenager balancing a ball on his head in the back garden.
6. The promising youth player in action.
7. At seventeen, scoring his first goal for United proper. The only goal in the game that counts most: the derby.

8. Celebrating a win with Phil Neville, their arms wrapped around each other like they never wanted to be apart again.
9. The fun-loving guy, one of the boys, larking around in just a pair of wet trunks, showing off a suspiciously large bulge. (Mental note: check other photos. Was it possible? Did he stuff?)
10. Looking moodily up at the camera, staring at it, unafraid.
11. The spiritual one: Ryan the free thinker, photographed in black and white, topless and looking upward into the harsh sunlight, hair spreading wildly over his chest.
12. The gritty one: ball under arm, unshaven, an ordinary guy like you and me, relaxing by a dirty wall. (Bet there's plenty of those in Worsley. But not in his mansion.)
13. Laughing with poor kids in Africa, and finally . . .
14. Tearing passionately at his United shirt in front of thousands of fat fucks cheering his every move.

The whole thing was perfectly arranged. Perfectly judged. And in pride of place, one of him taken from the back, the banner of his name, thick and brash across the top, above his number, and mine.

GIGGS

11

I walked towards home. Breathing was harder than it used to be. I felt a sharp, hot rush zip down and through my left leg and, at the last second, I decided on a different move. Even if it was just down to the Dog & Partridge, I had to be out of the house. I gave Guy a call, but he didn't pick up. Tried a couple of mates; they didn't pick up either. But some regulars would be in the usual seats. Half of them never left.

I took a left turn and headed towards the old place, thinking, I'm still young. Way too young to be talking about the good old days. As

Mum said the day after I got back from Plymouth, *You talk like you're dead already!* And I suppose that was true. That's what I was doing. Trying to die before my twenty-first birthday. But like I keep saying, people are fuckin idiots – good at repeating what they already know, sure, I'll give you that one for free. But they never think about why they know it. I limped back to the Dog & Partridge, still queasy, hood pulled down to protect me from the rain, walked in that welcoming door with the book under my arm, and ordered. *A pint of your finest English bitter, please barkeep,* I said, and parked my skinny arse on a stool. *Actually, Ricky, you'd better make it two.* The next person to walk in the door was my brother.

After I left Argyle, things were the same as always with me and Guy. It didn't seem to matter what was happening in the outside world. In the pub, we talked United most of the time. Talked about the next match, whatever it was. The league. The cups. Avoided my place in it all. Around that time Dad mostly talked United too, though he wasn't so shy with advice when it came to how I was getting on, the decisions I was making for myself. He called every few weeks to tell me off. Usually phoned up late, without warning. (Last thing he wanted was for me to be ready for him. Element of surprise, that's what appealed to the old boy.) So he asked plenty of questions, but if I wanted to know how *he* was, I'd have to work it out from the way he talked about the team. Sense it from his tone of voice when giving his opinions on the performance of the United midfield. As for Mum . . . well, she wasn't talking much. Her way of showing me what she thought of what I'd done.

But she didn't get it. Nobody did. Some people – who shall remain nameless – get all the breaks, all the luck, while others get shafted by the system. That keeps happening until they're kicked out of football completely and end up on their fat arse having to watch a whole new raft of young kids coming through on the TV. They don't know it yet, but they'll probably fail as well. They'll probably have their tiny hearts broken while the world watches on in tasty twelve-minute chunks, divided by three minutes of vaguely football-related adverts for razors and cars and energy drinks, documenting every juicy detail of the downfall. And let me tell you, DON'T START ME ON THOSE BASTARDS AT THE FUCKIN SPORTS CHANNELS!

The TV news is pretty bad, there's a lot of lies there, I know that. But at least the news tells you the world is scary and bad and that every single day unpredictable shit is happening. The Middle East is pretty fuckin depressing, but at least it's definitely there. The sports lot won't let you remember you even *live* in a world. Not for a single second, know what I mean? You can't *afford* to remember wars, earthquakes, murders, rapes and recession, or corporate greed or media bias or government corruption, coz you need all your energy to be incredibly *excited* about Super Sunday or Must-Win Monday or Seriously-Who-Gives-a-Fuck Friday which is always *just round the corner*, and *you wouldn't want to miss the bottom of the table relegation clash between Norwich and Southampton now, would you?* Stay tuned to find out if someone's maybe injured or maybe not, stay tuned to see if some knobhead who used to play for Derby County thinks Derby County have got a good chance in their next game. Stay tuned stay tuned – and, for God's sake, KEEP DRINKING BEER! That's what the little grey men say. And everyone agrees to carry on for ever and ever amen, praying to the box and the cashpoint, morning, noon and night, while getting royally –

It wasn't always like this, though.

Are you listening to me?

The game's changed – coz it's a different world now, right? Dirt-poor babies, kidnapped from the favelas and beaches of Brazil, the Ivory Coast, Ghana, Cameroon, Timbuktu, Disneyland, flown to Europe and before they know it they're stranded in the north of England, trying to convince themselves and everybody else that *eet has always been my drrreem to play for Weegan Athleteec*. Meanwhile, they have to learn, super-quick, how to be good clean boys, media-savvy millionaires, all smooth, acting like their life has always been like this. Like they were born to do it. Like they're not interested in drugs or loose women or gambling. They're not kidding me, mate! I know they're still dirt! But why should they care anyway? The likes of us can't touch them; we're not *supposed* to. They're kept nice and safe, well away from the public. Even average players are loaded now. Everything's about money.

*

I'm no conspiracy theorist, but like I say, don't get me started. It's all a way to keep the ordinary working man down. Ordinary, good men like my granddad, who worked hard his whole life, but died as poor as the day he was born. Men like my Uncle Si. Meanwhile, the rich and the lucky get richer and luckier by the second. The *milli*second. To grow these riches, they don't even have to *do* anything any more. They get richer while they sleep, wake up and get richer while they shower, shave, take a shit, eat muesli. All that money. Just growing and growing. Expanding for ever, coz it has to. Or else they might stop getting richer and start getting poorer. And we couldn't have that now, could we? These little grey shits who run the clubs and the channels and the papers, creaming off the good stuff and keeping us constantly frothing at the mouth about the next event with people kicking a ball or hitting one across a net or putting one into a hole – they don't know what it's really like to love what you do, to want to do nothing else, to stop the world for a while, press pause on everything outside those white lines and just be a player in a team, just *be*. To them it's just a series of banners for pies. That's why this country is dying. Maybe it's dead already but, I really wouldn't mind all this, I wouldn't, it's the *lies* that get me. And especially the lies they tell you in the after-game interviews, which are zoomed instantly round the globe, where

INTERVIEWER 1 FROM TV STATION X SAYS:

Well done [*insert player name*], you must be pleased with that result.

THEN PLAYER 2 FROM TEAM Y SAYS:

Thanks [*insert interviewer name*], yeah, I am. At the end of the day it's a game of two halves and fair play to [*insert opposition team name*] but even though we had our backs to the wall, they had all the possession, all the chances, hit the post twice and the crossbar three times in the last ten minutes, I think that when he sees the game tonight on TV, [*insert opposition manager name*] will agree we deserved to win the match.

THEN INTERVIEWER 1 FROM TV STATION X SAYS:

And it must be great to get on the score sheet. You've got a good touch for a big man.

THEN PLAYER 2 FROM TEAM Y SAYS:

Well that's a bit of a stupid question, Mr Interviewer. It's not even really a question at all, is it? But I'm contractually obliged to talk to you for the next minute and a half so yeah, obviously, it's always good to score. I thank God for that, a Catholic / Protestant / Islamic / Jewish / Sikh / Buddhist / Mickey Mouse God above all others who is most certainly on the side of me and my team in all our endeavours and very much against the players on the other team, even if they believe in the same God I do. But the most important thing is that we got the three points in the bag. That's where points belong. In bags. I do want the glory – of course, if I don't score I go home, sulk, drink myself stupid, shout at my children and beat my wife – but I can't say that without incurring a major fine or possibly a criminal prosecution. And, anyway, that's not the party line. So I have to tell you that I don't really think about records or personal fame and glory, and that when I rose like a salmon and put the ball in the back of the net today I WAS ONLY THINKING OF THE LADS. The laughing, joking, crazy, mucking-about-in-the-showers LADS. It was all about the lads, and full credit to them for getting the result we needed. You know Tim, the title race is a marathon, not a sprint, so we're just keeping our eyes on the prize. Taking one game at a time. Not getting ahead of ourselves. As for me, I just do as I'm told and like the Gaffer says, keep it tight at the back and loose up front. Don't think too much. Don't ask questions. And don't answer too many from people like you. Anyway, it's not really about me, is it? It's about the backroom staff, the tea lady, the cleaning lady, the supporters, the kids all over the world who follow this club, who understand the meaning of the word 'passion', who know what this club stands for and demand football duvets for Christmas and new kits every season in home colours, away colours and random third combination colours we don't actually need, and give us money money money, which I like to spend on convertible sports cars and swimming pools and tattoos which say THUG 4 LIFE on them and mansions in the country and jewellery for my wife-or-girlfriend, who is an aspiring actress/model who says she loves me for the man inside even though she's at least an eight out of ten and I'm clearly no more than a four and she won't have sex with me any more unless she's wasted and I remind her that if it wasn't for me she'd still be working as a waitress in a cocktail – sorry, mate, what was the question again?

SATURDAY 4 MARCH 2008
CHAMPIONS LEAGUE
LAST 16, SECOND LEG

UNITED 1–0 OLYMPIQUE LYONNAIS

RONALDO 41

(UNITED WIN 2–1 ON AGGREGATE)

ATTENDANCE: 75,521

GIGGSY WATCH – Didn't play. Not in squad.

Average Fan Rating: N/A

Mike had never been driven to a United match before, and his mouth felt like a sandpit. Maybe it was the suit he was wearing. Maybe it was all that space in the back of some stranger's car, the CD player blasting house music through fat little speakers, muting the noise of the crowd on the other side of the glass. Maybe it was the tiny television in front of him, the grinning Sky Sports News presenters, on mute, hyping the event. Or maybe it was the absence of a pre-match radio humming away in the background, those familiar voices debating the footballing issues of the day. Transfer talk. Team news. Some failed ex-player shouting, 'And I'll tell you another thing about what you need to succeed . . .'

'This is the only way to travel, Mikey,' said Terry, who was wearing a striped purple shirt. 'By limo! Mint, eh? Top! Let's ave it!'

Mike wondered whether his friend was joking. Or whether he was suddenly talking like this to make himself feel more like a real Manc, a real United fan – even though he was *obviously* from Cheshire, and since when did that count as Manchester? Terry's voice reminded Mike of Ledley, the man from the Liverpool bus, who he'd not seen since that glorious day. Whose five-a-side team he never turned up for. The car crawled along in the match-day traffic.

Terry had two other tickets spare, and they'd gone to Ellie and Jen, both nineteen years old. At a set of traffic lights they stood up, the top half of their bodies out of the car, waving at people walking past and screaming in fake American accents.

'YYYYEaah baby!' screamed Ellie.

'Check it out!' screamed Jen.

Both girls posed and pouted, pretending to be film stars – they'd never been in a limousine before, and suspected they might not get the chance again, so why not let loose? Just then a voice from the street shouted their way.

'Get yer tits out fer the lads!'

Both girls let out a dirty laugh.

'No way!' shouted Jen.

'No chance, you fat bastard!' shouted Ellie. She thought for a moment, then consulted with her friend. 'Should I give him a quick flash anyway?' she asked, holding the base of her top, as if she was about to lift it.

'Nah . . . let him suffer,' said Jen. 'Let him think about what *might* be under there when gets home and has a wank.'

Meanwhile, Terry sat across from Mike looking at the two sets of legs between them. He nodded.

'Not so awful to be alive, is it?'

Mike snorted. 'Terry, Ellie's your *sister*, man! Have some self-respect!'

'No! That's not what I meant. You didn't think . . .? Did you? Oh God!'

Mike thought, Would Terry fuck his own relatives? Or anyone else that agreed? Neither option seemed likely. Even in this limo, doing this thing, Terry didn't seem like much of a man. Mike thought about this as he looked at his friend. The limo continued to inch down the street.

When the wind started up Ellie and Jen gave up and dived back into the car.

'Why are you two so tarted up anyway?' asked Mike.

They both laughed.

'Don't be such a Mr Sulky Pants,' said Ellie. 'You scrub up all right too, you know! You look very handsome. Anyway, we *are* going to a party.'

Mike looked down at his newly polished shoes, wondering how he had become one of the prawn sandwich brigade.

In recent weeks, at home games, he and Terry had been talking in detail about how the current season was warming up nicely. They talked tactics. Style. Formation. Which led to other things. Sometimes Terry asked more questions.

'When exactly were you in the set-up?' he asked. 'What's Ferguson really like? What about Giggs? . . . I hear Ryan's a bit rude, actually. Never stops to sign autographs any more. A friend of mine says he heard he's in the closet. Such a shame he feels he has to hide it.'

Mike corrected him. Ryan, he reported, was the perfect heterosexual gent, a loving husband and father. Then he gave what information he could about his United days without being too specific. These days, he had a full routine ready to go whenever needed, with a regular script. It was important to come across as controlled, not bitter, totally at ease. And loyal. When talking about his playing career it was essential to look like he didn't feel anything about it at all, except maybe a kind of quiet, distant pride. To make people believe he didn't really care. And he was good at it. He was convincing when he smiled and answered Terry.

'They were good times,' he said. 'But then, so are these.' They swapped phone numbers.

The next day, Terry called Mike and offered up a ticket for what he called the 'full backstage experience'.

'My brother works for one of the sponsors,' he said, 'and gets tickets for all the European games. Whenever he's away with his work, he offers me the tickets. Very kind of him really. There's entertainment, plenty of food, and drinks flow freely. VIPs only, you understand. Last time he laid on a limousine as well, there and back, on his company. The Champions Club: it's the only way to see a game, Mike. I could really get used to it!'

The two men made plans, with Terry refusing to accept any payment for the ticket. That night, Mike borrowed a suit from Guy, who insisted his brother keep it afterwards. It had been another good week for Wilson Electrics.

When the limousine arrived at Old Trafford, the chauffeur got out, walked round to the other side of the car and opened the door with a sarcastic flourish. At that the little group of four burst out into the open and ran, in the rain, across the car park. Mike accepted a band attached to his wrist by a security guard. Then he went up the steps and tried not to think about being back in the underbelly of the stadium, flashes of memory surfacing from that different, other life as he once again stepped backstage at the Theatre of Dreams. Ellie and Jen had never been to a game before, but said they'd come back every week if this was what it was like. They joked all the way to the Champions Club entrance, high on the grandness of it all. Terry told them not to get used to it, tomorrow they'd be back working at the bakery. But then, tomorrow was a million light years away.

'Congratulations, sailor. You're my date for the night,' said Ellie, linking her arm in Mike's as they climbed the stairs.

On the next level was a second door, held open by two women who looked like air hostesses with identikit blond hair, red lips and fixed smiles. The women offered to take their coats, then showed them to the free drinks. And there were lots of them. Mike didn't know what to say; he could hardly speak around Ellie and Jen. When the girls got talking to two men at the bar a few minutes later, unattaching themselves and going off to sit on another table, Mike gave a smile and a shrug.

'That date didn't last long,' he said.

'They're terribly ungrateful,' said Terry. 'Unlike you. They won't be coming again.'

But Mike's mind was elsewhere. They were in. That was all that mattered. And no one had spotted him yet. He looked around and saw three men stood upright in front of him like soldiers at the palace gates, backs straight, holding ten pints to a tray, while two others behind poured fresh ones and loaded them onto the bar. No tills in sight. Not necessary. When he was offered a pint, Mike refused. His attention was drawn towards a vast buffet featuring cuisine from all over the world.

'Hey,' said Mike, trying to keep his voice down. 'Surely there aren't enough people here to eat all that meat?'

Terry grinned widely, as if imparting a terrible, delicious secret. 'Exactly,' he said. 'Ex-*act*-ly.'

It was two hours until the game started. Both men piled their plates high. Once Mike was finished, he took a moment to admire his multicoloured creation. His plate contained yellow rice, white potatoes, orange breaded chicken, brown lamb curry, yellow chips, a couple of kebabs and a token smattering of green vegetables. He followed Terry back to their seats, walking slowly, so as not to spill the kebabs. They sat down at a decorated table with their names on and picked up a knife and fork. Mike felt a brief flash of panic that someone would see his nameplate and remember him, but after a few minutes he forgot all about it.

The time passed quickly. Over-full from his meal, stomach aching, Mike picked his way through the goodie bag that had been left on the Champions Club seats. Complimentary programme. Champions League magazine. The branded pens and pencils, all pocketed, were welcome additions to his United room. He and Terry discussed the match to come, lingering on the details of what might happen until kick-off time was close. Mike got out his phone and messaged Guy.

ALL RIGHT R KID. BIG GAME 2NITE! IN CHAMPIONS CLUB, THE ONLY PLACE 2B! GIRLS EVERYWHERE. 2 IN OUR LIMO! PREDICTION?

Guy messaged back within seconds.

PREDICTION? A BLOODY REVOLUTION, FOLLOWED BY 30YRS CIVIL WAR. WHY, WHAT'S URS? BTW, JUST HEARD GIGGS ISN'T IN THE SQUAD 2NITE. UR HIS MATE, MIKEY. ASK HIM WHAT'S GOING ON!

Mike grinned; it was important not to rush his brother's return to the United fold – or else he might risk losing it. Better to let it progress steadily. Be patient. Not tease him about County. For now, anyway, there was a bigger issue. He wondered: was Ryan injured? Or dropped? Or finished? The thought made him light-headed, and he began to feel the effects of a long week at work. At that moment, the waiter came round and offered Mike beer, or wine, or spirits. For the fourth time since he'd arrived at Old Trafford, Mike politely refused.

'No thanks, mate,' he said to the waiter. 'I don't drink.'

The waiter winked. 'You did at school,' he said and winked again.

Mike wasn't paying attention. He was taking in the sea of tables, the serving spoons, the plenty. While the people around him all fed themselves fat, an entertainer played lounge versions of popular songs, mostly by Oasis, on an expensive keyboard. He was putting his all into singing a mournful version of 'Live Forever', but was being ignored by most of the guests. (Probably because the entire world knew Liam and Noel were City fans, thought Mike.) A compère followed the crooner, to little success.

'Half these people aren't fans of anybody,' said Terry, in a stage whisper. 'They're just representing their company. No one expects loyalty. These guys are being *paid* to be loud.'

Mike listened carefully for noise from the crowd outside. He looked around. Some things he felt he'd never get used to. What was really amazing was that, in this place, he could have been anywhere. In this large space, he and Terry, and Ellie and Jen, and the air hostesses, and the sponsors, were entirely cocooned from the outside world. It didn't feel like he was just yards from a grassy pitch and all those thousands of fans warming up before the action began. The stink of the toilets. The betting stand. The merchandise stall. The crush in the queue for drinks. Just then, the compère announced that the game was about to start. It was time to leave for the seats. Terry grabbed his sister and Jen, and all four headed for the exits.

To get to the pitch they had to pass through the Champions Club bar, along the corridor with action shots of great United Champions

League moments on the walls (Ryan very well represented, along with David Beckham, Roy Keane, Eric Cantona, Andy Cole), out of the warmth and finally into their seats in the cold. Just one little door, like a secret entrance into another dimension. It slammed behind Mike, and the roar of the crowd hit him hard.

While the other three wailed their way through the full ninety minutes, kicking every last ball in their heads and bellowing at imaginary injustices, Mike began to feel sleepy, and as he got sleepier, the tightness in his shoulders eased, along with the aches in his limbs. Everything seemed to slow and blur before his eyes, and even though this particular match was still undecided, he began to believe that the rest of the season was going to be a huge success. Mike had seen the future, and the future was good. Not having to worry about what happened next struck him as a huge relief. Why worry? Why stress? Everything was going to be fine. And without Ryan, at least for tonight.

Maybe Ryan's career was finally coming to an end, and maybe, once he was gone, just another ex-player like him and thousands of others, then maybe Mike would always be able to feel like this. As he sat there, seemingly transfixed by events on the pitch, but with his mind in another place entirely, he began to feel it was Ryan's very presence on the field of play that was holding him back, as if some cosmic balance was put for ever on tilt as long as that particular human being – that collection of skin, cells and bones – kept on playing for Manchester United. Another game, another season, another year. But maybe not for ever. Mike thought about how his old hero might feel tonight, down there in the team seats, by the pitch. Sitting there, like Mike once had, wondering what was coming. In his tired haze, Mike noticed that, even though he wasn't playing tonight, the old Giggs song was starting up again. Every time he heard it, that same image flashed in Mike's head: Ryan, standing above him, offering his hand, holding it out. Events on the pitch brought him out of this daydream. United had scored and were on their way to the next round. But then, Mike knew that already.

After the limousine dropped Ellie and Jen off, Terry turned to Mike as the driver started the engine up again.

'I've got a few more beers in the fridge,' he said. 'I'm having a good time. Want to come up?'

'Nah,' said Mike. 'Need some fresh air. Cheers though, top night. Hey, next time though, okay? For sure.' Mike put his coat on, opened the door and got out of the car. 'Bye, mate,' he said to Terry, looking back as he walked away. 'See you soon. Red Army!'

Getting out of the car had seemed like a good idea at the time, but once out of the comfort and into the rain, Mike wasn't so sure. Perhaps he should have had a drink with Terry. As he walked, Mike had to move fast to stop himself from staring at all the flashing lights in the pubs he was passing, each one just waiting for him to step inside and get drunk. Why had he put himself in this situation? He bit the skin on the inside of his mouth, kept his head down, counting the paving stones – one, two, three – thinking about anything but how good it'd feel to walk into the warmth and approach the bar.

Here's a story with a happy ending for you.

It was when I was doing well for the rezzies, that in-between time in summer 1992 before my debut. Scoring plenty, but no sniff of the first team yet. Back then, the whole family could see the prize, nice and close, but couldn't touch it. Back then, everything seemed to be a strange shape that we couldn't quite see whole. So when Dad asked me to join him out the front of the house after dinner one night, it felt like something important before anything had even happened, you know? Mum was on the phone to her cousin in the lounge and Dad had waited until they were deep into it before he moved. I picked my brand-new coat off the peg in the hall and Dad pushed me, finger on lips, out of the front door. He pulled it to, but didn't close it. When I got outside, Uncle Si was standing there, smoking. I thought he was working away until the following week. *All right, Mikey,* he said. *Shall we go for a walk?* I acted like this happened all the time. *Sure,* I said. *Why not. What the hell else am I doing?* We went down to the end of the road then stopped, just about still in view of home. Uncle Si sat on the wall. Dad hovered, standing. We stared out towards the road. I kept watching Uncle Si and even sat like he did, one leg cocked. It seemed the right thing to do. He sparked up a fag and we sat there for a couple of minutes. Dad lit one too and for a second I wished I was a smoker. It was cold that night, but though it was late, there was still some light outside. Winter was far away. Days were long. But I wouldn't have minded a bit of darkness, and I reckoned the others felt the same.

It was Dad who spoke first. *I want you to promise me something,* he said. (I told him I would.) *Don't fuckin lie to me.* (I told him I wouldn't.) *Mikey, don't ever forget what things are worth, okay? Coz . . .* He stuttered. *Coz your old man forgot . . .* And then he stopped talking. He finished his fag and put it out, not talking. (How long had it taken for him to smoke a single cigarette? It felt like we'd been there for years already.) He lit another one, still not talking. It was fuckin painful how long he wasn't talking for, but there was no way I was gonna interrupt him or even look up or admit this was happening, and Uncle Si was obviously giving Dad the chance to complete the sentence himself. Just when I thought we were gonna give the game up and head back inside, Dad looked to Uncle Si and shook his head. He just about managed, *I can't.*

A few seconds later, when he was sure Dad couldn't go on, Uncle Si took over. *Now,* he said, *it's no one's fault, Mikey, and we don't want you to worry about it. God knows you've got enough to think about just now, what with the team and everything. And we don't want to make things difficult, but . . . but your dad . . . owes a bit of money. You know. From bets. A lot of them. And this time, I can't make it go away.* Just then, Dad looked like he was gonna speak for himself, but then he decided against it. Uncle Si carried on. *And sometimes your dad thinks that, you know, this place, this city, it hasn't been as good to him as it might have been and . . . and maybe, somewhere, there's another home for him. Somewhere he could start again.* Another silence. A long one. It was hard to imagine anything on the other side of the silence. All this time, I avoided looking at Dad, and Dad avoided looking at me, and Uncle Si just smoked and looked up into the light above us all. At that moment, I realized I'd grown taller than them both.

After a while Uncle Si said, *This might be nothing, Mikey. It might. But I want to tell you* – we *want you to know – that from now on, if ever your dad isn't around, it's for a good reason. It's for his safety. The safety of the whole family. Do you understand?* He put a big hand on his brother's shoulder, as my dad let out a tear or two. *We all support you in what you're doing at United. And, Mike, whatever happens, I'll always look out for the family.* Then he looked back towards our house. *Please don't mention this to Guy. He's a good boy – the best – but he'd be angry, and we've decided it's not safe to explain. But we can trust you, can't we, Mikey?* (I nodded.) *There's a good lad. You know, we wouldn't ask if it wasn't absolutely necessary. And as for your mother, well. She's a remarkable woman, but to tell her, that'd be the selfish option. Don't you agree? Isn't it better to set her free?* Well, I didn't have much fuckin choice, did I? I nodded again as Dad headed inside, without saying a word. Before I could move, Uncle Si gave me a hug. Then he pulled away and said, *Right, well. Let's talk about how the fuck you're gonna break into that first team!* I unzipped my coat and went inside.

The next day I lost that coat somewhere between leaving for training in the morning and arriving home at night, and what kept coming back to me was Dad saying, *Promise me you'll remember what things are worth.* Uncle Si saying, *We can trust you.* The details of when I actually lost track of the damn thing were this weird blank in my mind. The more I thought about it, the less I could remember as I turned the thing over and over, so much it made me feel ill. Was it at the ground somewhere? At home? Had I left it in the changing rooms? I looked everywhere. I asked around. I even put signs up on the noticeboard at Old Trafford and on our street promising a reward for information or suspects. Like it was a tabby cat that had been in the family for years. A cat made of gold. When I told Dad, I did it knowing full well I was gonna get the bollocking of my life.

In the next couple of weeks he lost his mind quizzing me about that coat. He treated it like a fuckin murder investigation or something. Didn't matter what I said, he kept on with the interrogation – at mealtimes, at night, through the door when I was in the bath. Screaming like a crazy man. Trying to catch me out. Calling me a liar and threatening to disown me. In the end he gave up asking, but treated it like a personal defeat, an insult. As if this was the last and final thing he could bear. Maybe he thought I was hiding it and he was trying to break me. Or he thought I'd sold it. Maybe he really couldn't afford to buy me another. Maybe he was halfway out the door by then, in his head. All I know is, for weeks, whatever else was going on, we couldn't forget about that fuckin thing. Had it fallen into a black hole? Slipped into another dimension? Our brains had been swiped clean, then programmed to think about this one piece of clothing and nothing else. Which, in the circumstances, was a bit of a headfuck, don't you think?

It was spring by the time I'd saved to buy myself a new coat. Dad was long gone by then and I was more settled at United, but the lost coat wouldn't leave me alone. Coz if there was no sense to this mystery then what else was up for grabs? If this thing had just disappeared, then what kind of universe were we living in? I wore the new coat every day, even when it was hot, and I watched that thing closely, but the lost one still bugged me. Sometimes I'd be playing a match, daydreaming about being above the dressing rooms, looking down on them, hiding inside a cloud. I'd imagine having X-ray vision and big binoculars. Some nights I'd dream about finding that fucker in the alley by our street, and in the dream I'd present it to Dad, who'd hold it up like a trophy or a baby grandson. But in the real world, months passed, and nothing. I took down the signs. Sometimes Guy would make a joke of it, pretending Dad was still around, pretending to storm around the house, to go apeshit about it being gone. Then my brother would put a warm hand on my shoulder and say, *You've gotta let it go, Mikey. That coat, it's GONE.*

But I know it's somewhere. I know I'll find it one day. Whatever happens, this story's gonna have a happy ending.

THE LAW OF AVERAGES

Imagine: these are dark days. Spring 1999, and it's been months since you saw the inside of a warehouse or office or even the inside of a job centre. You're avoiding your landlord (cut the phone off just in case), and haven't seen Mum in ages – though Guy says there have been developments. She's been talking about Dad again, in that old voice, like he's just popped out to buy some fags and is gonna be home any minute. When it's not Dad, it's Uncle Si. (When Guy asks if you'll help persuade her to take an evening class or join a club, something *to get her out of the house, build her self-confidence*, you pretend you haven't heard. Which reminds you of someone.)

Speaking to Mum makes you want to get wasted, so you hardly ever speak to her. But at least, despite all this, you've been behaving yourself for a while – no risky jobs, no trouble. And you've been staying away from the bookies as well. These are real actual things of value, and you count the hours and days since you last gave in to yourself. Each time a day passes, you think about the numbers and feel good. Sometimes, at night, lying in bed in the blackness, you feel like you're desperately close to realizing something. Working something out. Something amazing that no one else has ever been close to. In your mind, in the dark, you reach out, grasping for the news. But this thing, you can't quite hold it. And even if you could, you're pretty sure you wouldn't understand.

It's the fourteenth of April, and another afternoon comes and goes. You've just finished a training session with the local non-league team, whose name you can't even bring yourself to say any more. Since your leg was just about good enough for you to play again, strapping on your boots and just *thinking* about turning out for that bunch of part-timers hasn't exactly been redemption. You don't know if you can go back next week. Today, running around on a non-league pitch, full of mud patches and dried up grass, you could hardly be bothered to breathe, never mind chase the ball. This team is lucky if it gets a few hundred in the crowd for each game. But you've got to play, or else you truly believe you might die. And at least there's always United. Always, always United. Whatever else happens, the Premiership rolls on. Old defeats are left behind. New challenges come into view. And there's always something exciting on the way; this season more than ever.

This season, this magical season, United's success has pumped life into you, and now you walk into the Dog & Partridge, all warm and friendly and safe and secure, and the FA Cup fifth-round match against Arsenal is about to start. Guy is there already. He's ordered for you. You settle on your regular stool and the game kicks off.

The game goes into extra time, and a big part of you wishes you were there in person. You had no money to go to the replay after blowing the last of your cash last week on paying off a big bill, but everything's okay coz who needs the real thing? From the second he says it, the commentator's report on what happens next is lodged in your brain for good.

> *Giggs gets past Viera . . . Past Dixon who comes back at him . . . it's a wonderful run from GIIIIGGS! . . . Sen-SA-tional goal from Ryan Giggs in the second period of extra time and the team with ten men go back in front 2–1!*

As the commentator takes a breath, Ryan whips off his top to reveal the official Hairiest Chest in the Western World. Everyone loves it, that chest, right down to the one curly hair, front and centre, just below the collarbone. The shirt gets twirled above Ryan's head and peace breaks out across planet earth. Enemies lay down their weapons and embrace. Dictatorships fall. Even wily old Premiership managers, who thought they'd seen it all, can't believe what they've just witnessed. The other commentator says:

. . . Well, words fail me! . . . STUNNED Arsenal fans, JOYOUS United fans . . . And if this is the last semi-final replay goal we ever see, well, it'll rank with some of the greatest EVER scored. He just bobbed and weaved and kept going, and when he needed a finish, my GOD did he GIVE US ONE!

You think, It's pretty fuckin mental, all these grown-ups, watching these beautiful things happen in another place, each colour magically beamed into this pub and thousands of others in nations all over the world. The idea of television suddenly seems impossible. Like a crazy joke. If someone told you the joke, you wouldn't believe it. Then you down your drink in one. The game's over in an instant, and it's victory. The TV blares out the gospel, the whole pub goes wild. Ryan has just scored the best goal of all time and Guy asks what you want to drink. *Special occasion*, you tell him. *Let's have something special.* Both of you know what that means. *Whisky*. When the Wilson brothers are out on the lash, together, like old times, all other things real or imagined slide away from you, don't matter, are gone.

After the game, the pub's buzzing. Everyone's talking about you-know-who, and some guy at the trough is saying it feels like Ryan's played for United since the beginning of time. He can't remember anything else BG: Before Giggsy. *Fuckin hell*, he says, *I was still married to my ex then.* This guy with his cock out, this bloke you've never even met, says, *It's like Giggsy and the club, they're the one and the same now. Don't you reckon?* You mutter agreement as you're shaking yourself dry. The guy says, *You can't go on for ever though. Nobody does. What is he now – twenty-six? Twenty-seven? I reckon he'll last another couple of years then Fergie will shift him on. Whaddaya think?* Well the main thing you think is that it's disgusting, the way these fat bastards, these lazy dickheads who haven't kicked a ball in twenty years, talk about world-class athletes like they're cattle. You want to grab this feller's head and smash it into a sink. He's still talking when you finish up at the trough and leave without washing your hands.

You dirty fucker.

Back out at the bar, Guy is celebrating, dancing with some lad you don't know, pints of beer raised like trophies to the skies and grins on both their faces. Everyone's mates. One nation under Fergie. And right now it feels like your big brother's as into the game as you are. There's just time for another couple of quick ones before the bar closes (Guy's had a good week – again – so he gets them in), and you chat about how 1999 is turning into a special year. It could yet be the best ever. Everything's ready, just right. (Are you talking about the team or something else?) Three men leave the table in the corner of the pub, the one by the front window. You and Guy have the same thought at the same time, and dive in there before anyone else can. Then you get down to serious business.

Guy admits Giggsy's goal was unbelievable, but despite everything he's not really a huge fan of Ryan, never has been – he's more of a workhorse man: from the Paul Scholes School of Grim-Faced Solid Dependables. In the days of Bryan Robson he was President of the Clayton Blackmore Fan Club. If he was alive in 1968 he would have preferred Bill Foulkes or Frannie Burns to the wayward genius of Georgie Best. He's always been that type. Never does the obvious thing. The smart thing. The easy, obvious thing that everyone else does. But on days like this he's good value, and you spar over whether Ryan's goal is the best goal scored, ever. By *anyone*. Each brother throws a punch, ducks, moves, making his argument. Voices are raised. You both talk over each other. There's nothing like it.

Guy's the proper philosopher these days, no doubt. And once he gets going, he starts up with the theories. Leaning in towards you, sneaking the odd sly look at the barmaid's tits as she glides by, picking up your glasses, he says, *Success on the pitch – true, pure moments of fairytale that'll go down in United history, become folklore – they're not really about talent at all. They're about* maths. *Know what I'm saying?* (You give him the face, but you're smiling. He carries on.) *By the law of averages*, he says, *if you play enough games, and if you get enough chances in those games, you're bound to score a goal like that in the end. Something special. Something memorable where the timing and the occasion and the weather are all aligned, like stars.* (You give him the face again. Is he an idiot? Is he fucking with you?) He says, *And Giggsy's played more matches than most. Hasn't he? So if you think about it – I mean, REALLY think about it – that means the goal against Arsenal wasn't special at all. It was ALWAYS gonna happen. You just didn't know when. All Ryan had to do was keep going. Not give up. You see?* Sometimes, when Guy's like this, you wish he'd stop trying to make you feel better.

A bit later, Guy gets talking to a woman you might know. You think about it: maybe she used to hang around in the park when you were younger? There were kids who never seemed to leave the place. They stayed all night, drinking, screwing, dealing. You look and look and you're sure that's where you know her from, but there's no name there. On your tongue. She's small and soft and she's laughing. She's wearing jeans and a simple white T-shirt like she's not trying to prove anything to anyone. Guy's still talking to her, and after a while he turns to you and whispers, *I'm gonna behave, Mikey. Gotta be good these days! But YOU should talk to her.* You ask, *Why?* Guy shakes his head and laughs. *I don't know what's wrong with you*, he says. *If you wanna win the National Lottery you've gotta get yourself a fuckin scratchcard once in a while!* You don't know what the hell that means, but when he pushes you over to this woman and explains she's called Gemma Black, you speak. *Hi, Gemma Black*, you say. *I'm Mike. Can I get you a drink?* She considers the offer, then after an age she accepts with a stiff little nod and then a *Well, what the hell else am I doing?* Later, you buy her another. (Guy presses a few crumpled notes into your palm on his way to the toilet and whispers, in his best New Jersey Mafia don accent, *For-ged aboud id.*) So you do. And you get another one for yourself too. Might as well.

By quarter past eleven the pub has started to empty out, people moving on home or to queues for clubs near by, and you three are pretty much the last to leave. You don't know why, maybe coz you get the impression she's not into the footie, but you decide to try and go until the end of the night without mentioning United to Gemma, or that you played for them, or what happened. She talks fast but she talks straight, and she says she doesn't want to think about the past. So maybe you shouldn't either. All that shit, you think, that follows you around. Maybe it doesn't need to. Maybe it isn't a shadow at all, and if you tell it to leave you alone, it might. When Guy gets his jacket he gives you a big bear hug and says, *He shoots! He scores!* Then he lopes off out the door of the Dog & Partridge, back to his dependable Clayton Blackmore girlfriend and solid Paul Scholes home and steady Frannie Burns job. You live alone, Dad's bound to phone late with something to say about the match, and you're not in the mood for his *I could have been a pro, you know, Mikey* and *Mikey, do you think your mother misses me?* and *You know, me and this barmaid, I don't think it's gonna work out after all.* So you decide to stay for one more.

Gemma came to the pub with friends but leaves with you. Not because you're a footballer, not because you've told her you have Giggsy on speed dial or that you've won a pile of medals. You have a laugh together. Like mates. (When she laughs she has this twang to her accent. Like she's from somewhere else.) And she's pretty sharp too, you reckon. Full of fight. She has an opinion on everything, and she must have a good opinion of you or else she wouldn't still be here, right? You head on to a club for one more, stand by the bar shouting over the music, and after a while there she's beginning to enjoy herself. You talk and talk about Manchester. Gemma says she moved here when she was about twelve, but always felt it was home. That, to her, the city *sounded* like home. And the two of you agree on everything that matters –

NEW ORDER [*from Salford*]

Early stuff good, later stuff bad

THE MONDAYS [*from Little Hulton/Salford*]

Hits very good, everything else very bad

THE ROSES [*from Altrincham*]

First album the BEST EVER, second one the WORST

OASIS [*from Burnage*]

Don't count. City supporters

THE FALL [*hundreds of members since being formed in Prestwich*]

Shit shit shit shit shit

THE SMITHS [*Morrissey: from Hulme, Manchester; Marr: from Ardwick, Manchester; The Other Two: doesn't matter*]

Brilliant. Obviously. Even though Moz is a poof. (Then you get side-tracked into talking about whether Morrissey is actually gay or just *nothing*. Is that even possible?)

and finally . . .

JOY DIVISION [*see New Order*]

Her favourites. Your favourites. The BEST.

Gemma says, *You'll think I'm daft but, to me, Joy Division sound like old Manchester, the one I miss, you know?* This is the kind of sentimental, rose-tinted crap you love, so you sing 'Love Will Tear Us Apart' for her, out of tune, loud as you can, in tribute. And at the end of all this, she's still there. Not rolling her eyes or heading for the door. Which makes you more relaxed. Which means she likes you more. When you start up the song a second time, this time you do it with the full Ian Curtis impression, shaking all over the place, then you do it à la Moz, early period, waving imaginary gladioli. Then you morph into Ian Brown, the swaggering walk-on-the-spot, all the attitude. The works. *Fookin nice one, mate!* you say. *Fookin nice one!* Gemma laughs and says, *You're an absolute idiot.* She smiles widely. *A cute idiot*, she says, playing with her earring with her left hand. You've never been called cute before.

After another couple of drinks, Gemma's mood turns. She says she gets lonely sometimes, especially since her ex-boyfriend scarpered back to Merseyside, where her family live. (You pretend you didn't hear that. You have to.) This is her first night out and feeling good in *months* and really she's not ready for anything new. She just wants someone to talk to. When Gemma starts crying, right there in the club, you don't act like a dick and tell her to dry her eyes. You feel like a new, clean man tonight, so you put an arm round her and say you understand. Which you really, truly, no shit feel like you DO. And she puts an arm round you as well, her other arm linking through yours, like she's hanging onto you. The alcohol on her breath smells like your own, the stale sticky insides of your mouth. You tell her she shouldn't be alone tonight. That she can trust you. She doesn't laugh, or tell you to *Shut the fuck up* or say *Is that the best you can do, Casanova?* You really love her for that, and for a second you think about telling her.

What are you so happy about, sunshine? asks Gemma, as you try to find the keys to your flat, an hour later. *Well*, you say, fishing around in your pockets, *I just met this girl, didn't I? This woman. And . . . and . . .*

me and Ryan . . . we're gonna be the same now. Just the same. Gemma smells good, she feels warm. She says, *You're not tough at all, are you, Mikey?* and when you lean in and hold each other on the doorstep it's good to not be alone. That's the main thing you remember afterwards: that it's good to be close to another human body. When you get inside you even forget about United for a while and your terrible mistake and, though you can't explain it at the time, that feels so good it's almost *too* good. You can hardly bear it. It's totally exhausting, but so is thinking about the same problem all the time and not being able to make it better. When Gemma kisses you, you close your eyes. Kiss back. Hope the feeling will last.

For a while, on this night, you've never failed. You're just an ordinary bloke who's got lucky at his local pub and can't believe it. That happens to everyone eventually, doesn't it? If you live long enough? It's the law of averages, right? If you fail and fail, and keep living? If you drink every night and talk to enough strangers? Even the ugly guys get lucky in the end. Even the ones with no chat, who have this strange spirit about them that nearly everyone stays well clear of. They get drawn to women like them. They're magnetted together. Sadness drawn to sadness. Anger drawn to anger. This magical night the two of you sit up late; Gemma smokes, the two of you sitting with legs dangling out of your window, looking down on the city, talking about her life. All the things that have gone wrong and how she's going to put them right. She wants to get out of her crappy job at the call centre, for starters, and into a better one. You tell her you want to help her do that, and you mean it. You promise to change too. (You know what that means. She can't know.) It's cold, but you keep yourselves warm for a while by hugging in the dark. When the rain starts, you go inside. Gemma leans in, pulls at your belt and says, *Come on. Help me forget.*

You and Gemma meet up two days later, back at the Dog & Partridge, where she's been drinking with a few friends. (A couple from Liverpool, but you don't say anything.) Then you meet up again three days later, at yours. And again, two days later, at hers. Basically, whenever there isn't a game on and she's not on shift at the call centre. (You arrange things around the matches, which is easy right now coz what else are you doing.) In between meetings you send her messages, and sometimes she replies. A few of the texts are really about her ex, and a couple of times she talks about *not going too far too fast*, but you promise that's not what you're trying to do. Why would you? Being with Gemma is like having a friend you never ever want to let go of. When the two of you hug, she feels like someone who's seen the world and can cope with it. You want things to go on for ever, just like this. Thinking about her makes getting up in the morning worth bothering with. So when Dad asks if you're getting laid or not yet, you laugh and say, *You're not gonna believe this, Pops. But I think I'm in love with a Scouser.*

Sir Alexander Chapman Ferguson:

Officer of the Order of the British Empire (awarded 1983)
Commander of the Order of the British Empire (awarded 1995)
Knight Bachelor (awarded 2000)

I tried the Gaffer three times. First, I wrote to him at Old Trafford, in late 1994, begging for another chance at United, saying sorry for the whole Argyle thing and trying to convince him I was back to full fitness. Surprise surprise, no answer. The second was years later, in 2003. A polite letter, all nice and neat in my best handwriting, reminding him who I was, and explaining everything as if we'd never even met. This time I'd asked around a bit first, and most of the lads I talked to said the same thing: the Gaffer's a good man. He dragged himself out of the dirt. If he can help, he will.

A month later, no reply. But I reckoned he didn't open his own post these days anyway – one of his secretaries probably read the first line then binned it. So I thought about going to the training ground myself, the personal touch, you know, but didn't want to be turned away from Fortress Carrington, famous worldwide for keeping away the plebs. Christ, I didn't even know where Carrington *was* – in my day, training was at the Cliff. Then I thought about going round to his house, just like he'd been to mine all that time ago. But my sources (a feller I met in the Dog & Partridge) told me there was tight security even at Fairfields – that's the mansion Fergie lives in, named after the shipyard his dad and brother worked at back in Glasgow, in case you don't know. The house is probably bigger than some of the ships they built. Anyway, I decided not to get arrested by storming it. Instead, I got his home address from my sources (another feller I met in the Dog & Partridge), and posted a letter, recorded delivery, with a so-big-you-can't-miss-it message on the front: URGENT: FOR THE ATTENTION OF SIR ALEX FERGUSON. I was a teeny bit wasted when I wrote it. Like 2002 and 2001 and, let's face it sports fans, most of the year 2000, 2003 was a pretty bad year. Course, I'm fine now, but every life has shit days, right?

Hello Boss!

I'm sitting here in my flat, eating egg and beans on toast – AGAIN! – and thinking, do you remember what it's like to be broke as fuck? Yes, it was ages ago. But we both know the only difference between men like you and men like me is a lucky goal here, an unlucky injury there, a penalty at the right or the wrong time. Right, Gaffer? These beans could be caviar. This toast could be steak. My cup of tea could be a glass of champers.

I read your book, you know, Fergie. Managing My Life. *It's okay I suppose, even though you've left out a few characters in the United story. (Not naming any names!) Still, fair's fair, there's some decent gossip and a nice happy ending and everything, but my favourite chapter was all about how you sat in your hotel room in Barcelona in 1999, after giving your last team-talk before the Champions League final. Stepping out onto the swanky balcony, looking up to the skies and wondering if you were going to go down as a great manager or just a good one. You knew you could do fuck all else. You just had to wait, and hope. But luckily, you were born to win.*

Tell me, Sir *Alex – I want to know if on that night in 1999 you thought about other times when you weren't in control. As a kid growing up poor in Glasgow. As a young striker, just like me, trying to make it. Your time at Rangers, when they made their top scorer train with the reserves. Then the kids. How about when you were running your own pub,* Fergie's, *clearing out the drunks, trying to scrape by and not knowing if you'd ever get another job in football? Being manager at East Stirlingshire, working part-time for peanuts, with no transfer kitty and no goalkeeper on the books? How about being sacked by St Mirren? The early days at Aberdeen? How about at United in 1990, four years into the job, no trophies and the fans calling for your head on a spike?*

Do you remember any of this shit or is it all too long ago now? How did you feel when United went thirteen WHOLE GAMES WITHOUT A WIN? Do you ever think of the players who had the talent, and almost made it, but didn't? The ones who never got a second chance? Hey, do you ever think of me? I was 'Little Giggs' Wilson, the winger you signed in 1991, who had all the talent but none of the luck.

DO YOU REMEMBER?

If you do, please could you send me some money? A few thousand should cover it, for now. If I don't get some soon I'm going to have to do something desperate, if you know what I mean. And no one wants that, do they? Besides, you're loaded! You won't even miss it! You're supposed to be a Labour man, Mr Ferguson, so how about a bit of solidarity for the working man?

Say hi to the wife for me.

With love and respect,

Mike Wilson

I asked all these questions and more, and never got a reply. Maybe he hadn't *seen* my letter. Maybe Lady F or Claire the secretary filtered his post. Funny really, but I didn't think too much about whether I was gonna get an answer. I just charged onto the next thing. Which I suppose says more than the actual letter itself.

SUNDAY 23 MARCH 2008
PREMIER LEAGUE

UNITED 3-0 LIVERPOOL

BROWN 34
RONALDO 79
NANI 81

ATTENDANCE: 76,000

GIGGSY WATCH – MadRed4Eva1985 says: Sorry to raise this again boyz n girlz but IT'S TIME TO RETIRE. Subbed yet again. Nani comes on for Giggs and 8 minutes later, BOOM. We won today but can't keep risking him in big games. It's no shame, it happens to all the greats, but wake up, folks. The team has moved on!

Average Fan Rating: 6/10

It was the first home game of the season that Mike Wilson hadn't attended in person, having been asked to take part in a stocktake at work. He'd already done sixty hours since Monday, and he was exhausted, but Brian had asked him to do another few hours as a favour, and asked in a way that showed there was really only one answer. So they agreed he'd start early and finish after the first half of the game, then come in early again the next day to finish off. Throughout that time, Mike checked his phone for updates every few minutes, between duties, and saw that, astonishingly, Wes Brown had scored a goal. Alone in the stockroom, Mike laughed out loud. He shook his head. In a world where even Wesley was a hero, he thought, as he counted the final pile of tracksuits, surely anything could happen.

Mike walked home during half-time, arriving just as the teams were kicking off again. He was exhausted. During the second half he fell asleep on the couch while the game played on the TV. He slept for twenty minutes until the sound of the crowd cheering the second goal woke him up, the United players in the screen jumping on top of each other as he opened his eyes. Liverpool players were standing with hands on hips, or looking at the ground, or up into the sky. A commentator was talking about fate, and the end of the season, and asking whether Alex Ferguson had finally constructed a team which could 'succeed even *without* the great Ryan Giggs'. Mike drifted back off to sleep again.

Hours later his phone rang, waking him a second time. His first thought was: what was the final score? His second was: what was the time? It was dark outside. He felt stiff from sleeping awkwardly, and he was sweating. He wanted to get in the shower. As he picked up the receiver he wondered, was someone dead? On the end of the line, his father's voice sounded small.

'Hello again, Mike,' he said. 'Son? You there?'

Mike noticed his father was drunk. Sometimes this happened. He said nothing.

'I can hear you,' said Gregory. 'Listen . . . just listen to me. Okay? I want you to know I'm sorry. I'm so sorry . . . But at least I'm still here. At least I'm still alive. Mikey. Son. Hey, are you gonna talk or not?'

Mike didn't reply.

'All right, all right. But you have to understand – it was – a thunderstorm, you know? There was a thunderstorm in my head.'

Mike focused on the difference in his father's voice.

'They were coming for me, son, for what I owed them. I'd been stupid. I lost a *lot*. And these guys, Mikey. They don't send reminder letters, know what I mean?'

It was distracting, this voice change.

'And, and at that time, your mother and I, we – she just didn't love me any more. You couldn't blame her. I didn't.'

Mike knew this man on the line had to be the same one who taught him to play football, who took him to practice, who thought the future was a win on the pools, but this was a tone he'd never heard before.

'It just seemed easier to go. And, and, you've gotta believe me, Mikey, I thought you didn't *need* me. You were gonna be a fuckin United superstar, y'know? I thought you'd look after your mum, Uncle Si would look out for you, and Guy would look out for himself.'

At that, Mike barked. 'Ha!'

'You can laugh, Mike, but your brother hated me. For breaking your mother. A man knows these things. And he's a such a by-the-rules type, he might have turned me in. So in the end I just thought, sod it – I could watch you grow up from here.'

Mike finally found the words he was looking for. 'Go fuck yourself, Dad,' he said.

Mike lay on the couch holding the phone for a few seconds, then put it down and got straight in the shower, where he turned the heat up so much that his arms and legs flinched. Finally he stopped and staggered, half asleep, to his bedroom. Then he fell down onto his bed.

Mike dreamed that Gregory called back later the same night.

In the dream, Gregory Wilson was sitting in just a pair of shorts, on a high stool under a hot sun, supping his next cocktail at a bar which looked more like a thatched hut. In the background, gentle reggae played while a dreadlocked barman sang softly along. In the foreground, the naked blonde from Guy's old bedroom poster jumped off a high diving board into a swimming pool, making a tiny splash on entrance.

'You watching the Liverpool match?' Gregory asked, scanning the pool for any sign of the blonde, fingering a slip of paper with a single word on it. 'You know, I really think something's happening this season.'

Mike couldn't make out what the word was on his father's piece of paper. Now they were in a pub with broken air conditioning and a Union Jack flag behind the bar. Ryan Giggs was wiping tables at the back of the room. As Mike reached out for his father's piece of paper, Ryan put down his dishcloth and a football appeared at his feet. He drew back his left foot and blasted it straight at Mike's face.

*

Mike woke up, groggy, dry-mouthed; the phone was ringing again. He imagined his father on the other end of the line, at the bar in the dream, saying to Ryan Giggs, 'I don't think he's gonna pick up.' Ryan replied, 'He's your boy. He'll pick up. I think he really misses you.'

I might have slagged him off in that letter, but I can see now: that was just coz I was angry. Deep down, I'd always known that the Gaffer got it right. Alex Ferguson always got it right.

In his autobiography he wrote all about how two corners from David Beckham set up goals first for Teddy Sheringham, then for Ole Gunnar Solskjaer. He wrote about how really those words didn't do those events justice. How the words didn't get anywhere near the events. Ha! Damn right, boss! You said it! Twenty-sixth of May 1999: WITHOUT DOUBT the most amazing turnaround in European history, Second World War included. *No question aboot that!* The most exciting Cup final ever. United's finest moment, happening on what would have been Sir Matt Busby's ninetieth birthday. United's Holy Ghost looked down from the heavens and *Behold: He saw that it was GOOD*. That famous old smile on show, he gave a dignified thumbs-up at the scoreline *Manchester United 2 Bayern Munich 1*. Miracle at the Nou Camp: it should have been the best day of my life. But while my old mates Ryan, Gary Neville, Goldenballs and the rest played the most important game of their lives, I lay there at home, woozy, light-headed, watching the bathwater turn from clear to pinkish swirls to red blotches coming from my wrists and spreading everywhere. Inside the nightmare, I wondered just exactly how much you had to cut your wrists to guarantee entry to the big training pitch in the sky. Thinking, all slow, that maybe I should have done it a little bit more. Just to be sure. Ripped hard at the flesh with a knife, like a real man, instead of slicing, all nervous, with the blade end of a pair of house scissors like a poof.

As the blood leaked out of me, a clear picture came into my mind. So clear it was like the rest of the world no longer existed, or ever had. There was only this one image. Right there, in front of me. It wasn't Mum crying at the TV soaps or Dad in his apartment in the sun, hunched over some ageing barmaid. It wasn't Ole Gunnar Solskjaer poking out a boot to score the winning goal, or Keano and Scholesy, both suspended, grumpy as fuck, wearing suits and not bothering to pretend they didn't mind missing the biggest match of their lives. It wasn't even the embarrassed officials taking the Munich team colours off the Cup and replacing them with United's at the last minute, or of Fergie dancing round the pitch in front of fans after the game. What I saw, in what could have been the final seconds of my roll-the-dice, lukewarm excuse for an almost life, was the image of Ryan Giggs's head screwed tight onto the shoulders of all the Bayern Munich team on cup final night. Onto the shoulders of all eleven players on the team, a ghostly glow around him, and he was doing his damnedest to kill Manchester United off. In the second half Bayern had hit the post and then the bar. We *should* have lost the match. But we (they) got lucky, we (they) didn't lose, and this was supposed to be the pot of gold at the end of the bastard rainbow. So what was Ryan's head doing on Helmut Scholl's shoulders, trying to chip the ball past Schmeichel? And why was it on Carsten Jancker's shoulders, doing an athletic overhead kick, disappointed as he watched it rattle off the crossbar? At that second I noticed that Giggs had become every player on the pitch. All the United eleven.

And the referee.

And both the linesmen.

The managers and the media.

The police.

The fans.

Multicoloured collages of colour flashed and buzzed in my brain as I felt weaker, dizzier, everything moving round and up and down, zooming in and out like a flying camera in my mind. Swooping. Dropping. Climbing. All angles at once. Why wouldn't Giggsy leave me alone? Why wasn't he with me any more? And why was he rising, rising, off the ground and into the sky, arms outstretched, head lolling on one side, hair longer and skin darker, and nailed, hands and feet, to two planks of –

I sat up.

And then, in between the gaps, the haze in my poor brain (stop pitying yourself, Wilson) in my stupid tiny mind (stop it), I had one more clear thought. In my gut, I knew: I wanted to keep existing. So I moved.

When I tried to get up, I slipped.

Actually, I hit my bad leg on the side of the bath, but the hot sting in my knee proved I was still alive, and at the time that felt like good news. (Ha! Good news!) I crawled through the hallway to the nearest phone, my four limbs numb, dialled 999 and told the operator, *The thing is, mate . . . United won the Champions League . . . but I wasn't in the team and . . . and . . . I SHOULD have been. And I couldn't think of anything else to do. It just seemed easier, to go. So here I am, know what I mean? . . . But I'm sorry! Come and help me, please.* A voice said, *So you want the ambulance service then, sir?* If some other twat had called 999 just before me and there had been no one free, then I would have had to wait, and I would have had to die. As it turned out, though, the ambulance angels flew down fast and I was conscious enough to tell the paramedic, more than once, that I couldn't believe *Jesper fuckin Blomqvist* had made the starting eleven for the final. *But that's Fergie,* I told the feller, who was Ryan, like everyone else in the ambulance. *You never know what he's gonna do next. He came to my house, you know . . . like he did with you . . . he called me son.* When the men carried me out of the bathroom and down the stairs, my telly was still on. Already, it was repeats. Nostalgia for what had happened earlier that same night, all happening just after the final whistle. The boys in the box were showing that magical moment, of the Gaffer being interviewed about the most dramatic final ever, him laughing, and admitting to the interviewer that he'd thought it was all over. Saying, *Football, bloody hell!* Then saying to him, *But you never give in!* And breaking out into a big, happy, granddad smile. It was those precious details that broke me, not being there, part of it. Not being close to the Gaffer when he smiled that smile, you know? As they wheeled me out of my flat and into the road, I thought about what it would have felt like to pick up my medal with all the other lads – jump up and down on the pitch, knackered but alive, singing CHAMPIONEEES while the confetti fell.

In the back of the ambulance, laid out on my back like I was already a gonner, surrounded by people in white pumping and blasting and rattling me left and right, I wept like a little girl. Didn't care who saw me. It didn't make any difference any more – I could feel myself shrinking by the second, shrinking and draining, leaking tears and tears till I had no energy or liquid inside me for more, though that's what I wanted. To keep crying, for ever. To never be ashamed of crying. To let go, let go, let go. The nearer we got to the hospital, running red light after red light, in a blur, passing all those cars, lorries, motorbikes, bikes, swinging between both sides of the road, the ambulance driver squeezing every possible second out of the journey, my football world seemed tiny and far, far away. Far away and irrelevant.

When I woke up, the Ryans were now a memory, maybe from my life, but maybe from someone else's – or maybe something I'd seen on the TV? Today, yesterday, last year? Did I make it up? I asked the questions, realizing even as I thought them that they weren't important. All that was left in my mashed potato mind was this thought: *I probably shouldn't have done this.* As they wheeled me through the hospital fast fast fast, heading for somewhere, I don't know where, the wheels of the trolley squeaking and groaning below like they wanted nothing to do with me, I hoped this wasn't the end. Or else Mum would never get over it. Then I hoped that maybe it was. Coz, if I did survive, Guy was gonna fuckin *kill* me.

Well, I did survive, just. I spent a week in hospital, then promised to go and see a doctor. But when the appointments came around, I couldn't face them. And I dealt with the attempt by just not thinking about it. Like it was some silly mistake that didn't need to be explained.

Six months later, I still didn't like thinking about it, but I was trying to change. Mainly coz I wanted to be a good dad to Little Ryan. I didn't know how, though, did I? I had no one to teach me what to do. After all, my own dad hadn't been any use, had he? Guy had a family of his own now, and as Sally kept saying, in her gentlest voice, I needed to *understand* that. Back then, everyone seemed to agree on one thing: that there was a lot that I needed to understand. So I didn't blame Gemma for keeping me away from the boy. She was a good woman and she was doing the right thing. Still, I was gonna be a good dad. Like I told Gemma when she came to visit me in the hospital after my attempt: *If it's the one thing I do with my life, I'm gonna be a good dad.*

Extract from the Salford Reds Fan Club Online Newsletter
1 April 2008

FERGIE'S WORST EVER XI?

You can't be right all the time, can you? In over twenty years of success, Sir Alex Ferguson has handed out United appearances to some of the world's greatest players . . . and some of the worst. Here, the Stretford End's own Teddy Linklater explores some of those who nearly lived the dream but ended up having a bit of a nightmare . . .

Goalkeeper: MASSIMO TAIBI

The £4.4m 'Blind Venetian' made just five appearances. Despite getting Man of the Match for his debut, the 5–0 defeat against Chelsea was, for some reason, more memorable.

Right-back: DAVID MAY

Gary Neville replaced him. United fans the world over rejoiced.

Centre-back: PAT McGIBBON

This Northern Irish defender was a youth team star, but was sent off on his only first-team appearance, a 3–0 League Cup defeat at home to York City in September 1995.

Centre-back: WILLIAM PRUNIER

Frenchman who lasted just two games after arriving on trial from Bordeaux in 1995. A 4–1 disaster at Spurs on New Year's Day 1996 sent him back where he came from.

Left-back: QUENTIN FORTUNE

Much maligned on the terraces, Quite Unfortunate played an inexplicable seventy-six times in this position and, sadly, others, before going to Bolton to 'further his career'.

Right-midfield: JORDI CRUYFF

Not as good as his dad. Probably not even as good as his granny.

Centre-midfield: ERIC DJEMBA-DJEMBA

So bad they named him twice. The £3.5m signing from Nantes played like a man worth £3.50 before being shifted on to Aston Villa, then Burnley and then Qatar. Yes, QATAR. Last spotted at Danish club OB. Next stop Accrington Stanley reserves?

Centre-midfield: KLEBERSON

Not all Brazilians can be as good as Pelé. Kleberson was the proof.

Left-midfield: RALPH MILNE

Fergie's self-confessed 'worst' signing, the word 'Milne' became a byword for 'shit' in the dark late eighties, before – praise be! – Ryan Giggs made this position his own. Seventy-three goals in 286 games for Dundee United, three goals in twenty-three for the only United that matters. Too busy boozing and gambling to pay off that hefty £170,000 price tag. Dogged by rumours of homosexuality, though these were never proven.

Centre-forward: DIEGO FORLAN, aka DIEGO FORLORN

A 'natural goalscorer' who took twenty-seven games to get off the mark for United. Became a cult hero after scoring twice in a 2–1 win at Anfield. Further proof, if it was needed, that United fans will forgive almost anything if you do well against the Scousers. Amazingly, Diego has gone on to great success at Villareal, Atletico Madrid, and is a hero in his native Uruguay. Massively talented. Failure in Manchester a mystery. Perhaps just couldn't handle the rain?

Centre-forward: PETER DAVENPORT

The late eighties were grim old times for the boys in Red. Peter Davenport was one of the main reasons why. Sold to Middlesbrough during a ten-game winless streak in late 1988.

And finally . . .

Sub: MIKE WILSON

If there's anything worse than being in the United all-time Worst XI, then surely it's being a SUB for that team, right? Apparently a versatile animal who was a fringe member of the legendary Class of 92, Fergie once said this boy was 'born to win'. Well, he played for the first XI just once, for two minutes, got sent off and injured in the same game. His career made Pat McGibbon look like Ryan Giggs. Last seen in Salford Job Centre . . . probably.

Post your comments on this article HERE:

GloryGloryRed329:

Oh I remember Pat McGibbon, he was SHITE!

IH8Scousers:

Teddy's right. Good old Diego Forlorn, forgiven everything for putting the ball in the Scouse net. Can't remember half of these names, though, must be losing my mind . . .

GloryGloryRed329:

How can you lose your mind when you never had one?

IH8Scousers:

Fuck you, knobhead.

Rooneysluckyboot12:

Well well well, Fergie doesn't always get it right, does he? Bloody hell, glad we got rid of the Djemba brothers – Eric Djemba and his lesser-known younger brother, Eric. Heh heh. Who the fuck is Mike Wilson, though? And where is he now?

CityMustDie_3:

Think he's dead, isn't he? I thought he was in a car accident a few years back.

Rooneysluckyboot12:

Nah, UR thinkin of another Mike Wilson I think. This one got done for lifting. Broke into a house in Hale Barns and got caught running through some bloke's garden with a telly in his arms. I read it in the *Evening News* . . . so it must be true!

IH8Scousers:

Yeah, that's right. A mate of a mate used to know him when he was a kid at Salford Boys. Never got over his injury. Real shame. Nice lad, apparently. And talented too. Football's a funny old game, isn't it?

Rooneysluckyboot12:
It certainly is, mate, it certainly is. Funny old game! Funny old game!

MadRed4Eva666:
I remember that match in 1992 and that was the worst tackle I've ever seen by ANYONE. Anyone know what happened to the defender? That tackle looked like a career finisher. Come on, people, why do we forget the real victims?

RonnyIsGod:
Can't even remember that guy Wilson – I think our man Teddy's just made him up for an April Fool. But Kleberson? No thanks, Fergie . . . I think he's a rent boy now. LOL x 1000.

CityMustDie_3:
OMFG – really? What's his number? Is he cheap?

RonnyIsGod:
Yeah. Cheap as chips. And dirtier than UR mum.

RedArmy_1001:
That sounds well gay.

RonnyisGod:
Cock lovin nigger.

BusbyBabesRIP:
Actually, if that's your attitude, mate, then you must hate Giggsy too, coz Giggsy's half-black. His dad was a black rugby player.

CityMustDie_3 – THIS ENTRY HAS BEEN DELETED

RonnyisGod – THIS ENTRY HAS BEEN DELETED

FergieforPrimeMinister:
Where's Wesley Brown on this list? Most overrated United player EVER. Only makes the team when everyone else is injured.

Heroesof99:
What?! Wesley's a L-E-G-E-N-D! And more apps than anyone so far this season.

CityMustDie_3:
Yeah, FergieforPrimeMinister, fuck off, don't mess with the Wes!

FergieforPrimeMinister:
No, you fuck off, knobhead. I'm gonna knock UR fuckin block off!

HungManc:
Anyone on here speak Polish? Or Hungarian? Hogy minden magyar vörösök odakint! Mi vagyunk a legnagyobb rajongók! Szeretjük Ryan Giggs!

CityMustDie_3:
Hungarians are gay.

EXTRA TIME

SQUEAKY BUM TIME

'I wouldn't swap my career with anyone's.'

Ryan Giggs

A DIRTY SIN

But it can't carry on for ever.

After nearly three weeks you can't hold it in any more. Don't want to. Can't remember why you needed to. But you have to get this right, so you tell her the two of you are gonna have a real treat. For the night, you tell her, you're gonna be rich. You're off to a posh new restaurant. Candlelight, nice soft music, the whole works – Guy reckons the food's the best on the curry mile. And when you get there, you remind her she can have whatever she likes. (She looks at you funny, says, *Don't talk down to me, please*, but it feels good to say it anyway.) Bubbly is ordered. Starters are ordered. You're in a smart shirt and trousers. She's in a dress. You make sure she's settled before you open your fat mouth and say, *Gem, I've got something to tell you.* She puts down her knife and fork and says, *You don't wanna get fuckin* married, *do you?*

It takes time to cover everything, your whole messy history, all the way from the red ball in the garden to your latest injury on the same old bad leg as always. It takes for ever to tell this story, which starts when the poppadums are brought out and goes on till the end of the main course. You know you're saying too much, you're talking too fast and her face says *no no no* while her head shakes so slow it's almost not happening. But you can't keep this to yourself, can you? As the waiters are pouring drinks you stumble, all clumsy, words jumbled. Something about Guy and Sally, and how you wanna live like them. How they're a total team, how they've always got their arms round each other, holding hands and sneaking kisses in public. Like they can't believe how complete the other one makes them. They're still working it out.

In time you talk faster, more direct, get closer to saying what you mean. As your chicken tikka masala begins to go cold, you can't believe it's you saying these words, but here they are, spilling out of your mouth. You tell her, *I love you, Gem*. You say, *You've got to help me.* You really truly believe she'll pick you up and take you on, so soon. After a few nights out, a couple of clumsy shags and some vague talk about the future, coz it's easier not to think it through, and coz Guy always says that *Love doesn't make sense, Mikey, you can't explain it*. As you talk and talk, you wait for her to crack a smile. Pull you towards her and squeeze. But at the end of your story she sighs, her mouth a tiny, tight O shape, her breath pushing slowly through the hole. She says, *It's been a laugh, Mikey, but . . . I told you I wasn't ready.* (Mouth back to normal now. Looks like a mouth again.) Then she says, in a gentle way, *Anyway, I need a grown-up. You really aren't one. I'm so sorry.* She gets up, thinks about saying something else, then leaves.

You phone Guy from the restaurant, the mess of the meal's leftovers in front of you, and even though he tells you he can't talk right now, he's at the hospital with Sally who's just gone into labour with their first kid, you tell him you've got no one else and you need him. (You actually say those words: *I've got no one else. I need you.*) You tell him what's happened and reel off every disgusting word you can think of to describe Gemma and what she's done. She's no longer a sparkling diamond, she's *a dirty fuckin Scouser, a filthy whore*. You tell him that thinking about her makes you sick. You tell him you're gonna win her back. You're gonna track her down and kill her. You're gonna cut her heart out. Break her into bits and mail the pieces to her family. (Guy tries to interrupt, saying, *The baby's coming, Mikey. It's coming early. Sally needs me. Do you understand?*) You fall down, right there on the street, in the dark, hand out in front of you, holding you away from the pavement. You're holding the mobile away from your ear, your cheeks wet, as Guy tells you to breathe deeply and stop saying things you don't mean. You tell him, *That's it. No more women. No more anything*. He says, *Mikey. Don't do anything stupid, you hear? I'm being serious. I really need to go now.* But where could he possibly have to be? What could be more important than family?

After the end of the world, you don't leave the house for days except to go to the twenty-four-hour shop and back for basics. You live off tins and biscuits and cheap beer. Anything you can get hold of. No matter how many times Guy or Mum try to get you to talk, you don't want to do that any more. (You tried talking, and look what that led to.) You don't answer the door. Don't answer the phone. Stay in bed till early afternoon and stay up all night every night, flicking between Sky Sports channels, drinking, playing *Football Manager*. You put on weight from living off shit and have nightmares about eating yourself to death. Meanwhile, in the game that lives in the screen, your latest make-believe career, it's 2008 and you're manager of Manchester United. In the game, you sold Ryan six months ago, to Portsmouth. He's retired now. In the game, you've just won the Champions League for the third season in a row.

One night that week, Guy climbs in the window and finds you asleep on the couch. You've got sweet and chocolate wrappers stuck to your trackie bottoms and MUTV is still on in the background. He sits down, close, wakes you up gently and tells you to *get a fucking grip, Mikey.* He says, *Have some self-respect.* Then he shows you a photograph of his baby and says, *Hey, Mike. You're an uncle. Meet Robbie.* But it's easy for him. Guy's got big eyes and smooth skin and he can talk to anyone. He's the sensible, strong man who's been doing a great job of building the family business since Uncle Si died. He's the boy next door and the clever teacher you secretly fancy and the mate you want to have a pint with and the useful handyman and the model you want a one-night stand with and the good prospect you'd leave your loving husband for, all wrapped up into one well-chiselled package. That's why he skipped from one girlfriend to the next with hardly a break from age twelve to twenty-one, and has been with Sally ever since. He can't understand what you understand: that you're the kind of man who only gets one chance. Your chance was Gemma. And you've had it.

This self-pitying bullshit goes on for another week before you properly brave the outside.

*

Imagine: a few weeks later, you see Gemma on the street. She's holding shopping bags. You smile, leaning in and giving her a big hug – you breathe alcohol onto her and tell her how well the team have been doing (you're on your way back from the bookies where you've had your first big win in a while). You ask her to if she wants to go for a quick pint. But she just presses a palm to your cheek and softly says, *Mikey Mikey Mikey, were you listening to me or not?* then picks up her handbag and walks away. She gives you this look as if you're supposed to know what's going on. That night you phone Guy (newborn in background), and ask how you can get Gemma to love you back, but he just keeps saying *What are we gonna do with you?* He never knows anything when you need him to. Guy's like the fuckin England team: raises your hopes then dashes them. It's all hat tricks and smiles against Kazakhstan and Jamaica, but when the heat is on and the men are separated from the boys, when it's shoot-out time against Germany in the World Cup semi-finals, he steps up to the spot and skies his penalty every time. You don't know what's going on inside Gemma's head, but she says she's already told you. All you can think about is answering that question, but you can't. You don't even know what the question is. Do you? That day could have been the last time you'd seen her if you hadn't taken a chance, once, on that first night together. You'd told her, *Don't worry, it's all gonna be fine*, then you'd lain down on the bed, in the dark.

When Gemma comes over a few days later to tell you the news, it's pretty obvious you have a different idea of what the word 'fine' means. You feel all light and heavy at the same time. (The drink doesn't help.) You wanna phone Mum straight away. You wanna phone everyone you know. You're gonna be a *dad!* Just like Guy. Christ, KIDS! That's the reason for sex in the first place, right? Why's she so surprised? What's wrong? One minute Gemma's right in front of you, in your hallway, strong and standing up straight and looking so grown-up and glowing and like someone you could share your couch with for ever, but the next it's all gone coz she falls to the floor, bangs her fist on the floorboard and says you've ruined her life. She says she's a stupid fucking bitch. She should have known better. She's a slag. She's a filthy slut who deserves to die. She hates herself. Why did she go to bed with such a dickhead? She collapses. One hand awkwardly outwards, holding herself up off the floor, she reminds you of something, but you don't quite know what it is. She beats her head with her hands and screams that she wants to jump off a bridge.

Gemma's parents make sure that doesn't happen. They say it's a dirty sin what the two of you have done, but a worse one to kill a baby, or yourself, or both. Their God would never forgive it. They lock her in her room with a member of the family at all times, to make sure she can't escape to that bridge and take a dive, headfirst, into freedom. Unlike Gemma's parents, you don't have a god to guide you. (Mum still has hers, but He doesn't make her any happier.) You don't have anyone to stop you from doing stupid, selfish, melodramatic shit when life goes wrong and you can't see it ever getting better. Half the time when you call Guy these days, he's too busy to talk – he's changing nappies and cleaning up sick. When Sally picks up the phone she says things like, *What is it now?* and *You know, your nephew might like to meet his Uncle Mike*, and *Do you know what it's like being married to two brothers at the same time?* All that baby business is doing funny things to Sally. She used to be all right. You wonder whether that will happen to Gemma too.

Meanwhile, a million light years away, Manchester United are about to beat Juventus in the second leg of a semi-final of the biggest club competition in the world. Flags have been waved. Songs have been sung. Confetti has fallen from the sky while all over the Stadio delle Alpi in Torino thousands of mobiles and cameras have snapped at the same time, making it seem like lightning is hitting the ground, again, again, again. With six minutes left on the clock Andy Cole scores the winning goal to send United through to the 1999 Champions League final – their first in over thirty years. You see the goal, and remember that pass, and wonder if life can get any worse.

So, the *real* beginning then.

On the thirty-first of January 2000 a bouncing baby boy was born in Wythenshawe Hospital, Manchester, after a long labour. He weighed seven pounds and four ounces. He had a wisp of brown hair at the crown of his skull, so soft it looked like candyfloss. Once he was out into the world Gemma was exhausted, and said she couldn't care less about the name. She said, *I'm dying anyway*. But the doctors said that kind of talk was normal for new mothers who were definitely going to live and, anyway, the name was important to me. The *most* important thing. So when Gemma said she'd go with what I wanted if I promised to leave her alone afterwards, I told her what she wanted to hear. *You'll never see me again*, I said. *I swear.* I was so high on it all that I nearly put in a request for the whole 1999 treble-winning team: which would have made him Something Schmeichel Neville Johnsen Stam Irwin Giggs Beckham Butt Blomqvist Yorke Wilson Sheringham Solskjaer Black. I'd heard of people who did that. But poor Gem, it might have killed her off after all. So I kept it simple and got a result: Ryan Alexander. For once I hit the jackpot. Gemma's granddad, who died years ago, was called Alex, and she liked the name Ryan anyway – she used to fancy him back in school, she said – so there was no fight, not about that anyway. A son. Mine. Perhaps that was all my luck right there. A lifetime's luck. In one. Ryan Alexander Black, welcome to the fuckin world!

Okay: that wasn't quite the beginning.

By then we'd been at the hospital nearly a whole day. All day and night, waiting. Going hours at a time without much news, except that there had *been some complications.* In the end they cut her open. I stayed at that place the whole time. I ate out of the hospital shop and drank coffee out of the hospital vending machine. Tried to get spirits climbing around me, not think about it all, what might happen. Just like in the early teams I played for as a kid, clapping hands and keeping Gemma's Gerrard-loving family up up up. Not sleeping, pacing up and down the hospital waiting room, wondering why it took so long to pull one person out of another one. Trying to concentrate on walking in a straight line, my lips tight together, I was pretty sure that if I opened my gob, I wouldn't be able to stop myself from saying, *If Gemma dies, do I get to keep the kid?*

The longer it went on, the fuller the waiting room got – there was her mum, dad, two sisters, an uncle, a few cousins too. It was the biggest family in the world. And they were nice enough (for Scousers), but in a way like they thought I'd never be able to look after a new little person who couldn't sit up or hold a spoon. I told them I was gonna be around, I was born to be a dad. (Said that sentence a lot.) Gemma's mum rubbed my back and told me I should get a decent job first. Softly she said, *Just provide for my grandchild, that's all I ask*. So I reminded the fat cow that it wasn't *hers*, she didn't *own* this unborn thing, nobody did, and threatened lots of things I didn't mean, coz I'm not just a fuckin CREDIT CARD, know what I mean? Well, Gemma's mum did NOT know what I meant. And neither did I. Hadn't had much sleep. I was a volcano. I burst and overflowed, then went quiet. I tried to explain afterwards, you know, but with some people you only get one chance. In the years after, I wished Gemma's mum would just give me the nice, friendly, mercy look that I'd never wanted when I had it in the hospital.

Little Ryan was a healthy baby, Gemma lived, and every day she was that bit more like the girl I bought a drink for in the Dog & Partridge on the day of the best goal ever. One by one, the doctors took out the wires they'd stuck in her, and as it became obvious that no one was gonna die, bit by bit the big family all went home. Both mum and baby stayed in hospital for what felt like months coz the doctors were worried about what they called *further complications*, but I was buzzing. Little Ryan was strong – whenever they let me in to see him, he was screaming the place down. (No baby dies screaming, do they?) And Gemma's bite was coming back. Meanwhile, one thing was obvious about the whole business – his mum might not want to admit it, but Little Ryan looked just like his dad. Right down to those little squashed-up ears. No need for a paternity test with those ears around! Whenever I saw him, I reached out and stroked them with my fingers.

Finally, Gemma and Little Ryan were allowed home. The day after they let her out, I phoned the house (again) and spoke to Gemma's mum (again), who wouldn't let me speak to Gemma (again), but did say that if I promised not to be any trouble then I could go round. For ten minutes. I promised what I needed to promise, and that night I spent those minutes at Gemma's flat, watched by her mum, who had her big arms crossed tight while I stroked those little baby ears with a huge grin on my face. *Yeah, I know,* said Gem, who was sitting up in bed. *Poor kid. What's he got to look forward to?* I smiled at her, then at Little Ryan, amazed at how small he was. I picked him up out of his cot, cradled the back of his tiny skull in the palm of my hand and said, *We made him, Gem. That's something, isn't it?* But Gemma isn't one for weak talk. *Yeah, well done, Einstein,* she said. *I wonder how we managed that? Fuckin hell, Mike, are you always gonna be like this?*

WEDNESDAY 9 APRIL 2008
CHAMPIONS LEAGUE
QUARTER-FINAL 2ND LEG

UNITED	**1–0**	**AS ROMA**
TÉVEZ 70		**(DE ROSSI MISSED PENALTY 28)**

(UNITED WIN 3–0 ON AGGREGATE)

ATTENDANCE: 74,423

GIGGSY WATCH – FergieforPrimeMinister says: Great Man unlucky not to get on score sheet, but his big-game experience was MASSIVE 2nite, esp as Sir Alex gave us all the shits by leaving out the big guns. Giggsy subbed again tho. Gaffer never seems to give him 90mins any more! Does he turn into a pumpkin after an hour or something?

Average Fan Rating: 7/10

This time the chauffeur agreed to put the radio on, and the pre-match build-up bled through small speakers into the back seats. Mike leaned forward and turned off Sky Sports News on the TV in front of him. He sat up straight. Then he spread his arms like wings across the back seat of the limousine. There was plenty of room. The girls had turned down a return.

'What, go to the football *again*?' said Ellie when Terry asked. 'But we've only just *been*!'

So now Terry wasn't speaking to his sister, and wanted no mention of her, but Mike thought it all seemed strangely quiet without her and Jen. Still, the smooth leather seats and warm smell inside the car were things Mike could get used to whether there were women around or not. They arrived at the ground, the driver held the door open again, and this time Mike bowed his head slightly and smiled.

'Thank you, Jim,' he said. 'Have a good night.'

'You too, sir,' said Jim. 'Up the Reds.'

Mike and Terry got out of the limousine together.

This time, when Mike was offered a drink at the door, he was ready. 'No thanks,' he said. 'Designated driver.'

And he did that, several times, each time looking directly at the palace gate soldier.

'No thanks. Designated driver.'

'No thanks. Designated driver.'

But, alone with Terry, Mike began to wonder. The old place, the thick atmosphere, made him want to become one with it. Also, Terry had offered this ticket for nothing again, and couldn't hide his disappointment when he found out he was going to be drinking alone. Mike thought, Would it be rude not to help Terry have a good time? It was one thing to say no once, twice, three times. But for ever? Who can say no for ever?

The next time the palace soldiers came round, Mike reached out a shaking hand to touch, slowly, nervously, uncertainly. The drink sparkled in its cool container. He sipped. Meanwhile, Terry was talking, but his friend wasn't really listening. Mike had broken his own rule, and had already forgotten why. Whatever it was, it hadn't taken much. He didn't know what to feel. He took his second sip, letting the liquid slip down his throat, making the world a fuzzier, friendlier place.

'Now,' he said, 'where did that buffet go? I've been saving myself all day!'

When the announcement came to go through to join the rest of the crowd, Mike was downing his third pint. Terry laughed and put a sweaty arm round him.

'Mate . . . Doesn't matter. Leave it. There's plenty more where that came from!'

Terry's arm remained where it was for a second or two. Then it moved.

Looking at the arm, Mike realized that they could drink for ever. Looking around at all the half-finished beers, wines and cocktails, it seemed there was an infinite supply, as well as the mountain of food.

'Right,' he said eventually. 'Till half-time then!' As they shuffled over to their seats, he hoped no one he knew had seen him coming from Corporate.

Mostly, the Old Trafford vibes were good. There was bit of native restlessness in the first half because of the manager's experimental line-up, and because of a debatable missed penalty for Roma, which could have let them back into the tie. But, aside from that, United dominated, the makeshift team coping well enough, with considerable guidance from one Ryan Giggs. (The talk of his imminent demise had died down again in recent days.) After the whistle blew for half-time, a relieved cheer went up from the crowd – they were that bit closer to the semi-finals.

As the punters in the cheap seats rushed to the bars and the toilets, Mike Wilson stepped back through the magic doors into the other side, where money lived, along with Terry. As the door closed protectively behind him, he noticed that, in among the cakes and meringues, mini cheeseburgers were freely available.

'Cheeseburgers?' he asked Terry. 'For *afters*?'

'Gourmet too,' said Terry, grinning widely. 'Different menu every time.'

'Well, they didn't have all this shit in my day,' said Mike. 'Good job I suppose. Else I would have been too busy eating mini cheeseburgers to play football.'

The queue for food was huge. People must have been lining up since before half-time. Mike decided to get another pint in. After all, it wasn't like you had to wait for *that*, was it?

Roma didn't threaten often in the second half, and Carlos Tévez scored a goal that put the result beyond doubt on seventy minutes. Mike gave a little smile when the ball hit the back of the net. Around him, the crowd celebrated this event as if a goal was the last thing they expected to happen in a football match – but Mike had known it was coming. There was no shock, only quiet pleasure. Tévez had chosen that exact second to score so Mike could enjoy the party afterwards, surrounded by all that money. And all that beer. Which he did, for several hours, toasting the team's future success. Mike told anyone who would listen that United were certain to win the Champions League.

'I feel it,' he said, several times, to strangers, pounding his chest each time. 'In *here*.'

On the way home, Terry and Mike talked animatedly about the game, and the season as a whole, as if they'd never get bored of talking to each other. It was all going right, they said. It was going to be a magical season. Like 1999. A magical season. But, as they neared Terry's flat, conversation stalled. The limo pulled up. Terry spoke.

'You know, if you want to come to another one of these, you can. If my brother has spare tickets again. Maybe the semis, eh? Better than having to listen to those blokes behind us in the usual seats, moaning on.'

'Yeah,' said Mike, the drink beginning to take effect. 'Cheers, man. Yeah. For sure.'

'We can keep going if you like,' said Terry, putting his hand on Mike's hand. 'You can see my flat.'

Terry guessed what Mike was thinking.'You know,' he said, 'you don't have to hide who you are, Mike. Not with me. I see you. I do.'

Mike thought about this for a few more seconds, looked at Terry, and noticed Terry's expression, which was all kindness. His shoulders, no tension in them. The top button on his shirt undone. Then he decided what to do.

'Nah, mate,' he said, keeping his voice light. 'Better get some kip, eh? Red Army!'

And he was gone. Walking, alone, giving Jim the driver the thumbs-up. As Mike walked, he imagined Terry watching, and he wondered whether Terry even had a brother at all.

The following morning, media outlets worldwide reported that Manchester United were through to the semi-finals of the Champions League. Meanwhile, Mike Wilson called in his first sickie at Sportswear Direction. He lay in bed, sweating, waiting for Brian to knock on the door and ask him what the fuck he thought he was playing at.

But no one knocked.

In the next few days, Mike waited for the cravings to hit again. He half expected to end up under a table at the Dog & Partridge by the end of the week, penniless, crying, singing himself to sleep. But that song never came. He didn't even want another drink. A few mornings later, walking to work at a brisk, steady pace, Mike thought about a future where he could have an occasional whisky at Christmas, maybe one on his birthday. Keep it under control. Behave himself. Not be the sad uncle in the corner sipping Coke who everyone whispered about. Mike really didn't mind staying off the drink, it was just *never* being allowed one. Life was too long for that.

Mike's experiences in the Champions Club had been worth it, he felt. That previous life of his, it was almost like someone else's life, that he could look at, and understand, and empathize with. It had been good to go back to the inner sanctum of Old Trafford, without consequence – two nights out, two games, and the world hadn't come to an end – no ex-player alarm system had gone off. Alex Ferguson hadn't dragged him out onto the street and told him never to return. But he had no desire at all to go back to the Champions Club. Soon Mike would be back where he belonged, in his usual seat. Terry was a good guy. He'd understand. That whole week he slept more easily than normal. He slept right through the night, every night. And Ryan was often in his dreams.

UNITED IS COCA-COLA

Whisper it: *Sometimes you think about giving up the game for good.* It's now 2005, thirteen long years since you burst onto the Old Trafford turf, and you can finally admit it: things have changed. In the last few years, since you started to put life back together. Since then, unexpected things have surfaced, things making you suspect you might not be in control of your mind after all. A desire bigger than anything you can describe or understand seeps into your cells when you least expect it. You could be in bed, trying to sleep. You could be getting up, bleary-eyed, shovelling breakfast down half awake, before heading out to work (wherever that is this month). You're not on guard, not expecting anything to happen. Why would it? But before you know what's happening, you're dreaming.

The first time you clearly remember wanting out is one day when you're lacing up, about to turn out for the local amateur team who still let you play with them sometimes. When you're fit enough. And when they're a bit short. You've not heard from the guys for a while until you get a call early one Sunday morning from Bobby, the team captain. *Hey, superstar,* he says. *Fancy rolling back the years one more time?* And, it's amazing: you don't. Some time leaks by. As he's waiting on the other end of the line you notice your boots, still mud-caked from your last mediocre appearance, slung in the corner of the kitchen cupboard with your shin pads. Bobby says, *You injured, champ? Or dumb? Or what? We're a man down here! Do you wanna play or not?* You open up to tell him NO, but you've not seen another human being in three days, you've been saying yes all your life, and the noise that comes out of your throat is a lie.

A couple of hours later you're in the pissing rain, hovering on the touchline, waiting for the ball, playing in front of about ten people. Including subs. One of the men, maybe the manager of the other team, is shouting like his life depends on victory. You wouldn't say this to him, it'd break the poor bastard, but he's making no difference to events on the pitch. No one's listening. It reminds you of a thousand long years ago when you were a kid, and Dad was right there, close by, living every moment with you. Standing with Uncle Si, screaming. Now you think about it – now you *can* think about it – you realize Dad was useless too, and you were growing *despite* him. You were young then, and bursting with energy. But now you feel ancient: your bones ache and sometimes your bad leg feels like a dead weight you have to drag around like a ball and chain. (The pain comes and goes.) When you bend down to retie your laces that old knee wants to buckle, and you feel like sinking into the mud for good. Dropping down into another world.

But then, another change. The ball comes your way, the old magic pulses through you, and you're hugging that comfort blanket again. Other players call your name, just like they used to, but you're not gonna pass the ball to these monkeys. These amateurs. Are you? You're miles out, right on the halfway line, but this is the lowest of the Sunday league low, you're a professional athlete, a fuckin MANCHESTER UNITED player and there's no way you're gonna give up the ball. You head right for goal, powering through one, two defenders, stumbling over one, two tackles, and soon you're at the edge of the area. Do you shoot? No, you keep dribbling. As the keeper comes out to your feet you go right round him, take the ball to a yard from the white line and just tap it, ever so lightly, inside the dirty white post. Grinning like fuck. *And Wilson does it agaaaaaain!* shouts Bobby. *Is there no END to this boy's talents?*

Later on, at the pub, the team are sitting around at a couple of corner tables, talking the game to death, analysing it like the match actually matters. Bobby's the worst of the lot. Talking about your goal, he says it reminded him of that amazing solo one scored against Arsenal back in 1999, the year everything went right. (For the team.) *I swear*, says Bobby. *That goal . . . it was better than Giggsy's!* Everyone else agrees, and they toast you. *To Mikey Wilson!* they shout. *Better than Ryan Giggs!* Then they clink. There's a purity to it, you think. These guys, who leave their wives and kids on a Sunday morning, hoof it around, and dream. You raise your arms, join in the toast to yourself, forget you ever wanted to stay at home and ignore the twinge in the back of your leg.

A few months later it happens again. It's summer now, the days are too long, exhausting, there's been no football for weeks, and your hours at (yet another) new office drag. Meanwhile, the boys in the box are struggling to make like they care about cricket and tennis, MUTV is round-the-clock repeats, there's fuck all to talk about for days on end, and one day, out on the local playing fields, you start thinking of what it might be like to escape your flat and fuck off out of Manchester for good. You daydream a lot. Mostly of ways you can steal away to a better life somewhere else, Little Ryan with you. (He's five now. In school. You see him a couple of times a month for a few hours, under supervision.) Sure, Mum would worry at first, and you'd have to live quiet for a while until Gemma gave up the chase. But Mum would get over it, just like she did with Dad (she's just joined an over-fifties dating company and she's starting up her own homemade jewellery business online; she's gonna be just fine), and soon enough you'd get settled somewhere hot, with a beach. Somewhere they'd never heard of football. Maybe you'd buy a little cocktail bar at the beach and you could run it. Start a new family tradition. Get free of the old one. For a while you forget that's exactly what Dad has done. Then you remember. And laugh.

The thought of leaving grows. And more than once you stand outside Gemma's place, hands in pockets, for an hour or so, watching the door, looking for movements and considering one of your own. You're there just a bit too long not to be noticed by Gemma's mum, who stands at the window, looking out, making sure you can see her phoning the police. You never actually do anything about leaving, but something can't be unborn. The idea that you might not follow the team this season. Not just give up the ticket, but not watch the games at all. Put the TV and the radio in the bin. Cancel the subscriptions. Clear out the United room. Just pick up Little Ryan, leave, and start again, music playing loud in the car as you speed off into the distance. When you think of this you shake like you're doing cold turkey already.

Then it passes. You can't believe you ever considered it.

The first day of the 2005/06 season is the same as always. You put on the shirt, buy a programme, place your bet (one pound these days, no more), and head towards the ground, like last year and the year before. Ryan is about to start his sixteenth season in the first team and his pre-season form is good. As you pass through the turnstile and head towards the seats, you talk with Guy about the team and avoid everything else. Some graffiti on a wall by the chip shop reads, *United is Microsoft. United is Disney. United is Coca-Cola.* Guy says, *Must have been done by someone against the takeover. Or a City supporter.* Guy's smiling, but you HATE Manchester City. (Why is that, though, really? Why?) You pin a badge to the lapel of your jacket. The badge says 'Love United, Hate Glazer'. Guy shakes his head, laughs, says, *Right on, comrade!* You answer, *Right on*, and melt into the crowd.

After the game, walking back down Sir Matt Busby Way, you say, *I've been thinking, bruv. One day, maybe once Fergie and Giggsy retire, I might stop all this. Once they're gone, that might be easier.*

Guy's a good lad. He doesn't say anything back.

David Robert Joseph Beckham:

Officer in the Order of the British Empire (awarded 2003)
United Nations Children's Fund Goodwill Ambassador (2005–present)
Time Magazine's 100 Most Powerful People in the World
(first appearance 2008)

We never really knew each other. Goldenballs was a shy boy then, and the few times we did speak, I usually took the piss out of his voice. That was back in the days when it looked like it'd be me, not him, who'd end up doing Nike adverts, marrying a pop star, starting up a football academy in my name and trying to crack America armed with just a smile and seven hundred bastard support staff.

Beckham's success was everywhere. After that day he scored from the halfway line against Wimbledon (so lucky!), he was like the new Giggsy for a while, until he suddenly inflated and got bigger and kept getting bigger and more famous than Ryan had ever been. Where Ryan had a hundred screaming girls following him, Goldenballs had a thousand. Where Ryan did low-rent adverts for Quorn, stumbling through the simplest of lines, Beckham was smooth, a different animal. A natural in front of a camera, modelling for Versace and Calvin Klein and Armani – all those fuckers – posing in tight underwear, blown up on billboards so big that his cock looked ten foot long. I never saw the appeal myself. Too girly. Too weedy. All sarong and no trousers. Giggs was the original: Becks before Becks. He had it all, first. The celebrity girlfriends, the million-pound boot contracts, the sponsorship deals in the Far East, all while David – whose penis now commands over 300,000 results on Google by the way – was still out on loan at Preston

North End. People have got short fuckin memories in this game, I'll tell you that.

As we got older I got bored of seeing Beckham's mug on my TV, on billboards, on packaging for everyday items. *Buy shit!* he said. *Buy more shit! Buy even more useless shit I can afford and you can't!* If ever there was a footballer born to line the pockets of the men in grey suits, it was David Beckham. I was getting really fuckin tired of it, so honest-to-God tired that I didn't really even wanna get in contact. But I'd already ticked off most of the others and was way past thinking straight. Scholesy: no answer. Butty: no answer. The Neville Sisters: no fuckin answer. The longer it went on, the more I could only think about one thing. This letter from 2004 proves it. All right, at least I was sober this time, and I wrote it in my best handwriting. Neat, just like him. A nice neat boy. Squeaky bastard clean.

URGENT: FOR THE ATTENTION OF DAVID BECKHAM

Dear David, OBE (Great! Now best mates with the Queen!),

The guys in my local, the Dog & Partridge in Salford, said you'd never be the same after Fergie smacked you about in the dressing room after that Cup tie against Arsenal – but I knew you'd be okay. Is your eye all right now? It seems like it from what I've seen on the TV, and all publicity's good publicity, right? So your sponsors won't mind too much. Anyway, I'm sure you'll win lots of trophies now you're at Real Madrid. Some guys on the forums say you're a traitor for leaving United, but me and the Stretford End understand you wanted to stay, and that you've given your best years to United. If you hear some fans singing that song about your wife 'taking it up the arse', or the one about Cristiano Ronaldo making you 'look shite', just ignore them. It's only a bit of a laugh. And anyway, at least one of those two things is true, so best not to make a fuss. eh?

My name's Mikey Wilson – I'm the one from the Class of 92 who got moved on to Plymouth. We used to be in the United youth team together, remember? Then the rezzies, and I played for the first team as well. I was a striker – the Gaffer once said I was 'born to win'.

They used to call me 'Little Giggs' in the early days because I was a bit younger than Giggsy and played the same way, but I always thought I was more like you. Here's a photo so you can see. My mum says we have the same cheekbones. What do you reckon? Anyway, I got injured on my debut for the first team.

I never really recovered. It's not easy to write this, David, but I hope you'll understand and take pity on an old mate who just needs a break – in a way, our situations are the same. The Gaffer called time on my United career too early, and the same happened to you I suppose. Anyway, I need a job – do you need a security guard, or PA? What about a coach for your academy, or maybe your children need a babysitter? I'd do anything, and I promise I won't steal any of your stuff and then try and sell it on eBay. I do live in Manchester, but I'd move for you guys, no danger. (Maybe if I was working for you, my ex would let me bring our boy.) If you can't give me a job then please send cash as I'm clean out of funds, and unlike you I can't make a living from the game we both love any more.

Say hi to Victoria for me.
With love and respect,

Mike J. Wilson

PS There's a second photo of us here, in action for the rezzies against Everton in spring 1992. My mum wants it back, so please send to the above address.

PPS You can keep the photo of me on my own if you want.

Well, say what you like about Goldenballs, but he was the only one who got back to me. Sort of. And the only one who gave me anything.

Dear Mike,

Thank you for writing to David Beckham! He is very happy that so many young people want to get in touch, and is just sorry that because of the many thousands of letters he receives every year he can't write back to everyone individually. Please accept this Real Madrid badge, a packet of official FA stickers of David and his England teammates, and a discount voucher for the David Beckham Fan Club, also an entry form for a competition with first prize being lunch and a training session with David!

Thanks again,

Fi Bingham
Assistant Communications Director
The David Beckham Fan Club

Yeah, it was a low day when I got that letter. But I kept the fuckin badge, for sure. And the stickers. And I went in for the prize, just in case.

Name – Mike 'Little Giggs' Wilson (the one from the Class of 92)
Age – too old to enter this competition
Why I'd like to meet David – Because if he doesn't make me rich I'm going to hang myself from the Old Trafford gates.

I didn't write to any of the other players for months afterwards. There's only so much one man can take. Still, in the end, there was one more I had to try. And I knew he wouldn't let me down.

TUESDAY 13 APRIL 2008
PREMIER LEAGUE

UNITED	**2-1**	**ARSENAL**
RONALDO 54 (PEN) **HARGREAVES 72**		**ADEBAYOR 48**

ATTENDANCE: 75,985

GIGGSY WATCH – InArseneWeTrust says: 89th minute sub and still an Average Fan Rating of 8/10? RU SERIOUS?!? OMFG, this site is sooooo biased. Did he even touch the ball? CHEATING NORTHERN SCUM.

Average Fan Rating: 8/10

Mike's usual match-day outfit wasn't quite the dress code for Netty's Olde Biscuit Bar, but Debbie Carlsson didn't complain. He'd agreed to sit in her favourite spot, by the big windows, and that was enough for her. She told him she liked how the windows attracted the light and how, in the afternoons, it was good for watching people go by the park. Mother and son drank cappuccino and discussed how Guy and Sally were going to be parents again soon, and Debbie talked about how a Christmas all together was finally a real possibility. Her and Derek. Mike (and maybe Little Ryan, for part of the afternoon). Guy and Sally and their three little ones – Robbie, Millie and the one on the way.

'I can almost smell the turkey,' she said.

'What are we doing here?' replied Mike. 'This isn't exactly your kind of place, is it?'

'Well,' said Debbie, 'it didn't used to be. I'll give you that, Michael.' She faced him, unafraid. 'But I bring Derek here now. We met here you know, at this very table, the first few times we dated.' She laughed.

'Well, we never called them "dates". Derek called them "coffee meetings", but we both knew that wasn't quite true.'

'Mmm,' said Mike.

'Derek never said anything about it, though. About how I wasn't ready to call them dates yet. That's one of the things I like about him the most, you know – one of the many things. He pays attention to what's important to me, and responds to it. Women like that, Michael. To be responded to.'

Mike noticed his mum was sitting up straight, still holding onto her handbag as if it was attached to her hand with glue. Why didn't she just let go?

'Well, this place is miles from the ground,' he said. 'We'll have to get the Metro in. And it's Arsenal today so it'll be mental.'

Debbie's reply was gentle. 'That's fine, darling,' she said. 'I've been on public transport before.'

There was something about his mother that Mike couldn't quite identify. It had been coming for a while, in stages. It was years since her darkest days, but this part of the transformation, the part that Mike couldn't name, this was new. It didn't even feel like that long since he'd seen her. Was it new clothes? A new way of speaking? He was sure his mum seemed to be getting posher as she got older. Or at least, she wanted to be. He watched her eat her slice of carrot cake and couldn't help but notice the controlled way she pressed her fork into the flesh of it. He thought, This was going to be a disaster.

Mike had been so shocked at her offer of company that he forgot to refuse it. Debbie had hardly ever gone to football matches before. Or shown any interest. Even when her son was playing for Manchester United, she said she couldn't bear to watch and only came that once. Eventually he'd given in.

'Course, I'll pay for your ticket,' he said. 'Just this once.'

And she'd smiled. 'Thanks very much, Michael, you're too kind. But I'm a working woman now – I can pay for my own. I'll even get yours if you're nice to me.'

Why was she making this so hard? He felt like getting up, walking out and going to the game alone. Maybe he wouldn't even go to the match. All this behaving himself was making him thirsty.

In the next few minutes Mike fended off several different approaches. Debbie started with gentle nudges, asking in an encouraging way about whether he was seeing Little Ryan soon, also whether he was seeing anyone special. Mike gave her nothing. Then she took out a series of photographs she'd taken of Little Ryan when the boy had visited her the previous weekend, photos in which he was jumping on the mini trampoline she'd bought for him and playing in the back garden with Derek. Again, Mike's answers were short. They made no acknowledgement of effort. She could suffer, at least for a while, for coming to an arrangement with Gemma without telling him. Then Debbie tried a more direct route.

'I'm happy to help you, Michael,' she said. 'I *want* to help. So does Gemma. But you don't answer the phone, you don't talk. Are you drinking again? Tell me. Please.'

Mike didn't answer. He stared out of the window. 'Do you think about Dad any more?' he asked. 'Do you ever wonder where he is?'

Debbie wasn't going to answer that one. At least, not now. Not in this place. Instead, she made another leap. 'Michael, you look good,' she said.

'What?'

'You look good. I mean, have you lost some weight?'

'Er, no,' said Mike. 'Yeah. Maybe a bit.'

'That's a nice haircut as well. It's nice you have a nice haircut.'

Mike let his head rest on the table in front of him. 'I had to let it grow, for work.'

Debbie stroked her son's head, threading her fingers through his hair slowly. 'Well, I like it. And I want you to know, we all think that . . . What you've done this year, it's amazing.'

Mike nodded weakly. He was a grown-up now, just like Guy, and like Derek – a man whose only interest seemed to be making his new wife happy in small, sensible ways. Mike thought of what he might do for Christmas this year. Maybe go away. Far from everyone. If he was alone, he could do what he liked, and no one would know.

'I'm a married woman now, Michael,' said Debbie. 'But don't you think this has gone on long enough? I'm sorry but your dad, wherever he is, is not worth waiting for. I should know. I wasted years waiting for him.'

'You never know what's gonna happen.'

'I do, Michael.'

'What if he's just waiting for the right time to come back?'

'Well, if that's true – and I doubt it – then the right time has come and gone.'

Mike bit the inside of his mouth, gripping the flesh tight between his teeth.

'I don't like to admit it,' said Debbie, 'none of us do, but your father probably isn't . . . of this world any more. After all, he was a big drinker, wasn't he? And the doctor was always saying he had to stop, for the sake of his liver. His own dad died of a heart attack really quite young. So did his poor brother, of course. And your father was an angry man.'

'He's still alive,' said Mike. 'And he's coming home.'

'Michael, please. It's been fifteen years. Not this again.'

'Not what?'

'He left us, Mikey. We needed him and he left. *You* needed him. Have you forgotten?'

Debbie smiled sadly, but it wasn't the sad smile her son remembered from when he was a child. It was a different kind of sadness, that didn't seem so sad at all.

'Come on,' said Debbie. 'Your old mum does remember how to have fun, you know. And I've got a good feeling about today. Arsenal are vulnerable at the back.'

She reached into her handbag and, with a grin, pulled out a United scarf which she tied around her neck. Then she took off her jacket to reveal a faded United top circa mid-eighties, one that Mike was fairly sure she'd found in one of the old bags of clothes he'd left behind when he moved out of home. She flicked the collar upwards, à la Cantona.

'You look a hundred years old,' said Mike. Then he smiled.

They got the Metro to the ground. It was so busy that Mike and Debbie had to stand near the doors, pressed right up against them, holding onto the bars above while the crowd around them started up with songs, banging on the windows to the beat. Anti-City songs. Anti-Liverpool songs. Anti-Leeds songs. Debbie couldn't remember the last time she'd taken the Metro, and the noise was giving her a headache. But she was sure to talk exactly as she had done in the coffee shop, only a little louder, just enough so she could hear herself.

'You know,' she said. 'I really don't mind if you never get married. You can do whatever you want.'

The tram jolted.

'I'm just saying. Just because everyone else is doing it, doesn't mean you have to as well. Do you remember my Uncle Benny? He was always such a happy thing! He put his long life down to not having a woman nagging him all the time.'

Mike was sweating again. He always seemed to be sweating. On one side of the busy carriage a young mother tried to hold her two children close as the Metro lurched forward and back. Behind him, a middle-aged man and two big men in baseball hats stood, expressionless, as if they couldn't hear what was being said. A drunk started stamping his feet and shouting.

HELLO! HELLO! We are the Busby boys,
HELLO! HELLO! We are the Busby boys,
And if you are a CITY fan surrender or you'll DIIIIE!
We all follow United . . .

'Lovely song, that,' said Debbie, and grinned.

Mike kept his voice low. 'Listen,' he started. 'I've got to say –' He took a deep breath and let it out. 'I used to steal from the newsagent's at the bus station, on my way back from school. I gave away some of the things I stole, but I kept some of them too. I stole from your wallet.'

'I know. It's okay.'

'No. I did bad things, Mum. I broke Jay's jaw once, for no reason. That was why I was suspended from school, the second time. There are other things too. I should say them.'

Debbie put her hand lightly on Mike's arm. 'It was a long time ago. You're a good boy now. Let's forget it.'

'I stole a hundred times. I can't forget it.'

'Yes you can,' she said firmly, holding her son's elbow tight, pincer grip. 'You must.'

After they got off the Metro, her manner changed. Like an excited teenager she walked fast among the bustling crowd, even breaking into a skip when the ground came into view.

'Wow, I should have done this years ago,' she said. 'And look, there's lots of families, aren't there? Oh Mikey, we should get *ice cream . . .*'

Mike almost lost her when she ran through the crowd to the other side of the road and bought a couple of badges and a flag.

Once they were inside the ground Debbie purchased a programme (for Derek, she said), another coffee (she drank a lot of coffee these days) and placed her one pound bet on the scoreline, another for Mike. (She supported 'sensible risk-taking', and approved of his recent one-pound-a-game strategy.) After some detailed deliberations she went for 2–1 to United, which Mike said was sacrilege because it suggested Arsenal were actually going to score. He'd gone for 4–0. But his mother was certain.

'I *know*,' she said, pounding her chest. 'In *here*.'

In the minutes before kick-off Debbie started analysing the game ahead. She didn't like Ronaldo, she said, because he didn't have a kind face. Though he did score a lot of goals. The same went for Wayne Rooney. She quite fancied that dishy Ryan Giggs, though. It was a miracle he was *still* playing, didn't he think? He was on the bench today, wasn't he? She didn't wait for answers: she was deep in the manager's programme notes before Mike could launch into a United history lesson. Halfway through reading what Alex Ferguson had to say on the coming adventure, she looked up and spoke, to no one in particular.

'I remember when he came to our house that time,' she said. 'What a gentleman he was! I remember, he told you to respect your mother.'

The teams came out and Debbie stood to applaud. 'Come on, you fuckin Reeeeeeds!' she screamed.

She looked over at her son, with a fierce look in her eyes, then sat back down and began to read the match report on the reserves game from last week.

A couple of hours later, the atmosphere among the fans leaving the ground was happy, full of jokes and hopes for the coming weeks. United had come from behind – again. They'd beaten a key rival – again. They were battling away at the top of the table alongside Chelsea, fighting for the title, and were still in the Champions League too. As in 1999, Mike had the sense that the jigsaw was beginning to complete itself, and something glorious was about to happen. A lot had changed since then. It had been a long time since he'd come round after his suicide attempt in 1999, making promises he wasn't ready to keep.

'No more,' he'd told Debbie back then, shaking his head, hands still trembling, despite the bandages. 'I'm gonna sort myself out. I have to, don't I?'

Nine long years later, Mike was finally keeping his promise. He was coping better, working hard, staying sensible. He'd even had fun watching Manchester United with his mum. Coming away from the ground with the winnings from guessing the score correctly, Debbie had a flush in her cheeks Mike hadn't seen in years. In fact, he couldn't remember if he'd ever seen it before. Facing forward, not looking at her, walking through the crowd as he had done so many times before, he admitted something to himself, then said, 'I'm happy you're happy, Mum. You've done so well.'

At first Debbie Carlsson did nothing. She didn't even reply, she just linked her arm through Mike's and kept walking through the crowds, holding onto him. Mike noticed she was holding tighter than before.

When they parted ways that night Debbie faced him and zipped up his coat.

'I've got a good feeling about this season, you know,' she said, in a quiet voice, readjusting the scarf around her son's neck. 'I really think we could be Champions of Europe.'

FANTASY PRESS CONFERENCE

Imagine: all these years later, it starts up again, like a curse that's been sleeping, just waiting for the right time to return. Even though you're the only one in this lot who had a real career, even though they started out respecting you and calling you *Guv'nor* and putting your name in capitals on the team sheet (a scrap of paper torn out of Bobby's accounts book), it's not long before they're all taking the piss and calling you *that name* again, especially when you go in for tackles, all soft, like the last thing you want to do is risk your bad leg one more time. Sometimes you wonder if Bobby is in the closet or something – like old Jay Gibbons (now Jason Gibbons, Chartered Accountant), he's always accusing everyone else. He's got a wife and kids, but people pretend their whole lives, don't they? You hear about that shit all the time. People lie for decades rather than face themselves. Still, you might as well forget it. You'll never know the truth. You just don't get *them* admitting they exist, do you? Not in this game, folks. You only know of one, Justin Fashanu, and he ended up topping himself. The football world isn't ready, and never will be, so it would NEVER NEVER HAPPEN that

THE FACELESS OFFICIAL FROM THE PLAYERS FOOTBALL ASSOCIATION SAYS:

Thank you all for coming to celebrate this wonderful occasion – wonderful not only for the players concerned but also for us here at the Players Football Association, because today we're here to witness a world first! It really is an honour. So: we'll start with a brief statement from TEAM A midfielder FOOTBALLER 1, then a further statement from TEAM B and England full-back FOOTBALLER 2, then a joint reading from both. We'll be taking questions from the floor, but only a few. As I'm sure you all appreciate, the happy couple can't hang around here all day. Now I'd like to call on FOOTBALLER 1 to begin.

[*assembled media scrum breaks out into spontaneous applause*]

THEN APPARENTLY PREVIOUSLY STRAIGHT FOOTBALLER 1 FROM TEAM A SAYS:

Thank you. Thank you. [*reading from a script*] I want to take this opportunity to publicly state the nature of my relationship with FOOTBALLER 2 [*looks across lovingly at* FOOTBALLER 2]. We were hoping to keep this a secret until after the happy day [*laughs*], but following much speculation on the terraces about whether or not I *take it up the arse*, specifically from FOOTBALLER 2, we've decided to announce here today that we are very much in love and have recently set a date to tie the knot.

THEN MEDIA HACK 1 SHOUTS OUT:

Give us an invite, will yer?

[*cue assembled media scrum laughter, followed by a standing ovation, and calls of 'Me too!', 'And me!'*]

THEN APPARENTLY PREVIOUSLY STRAIGHT FOOTBALLER 1 FROM TEAM A SAYS:

Please, sit down everyone [*they sit*]. You're too kind. But you'll put me off – God, I'm a wreck! Now where was I? Ah yes . . . [*reading from script again*]. We're so grateful for all the messages of support we've had from the FA, supporters groups and especially the press, but all rights for pictures at the wedding have been bought by *OK!* magazine. So, apart from the two hundred celebrity guests and the several dozen casual workers on minimum wage, who don't count because we've bought their silence, we'd very much like to just have a quiet family affair in our massive hired mansion in the country. [*assembled crowd say Aaah!, Oh no! etc*] So please don't climb over the walls! After the wedding and honeymoon, which will take place shortly before pre-season training, we request the space to return to the sickeningly intense and highly sexual love that we've found together. So please respect our privacy . . . except in the pages of *OK!* magazine, which by the way is an excellent read. I'd now like to hand over to my life partner, FOOTBALLER 2. [*they hold hands*]

THEN APPARENTLY PREVIOUSLY STRAIGHT FOOTBALLER 2 FROM TEAM B SAYS:

[*speaking without a script*] Well, I think FOOTBALLER 1 has said it all really. I just want to take this opportunity to tell him publicly how much I love him, and how ever since I first laid eyes on him during that league match one misty October afternoon last year, there's only ever been one set of thighs for me. I'll always remember the moment when he tackled me from behind – I wanted to have my way with him right there and then! And why not, eh? [*laughs, whoops and wolf whistles from the assembled crowd*] But seriously . . . thank you, FOOTBALLER 1, for making me complete.

[*another round of applause and 'Aah's*]

THEN APPARENTLY PREVIOUSLY STRAIGHT FOOTBALLER 1 FROM TEAM A SAYS:

Thanks, FOOTBALLER 2, it means so much to me, for you to share that with the room, and with the world. Now, we would like to conclude our statement with a joint reading from our favourite love poem, 'Glad to be Gay', a tribute to the song of the same name by the current poet laureate, a close friend of ours. She cut short her holiday to compose the following especially for us . . .

THEN MEDIA HACK 2 SHOUTS OUT:

Give us a kiss for the cameras! Go on!

[*another massive round of applause*]

THEN APPARENTLY PREVIOUSLY STRAIGHT FOOTBALLER 1 FROM TEAM A SAYS:

Okay, just one! Then the poem.

[The couple look embarrassed, then smile and kiss. This starts off soft and shy, then becomes long, hard, strong. Overtaken with passion, the two players begin to tear off each other's clothes, pushing the representative from the PFA out of the way. FOOTBALLER 1 *bends* FOOTBALLER 2 *over the table in front of them, pulls down his trousers, slips a hand tenderly between his legs and whispers 'I'll always love you' as the assembled media clap and shout 'Go! Go! Go!' and – and – and –]*

Course, it'd never happen, right? And thank fuck for that. Whenever Bobby calls you a poof, you call it him right back, and try to think of something clever to say that'll make the rest of the lads laugh.

Recovery was slow after Little Ryan was born. In 2000 I usually managed a few days without a drink, then a few days back with it. A couple of good weeks, then a couple of bad ones, returning, in shame, to you-know-what, the ex I couldn't quite stop fucking one last time. Actually, there were a few exes on the go, if you want to put it like that. Booze. Bets. Football. Mum suggested I join a club of some kind to take my mind off what I wasn't doing. Guy said that only work would set me free. Okay, my leg was no good for football but I could still walk on it, and as Gemma's big sister told me at Little Ryan's first birthday party, one of the few times I was allowed to go round in those early days, *You don't need to be able to* run *to sit at a desk, Mike. You just need a backside, and you're a pro when it comes to sitting on yours.*

Well, it wasn't at a desk, but in 2001 I did get a real job – night shift in a warehouse, sorting papers and magazines for all the newsagents in Manchester, shifts from eleven at night till eight in the morning. The place was massive, like a country all of its own. I walked to the bus stop and back every day from the flat I'd just moved into, one I shared with two fellers I met through an advert. Neither of my flatmates talked much. Nobody asked questions. And it was all right at the warehouse: having a name badge, eating sarnies in the staff room at break, complaining about the bosses and the government with the other boys and holding a pay slip at the end of the month. It was like being back on a team. I walked a few miles most days, even at weekends, and shaved before every shift. I ate well. None of that shit that smells expensive, but always makes you feel cheap afterwards. After I went a whole month clean, Gem let me stay on the couch at hers for a night. *Just to let you see what you're missing,* she said. *And that you don't have to miss it at all.* She even let me change Ryan's nappy. Me! A nappy changer! The little bugger stank up the place, but I was grinning ear to ear. Gemma stood behind me as I was doing it. I thought about what could have happened between us if I'd just never told her about United, my past. Fucked it all up on the curry mile. She rubbed my back when I was finished and said, *You're doing really well.*

Still, sometimes the routine was too much, and there were whole days when I thought about fuck all else apart from giving up. The bloody Manchester rain, pounding down on me as I walked. Tired legs. Damp, squelchy shoes. Damp socks. Monday to Friday, from leaving the flat at eight at night to getting home at seven in the morning. The wind was the worst, and as I walked, head down, both hands deep in my pockets trying to get through a gale, sometimes I thought: surely Manchester was the only place in the world where it was raining. Surely it was taking up all the world's rain supply, and there were countries where it was so hot, so dry, that you PRAYED for a fraction of the rainwater that Manchester was hogging. Every day I put my hood up and pulled the string tight, leaving only a small gap for me to look through as I walked through the wetness – but I was always soaking. And I couldn't even warm myself in the pub at the end of a hard night's work. Even if I wanted to, the Dog & Partridge didn't open before nine a.m.

Some days I passed by it on my way in to a shift, around closing time. Trying not to look in the window for the regulars. To think about something apart from what I wasn't doing, I'd daydream about what things I'd change if I was Mayor of Manchester. Paint City's ground red, for starters. Maybe change a few of the road names. Add a few more. Bobby Charlton Avenue. Duncan Edwards Road. Giggs Street. Who the hell were our streets named after anyway? Dead men in grey suits, mostly. I'd put that right, no danger, and I'd stop those rich bastards knocking down bits of the city's great past too, putting big new shiny pieces of the future in their place that didn't make the place any brighter, just made it feel less like home and more like an international roundabout. Manchester was changing too fast. *The city's something else now,* I told Mum, standing in front of her in my new warehouse overalls. *In the old days, you could leave your doors unlocked.* She laughed at that. *Ha,* she said, smoothing a crease in my outfit. Then quietly, *People round here have always been thieving bastards.* And that's when I decided to finally get a place of my own.

But better not to think about that. Better not to think about the city now, or then, or the concrete blocks in the college where I went to night classes twice a week, or all the boozing I was missing with the regulars in the Dog & Partridge, who sat around playing darts and having a laugh, getting slowly fatter with every pint and packet of crisps, happily, slowly inflating. Better not to think about all the games I was missing playing in or watching. Better not to think about United at all. Life there. Life without it. I was never far from the bottle or the bookies, but the longer I lasted, the easier it became to live without, and the more nappies I got to change. I even went a while without thinking about it at all, or why I wanted to do it in the first place. A whole year passed. And I tell you, recovery is a pretty unglamorous business. But this year was the first year in a long time I could really remember, with some pretty sound moments in it as well. Ones that made me want to work towards more of them. As for the team? Even when I wasn't watching, it dared to carry on. There's never any end. And United were successful *every* season now. You can't win the Champions League all the time, every fucker knows that, but success was now standard. By 2001, Ryan's trophy room? It was bursting. Our lives were very different. Even our daily diets had little in common.

On the wagon, you do what you need to stay on. It's starts out with a little sugar on your breakfast cereal, then a heaped spoonful, and it ends up with night after night in front of the box stuffing your face with pizza, with sweets, with chocolate. I never knew I had a sweet tooth before, even in the old bus station days – but it must have always been there, waiting to do me in. In six months I went from being the fittest I'd ever been – full proper abs (not really), like the guys on the front of *Men's Health* (liar) – to just being this total slob, vegging out every day after work. Living off crap. Compared to working in the warehouse, training with United was a piece of piss. I came in so emptied out that I felt like I'd earned doing whatever the fuck I liked once I was finished, know what I mean? I felt like no one should deny me, well, ANYTHING. Sitting naked in front of the TV, shouting at Sky Sports, tanking can after can of Coke and dipping into the biscuit tin just that once more. I'd earned it. Energy: gone. Motivation: gone. Point to living: you're fuckin joking, right? But I didn't notice. You don't, do you? Us human beings, we're a fuckin mystery to ourselves. Besides, when you're tired, there's only so much you can think about at once.

All I could think of that whole time was that that I had to KEEP THIS FUCKIN JOB, and STAY CLEAN and CLEAR DEBTS and BE GOOD and then Gemma would have no excuse to fuck with the new weekly arrangement. Having my boy over every Saturday. Taking him to McDonald's and the footie. Having him stay over once a month (with supervision). Even getting the odd whole weekend (with supervision). These were the best things in the world. Gemma had been pretty fuckin clear, though: the boy was better off with no dad at all than with a deadbeat dickhead who wasn't living in the real world. (She used that on me a lot – *not living in the real world*. Well, where was I living then?) She was trying to bring Little Ryan up *right*, she kept telling me. (Like anyone would try to do it wrong.) Until I could prove I could help her do that, and could be relied on to do that, I could forget about independent access. She said those words a lot. Given that choice, I went for the behave-yourself-work-hard-get-fat-be-miserable route every time. For weeks on end, after every shift, I sat on that couch telling myself I was getting better when the truth was pretty fuckin obvious. Guy could see it. Even Mum could see it, and back then she was in dark places of her own – but I wasn't ready to listen.

And then I slipped again.

Anyone who tells you all booze is the same has never been a serious drinker – whisky, cheap whisky, is the worst. It brings out the darkness. The bitterness. The bad. Which, after Dad started calling more regularly, seemed about right. Up until 2001 he'd call about once every couple of months, maybe not even that much, and only when he was feeling homesick. But now he was phoning all the time. Twice, three times a week. He'd call to ask me quiz questions. For relationship advice. Sometimes he'd call late at night, drunk, full of poison, and I didn't know what to do except suck up what he had to say, join in with a dram of the old Scotch, then spend days afterwards wondering whether any of what he spat out was true, or whether he was just reminding me he was still in charge. Those games – they were why Guy said he never wanted to hear Dad's name again. *That angry man*, as he called our father, if he came up in conversation. When Dad got into a rhythm, that temper made him say dark things. It flared suddenly, before fading fast. It reminded me of my own.

So, anyway, whisky. Before 2001 it was only ever out on special occasions, whenever me and Guy had a good excuse to raise a glass. Or at Christmas. Or when Mum handed out the occasional medicinal one. But around 2001 it became regular. It was whisky that got me started fighting, usually after away games, where I could safely get banned from pubs I didn't have to go back to, where I was always alone, and where Gemma couldn't see me drifting from the man she wanted me to be. (Guy didn't come to away games after Robbie was born.) I'd order one whisky, straight, each time I ordered a pint, and after a few of both I was numb. It didn't matter who I hit. A spilled pint, accidental knock on the shoulder, heading for the toilet or the exit. I didn't wait for explanations.

Most of the time I had a clear mind. A clear head. Like I wasn't even on earth. I was on some other planet where you can climb out of yourself, watch yourself, all calm, from far away. You know? But sometimes I'd be laying into a feller, maybe he'd be on the floor outside a pub. I'd be kicking him, maybe he'd be wearing his team T-shirt – for Barcelona, or Inter, or whoever. Calling me names. Saying he was gonna kill me. Or asking me to stop. And I'd be looking down on myself from above, looking at myself like when the boys in the box show you a goal fifteen times, replay after replay after replay, from every possible angle. Real time. Slow-motion. The works. And I'd be thinking about all of us, spending all this time and money on teams that didn't care if we lived or died. About how our clubs would go on, not caring if we'd been lifelong supporters, not even knowing. Just taking our money, keeping on taking, selling us kits, scarves, badges, flags, T-shirts, computer games and match tickets. Selling us new heroes for new seasons, writing old ones out of the story. Even if we couldn't be there, we paid to watch the games on TV – and we even had a club station now: an official mouthpiece of the State, a round-the-clock propaganda channel. When I was kicking out, watching the steel toe-caps do their work, I thought about all of us, giving all that love and passion and energy to something that didn't notice we were alive, that was programmed to *just – keep – taking*. Something you couldn't affect, couldn't change. No matter how much you prayed for victory, talked about tactics, phoned the radio phone-ins, wrote on the message boards, discussed the best way forward with everyone you met, travelled round Europe to follow follow follow the team – they didn't care, did they?

The little grey men, they can't care. Coz caring is potentially unprofitable. People talk about *ordinary supporters*, the *real fans*, but we're dumb fuckin sheep, all of us, for doing all that following, for letting ourselves believe we matter. Even if you were a *player*, they still keep you away. Coz over time the names change, the owners change, everything changes (not Ryan though), except that the game goes on, and it goes on with or without you. Even when your team wins something big like the title or the Champions League, the celebrations last for a few hours and then they just start selling the whole fuckin circus all over again. Nothing ever counts for long. Not the awards, not the names on the shirt. (Stop it stop it stop it.) These whores, they kiss the badge, soak up the songs, declare undying love, then next year they're doing the same in Italy or Spain, or anywhere that'll pay them most. These days, all you've got to do is look at the City line-up to see more evidence than any man could cope with. Like kids in Argentina are growing up hoping they'll play for City! Seriously! The *lies* are what bother me. I can't bear lies.

So all the time I was kicking the guy on the floor, I was really kicking United. You know what I mean? BANG – take that, football. BANG – take that, United. And again. And again. Sometimes, if I was drunk enough, the guy's face would eventually turn into Jay's face. Or Ryan's face. Or Dad's. Sometimes they were the same thing.

WEDNESDAY 29 APRIL 2008
CHAMPIONS LEAGUE
SEMI-FINAL

UNITED 1-0 BARCELONA
SCHOLES 14

(UNITED WIN 1—0 ON AGGREGATE)

ATTENDANCE: 75,061

GIGGSY WATCH – RyansHairyChest says: Hats off to the L-E-G-E-N-D. 759th app 2nite, same as Sir Bobby's record. Solid in defence, good under pressure, all 18 years of United experience needed as we held off the Spanish charge, Giggsy was ESSENTIAL to reaching the final. Anyone who disagrees can come round to mine for a beating. Where are you now, @RonnyIsGod?

Average Fan Rating: 8/10

At the final whistle, fans on all sides of the ground jumped and thrashed and cheered as loud as they could. Mike Wilson was with his son. Standing up out of his usual seat, picking up his boy, he stood and yelled at the sky.

'We're going to Moscow!'

As he shouted, he imagined Guy Wilson sitting alone in his living room in south Manchester with a cold beer, quietly toasting the result and finally giving in to United again. Mike imagined Guy's son, Robbie, loyalties already clear, running around the room, screaming happily. Those big European nights at United, thought Mike. They were made for families. He wished Guy and Robbie were there. Robbie and Little Ryan were going to be best friends. But with or without those two, United were back in the Champions League final, following a display of defensive perfection against the best attacking team on the planet. Mike wondered what his older brother was really doing at that very moment, and whether he missed the Three Unwise Men. Guy always used to joke that he found it hard to concentrate on a United game when they weren't providing commentary.

As if in reply, at that very moment, two of the Three Unwise Men stood to applaud United's victory, but with rueful smiles on their faces. Bill wrapped his scarf around his neck, turned to Dave and whispered.

'John would have enjoyed this,' said Bill, shaking his head.

'You're right,' said Dave. 'John was a Red.'

Mike thought of how the bars of Manchester were about to explode, and he thought about drinking. Tonight the city would be buzzing, everyone talking about United's heroes, messages zipping through the sky as people called and texted friends and family to share the news. Share how close it was. How they nearly didn't make it. And talking about how it was a night for the Old Guard, bawling to be heard over the music in one of the bars down at the Locks, in the Northern Quarter, Deansgate. Mike imagined the city of Barcelona, all quiet, and their supporters in Hong Kong, in Sri Lanka, in Indonesia, their insides aching, while the Old Trafford crowd broke into song.

This is how it feels to be City,
This is how it feels to be small,
This is how it feels when your team wins
NOTHING AT AAAALLLL!

Mike imagined scenes all over. He imagined Guy and Robbie, and two of the Three Unwise Men, and Gregory watching at his bar, and Debbie and Derek half watching at Derek's brother's house while waiting for the coals to heat up the barbeque, and Terry (for some reason he hadn't turned up to the game today), all wondering the same thing: why was it that United fans always sang songs about Manchester City at times when City were nowhere to be seen? Mike kissed Little Ryan's forehead and said, 'You BEAUTY.'

Mike looked at his son and wondered, in the midst of all this imagining, all these dreams, was this real? Yes it was. His boy, at his first ever match. With his dad. Two buddies together, taking in the game. It took him back to his own first visit, that first walk up the steps. To see Little Ryan's eyes open wide at the sight of it all was amazing. As the crowds started to disperse, Mike picked him up, held him high and pointed out the Republik of Mancunia sign draped over the side of one stand, the sign reading FOR EVERY MANC A RELIGION, the running total of how many years it had been since City won anything, and the Giggs banner: TEARING YOU APART SINCE 1991. All the landmarks. He'd already bought Little Ryan his first kit – a bit big for him yet, but he'd grow into it – and Mike could see the magic starting up inside the boy. There was no way his kid was going to be a Liverpool supporter.

'Dad! Dad!' said Little Ryan, jumping up and down. 'You won!'

Mike was hoping the boy would start referring to United as 'we' soon.

While the rest of the crowd was jubilant, singing their way to the exits, the remaining Two Unwise Men were finding it tough to come up with anything to complain about. Close to winning yet another league title, and in a Champions League final as well. Life was too good. So good that they'd even forgotten to leave early to beat the traffic. They had to revert to safe old ground, shaking their heads in unison at the posse of embracing United players who faced the crowd, hands linked in a chain, once the game was over.

'It's a disgrace the way they celebrate these days,' said Bill. 'They're all bloody over each other, these lads!'

'Like a load of bleedin poofters,' said Dave. 'I tell yer, in my day, you went about as far as a manly clap on the back. Nowadays, well!'

Bill grunted, in the way John used to.

The singing of the crowd drowned them out.

This time, it was a different song. The crowd was half gone now, and Mike and Little Ryan were on their way out too, but the song was still loud.

If I had the wings of a SPARROW,
if I had the arse of a CROW
I'd FLY over Maine Road TOMORROW,
and SHIT on the bastards below, below,
SHIT on, SHIT on, SHIT on
the bastards below, below,
SHIT on, SHIT on, SHIT on
the bastards below.
You're the SHIT of Manchester,
YOU'RE the SHIT of MANCHESTER!

Mike joined in, holding his arms in the air as he made his way down the steps towards the exit, knowing Little Ryan was looking on. He hoped the boy wouldn't tell his mother too much of what he'd heard. And he wondered when fans would change the words to accommodate City's new ground. The City of Manchester Stadium. How would that fit into the song?

The City sing, I don't know WHY,
Coz after the match you're gonna DIE,
Let's all laugh at City, HA HA HA HA,
In your bitter blue WORLD,
You don't go to WEMBLEY, you don't win no CUPS,
You hate MAN UNITED and hope for FUCK UPS,
In your BITTER BLUE WORLD!

As the song died away, Little Ryan looked up at his father, and grinned. 'The song has got swears in it,' he said. 'They just said "fuck".'

'You know a lot of bad words for a seven-year-old, sunshine.'

'I'm eight. I've been eight for ages.'

'Yes you are,' said Mike, putting his arm around his son's shoulder. 'Yes you fuckin are. Now come on, let's make a break for it!'

The boy took his father's hand, and the two of them started running towards the car park, through the mass of happy faces.

'Dad, can I come to see United again?' he asked, as they ran.

The question made Mike so complete, so fast, that he forgot to reply. He was daydreaming again, even as he ran.

He was thinking about last week's conversation with Gemma and her new husband, Colum, the three of them, like friends, making future plans over coffee. Running, holding his son's hand, Mike thought of his promise, and how Colum really seemed like a nice guy, and how it was okay, this new arrangement. This reality. He thought of the affectionate smile Gemma gave him, like she was his sister, mother, like she was his friend. He thought of how he'd agreed to pay maintenance for Little Ryan while his baby half-sister, Alice, cried in her pram, and of how they'd shaken hands on regular Saturday visits, with possible weekends after good behaviour. Father's good behaviour, not son's.

Then Mike came out of his daydream, and remembered his son's question. He slowed to a stop, the crowd still rushing around them and, just then, began to fear how Little Ryan might remember this day as an adult. He didn't want there to be any doubt. He kneeled down and held the boy's arms.

'Listen,' he said. 'I want you to know that . . . that I don't ever need you to *do* anything for me. Okay? I'll always. You know. Take you to matches. You can come whenever you like.'

Then he pulled his son towards him, hugged, and released. Little Ryan looked up with an expression Mike could not decode – maybe it was love, or admiration, or confusion. Maybe it was something else. Surrounded by celebrating fans, both stayed still for a moment, as if they were alone, in a quiet place. Then Mike changed his tone, and they began walking again.

'Now!' said Mike. 'Did I ever tell you, our family have been sitting in the same seats at Old Trafford for over sixty years?'

Mike told the story of how Great Granddad Peter got the tickets after the Second World War; as he talked, always holding the boy's hand tight, being careful to look out for traffic as they peeled off Sir Matt Busby Way, crossing the main road and heading for the Metro station. He had to get Little Ryan home safe, and at the agreed time.

NO MORE ROY OF THE BLOODY ROVERS

Imagine: it happens, for the third time in a single lifetime, and this time that's it. No coming back. No more magical returns from injury. You falter, clutch your leg tight, cry out, and fall. Like a death, in that moment between faltering and falling, your whole football life flashes before your tired eyes. From the red ball to this moment, on a cold, ordinary day in 2006, on a lumpy pitch in Salford, playing for a team of amateurs, in a game no one cares about. Except your boy.

Since kick-off, he's been standing on the sidelines, cheering you on, saying to his Auntie Sally and Uncle Guy, *Did Dad really play for United?* He's been holding Sally's hand on one side, Guy's on the other, his little mind spinning. Trying to marry the image in front of him, the man in front of him, with the ones he's seen on TV and at Old Trafford. And now he's watching as you fall, his eyes bulging, then looking up at Guy and Sally, asking with his eyes whether this is really happening or not. This – after everything – this is the end of the bastard road.

Meanwhile, *he* is doing just fine, and probably always will be. He'll probably play on until he's forty. Win everything – yet again. Then come in as assistant to Sir Alex, who'll groom him for managerial success. (In the meantime, he'll keep playing the odd game, the not-so-secret weapon all the other teams fear.) When Sir Alex is on his deathbed, *he*'ll get asked to lead the team into the future and he'll be the United manager for the next fifty years. He'll probably be the most successful one of all time, winning everything so many times that all other teams give up and disband. Go off and play golf or something. Then he'll run for prime minister, and achieve world peace in just under a year, setting up a new Manchester United colony on the moon.

That's the worst case scenario for Ryan. But what about for *you*?

The first six months out were the worst. All those hours on the treatment table, hearing players laughing outside while I was bored shitless in the gym, slowly building strength. When you're injured you're a ghost. Players ignore you, mostly. There's always the next game, a title or a cup to chase, or international breaks when no one's around except you and the other losers on the fringes. There's the goal scorer of yesterday's match to congratulate, the new jokes and new songs and new everythings, while you're stuck in that room not being the new anything at all. The boys don't wanna think about you coz they know it could be them next. Every time they slide in on a fifty-fifty ball they're gambling on turning into you, so I don't blame anyone. All right, there are others coming through the gym, but usually for a few days or a few weeks at a time, then they leave, fit, off to rejoin the fun. And the whole time, the whole time I was in there, I really couldn't care less if I saw anyone, except one person. I just wanted him to stop by once. To see how I was – that's not too much to ask, is it? Eh? To pop his head in and ask how I was doing. It wouldn't have taken him long to say sorry for that pass. Wouldn't have cost him much.

By the time I came back from my injury in summer 1993, all my lot had moved on, up, some I'd been playing with were ahead in the queue to break into the first team, and there was no longer an opening for a pacy striker who played the game beautiful, the way it should be. Meanwhile, a certain Welshman had made a place in the team his own shortly after my debut, and had been doing pretty fuckin nicely while I'd been gone. And, of course, the team had won something by then, so we were suddenly living in a different universe. Those who'd been part of it were heroes. The rest of us were shit. Ryan had ruined me.

It was about three weeks after I started training again, and three months after the debut against Oldham, me and Ryan were on opposite sides in a practice game – it was first team against reserves. We both went in for the same ball, a hard tackle, you know? Your classic fifty-fifty. He got up straight away, strong and healthy, while I just lay there, not able to move. He held his hand out to help me up, but I couldn't accept it. I wasn't ready to stand, not just yet. And that's when it happened. He looked at me, in that way you'd look at a lame horse, just before saying, *He's fucked, lads. Might as well shoot the poor bastard dead.* And I wish they had.

TUESDAY 11 MAY 2008
PREMIER LEAGUE

WIGAN ATHLETIC 0-2 UNITED

RONALDO 33 (PEN)
GIGGS 80

ATTENDANCE: 25,133

Giggsy Watch: RedDevilStatAttack says: By coming on as a sub after 68mins, Ryan Joseph Giggs equalled Sir Bobby Charlton's record of 758 appearances for Manchester United. But Giggsy's no bit-part player kept on for the sake of sentiment. In this match, more than any other player, he helped shape the future. Just when it was needed, Ryan popped up to score United's crucial second goal, securing United the Premier League on the last day of the season, breaking Chelsea hearts with it. Not bad for a wrinkly, eh?

Average Fan Rating: 9/10

Mike Wilson had to admit: as stories go, you could do worse. He grinned widely, and looked over at Terry, who had agreed to make the journey to Wigan with him for this special occasion. Terry grinned back.

'You know, mate,' Mike said. 'He could just stop breathing, right now. Don't you think? Wouldn't that be beautiful? You die on stage, you're never forgotten.'

Terry thought he'd misheard something. 'What are you on about?' he asked.

'Well, the image, eh? It'd live on for ever – and no one could ever forget him. What else is there left to do? United waited twenty-six years without a single one, and he's gonna have ten league titles in his fuckin toilet!'

Terry said, 'What?'

'Seriously, don't you think it'd be magic? A fairytale ending. He should just pick up his medal, and go right there and then.'

'Die on the pitch?'

'You know. Pick up a knife and stick it in his chest. Hara-kiri. Like . . . er . . . you know. Who does that?'

'The samurai. Are you mad?' Terry could no longer disguise his smile. 'It wouldn't be right,' he said. 'We're not at the end of the season yet.'

A few rows below Mike and Terry, an elderly woman was missing all this. Mike watched her. She was listening to the radio through headphones, like he used to when he was alone. Mike imagined what she was listening to. Perhaps a radio commentator calling Giggs's goal 'the perfect way to the perfect ten for Man United'. Attempting to sum up a whole career armed with only a few notes he'd made before the game, just in case. He was probably saying, 'Football does have a way of rewarding the good guys . . . this is a fitting end for one of the best players in football.' Or something like it. A wobble in his voice as he reeled off the clichés. He was probably saying, 'You couldn't write this . . . you just couldn't write it. Well done, Ryan. We salute you.' And that would be fine. Sometimes things were repeated because they were true. The woman, and Mike and Terry, and the United contingent at the JJB Stadium, all applauded. Ryan's hair had dots of salt in amid the pepper, his scalp had hints of baldness, but he still had it all. He had it all. And Mike Wilson didn't. Why?

Earlier that day, he'd told Gemma he understood.

'It's fine,' he said, standing on her doorstep, not able to get inside, bubbling up but not showing it. Trying to sneak a look past her into the hallway, to see if anyone was back there somewhere, afraid to come out. Trying to prove he could stay calm. He had to do that or else she'd use it against him.

But actually, wait a minute, thought Mike, sitting back down with the others as the goal celebrations were dying down. It was *not* good enough to just say she forgot about today, it was *not* all right to let the boy go off to his nana's birthday. *She* saw him all the time. *She* was round the house every night, feeding him, playing with him in the garden, tucking him into bed, reading him bedtime stories and telling him what a waste of time his father was. And this was part of a growing pattern. A concerning one. Never mind today, he was supposed to be taking Little Ryan to the European final in ten days' time – he'd promised the boy he could watch the team whenever he liked – and now, on the most important day of their lives, he'd be without his son again, in Moscow. Because Colum – a stranger, basically – didn't want him to go so far away with *a man who's been hanging around outside the house, like a paedo or something.*

At that moment, Mike thought, he was watching a team he was no longer part of. Sixteen years ago, he wasn't really a part of it then either. Just a visitor. Most of the players wouldn't remember him, and not even Ryan Giggs did when he tracked him down last week, to that hotel bar in Salford, the one all the fan forums said he hung out in. Ryan hadn't been in there the first three times, but the fourth time, Mike got lucky.

On that day, he ordered a lemonade at the bar, pretended to almost pass by, then pretended to be surprised to see Ryan Giggs. He went over and said hi in a casual way. Ryan looked at the woman he was sitting with. It might have crossed Ryan's mind that perhaps this strange man was a stalker. He might have worried this man was a friend of his wife's. Or worse, a journalist. Or maybe he recognized him from all those years ago when he gave Mike that magical tour around the Theatre of Dreams – and he wasn't worried at all. But whatever the look meant, he relaxed when Mike explained that they'd been in the same team once, told him he thought he was the greatest player ever, and explained how the coaches used to call him 'Little Giggs' – Mike even gave him the dates of a few of the games they'd played together, reeling off some names, ones Ryan hadn't heard in years. He smiled and laughed.

'Sorry, mate. Of course I know you. It's just been a while, you know? I've played with a lot of lads over the years.'

He lied out of kindness, so it was okay. It really was. Ryan asked how Mike's career was going, whether he was still playing, and Mike told him he was working with a good non-league club these days.

'Getting my coaching badges,' he said. 'You know, working my way up.'

Ryan didn't doubt it. He wished Mike well, looked right at him as if they were equals, and spoke with respect.

'Nice to see you again,' said Ryan Giggs. 'Well, take it easy, Mike.'

'You too. And hey, good luck in Moscow.'

Then Ryan Giggs offered his hand and Mike shook it, palm all hot and wet, heart beating hard, looking at those dark pupils, that stubbly jaw line, and the cute smile starting at the corner of his mouth. Then Mike left, walking over towards a table at the other end of the bar. Then he just sat there, remembering. Looking. Wondering how one human being could have got everything so right in a single lifetime.

Alex Ferguson had once described seeing Ryan Giggs playing football at just thirteen years old. He described it as if it was a heavenly vision, not a scouting mission. He'd got all poetic, famously saying that back then it seemed like the boy was 'floating over the ground, like a cocker spaniel chasing a piece of silver paper in the wind'. In that hotel bar, with Mike watching, in 2008, Ryan and the woman got up from the table, heading for the door. Then the most successful club footballer of all time waved, turned and floated away out of sight.

'He really recognized you?' said Gregory, chewing while speaking to his son on the phone, the night United became the 2007/08 Premier League Champions.

'Sure,' said Mike. 'Why wouldn't he?'

'Thousands wouldn't believe you,' said his father, burping. 'But I do.'

'Right. Right. Are you wasted?'

Mike heard Gregory wipe his mouth and then swallow.

'Listen. Mikey,' he said. 'I've got something to tell you.'

'Yeah?'

'Yeah. Listen. Things haven't really been working out for me here. And I've been thinking. You know. That maybe it's time to –'

Mike interrupted. 'Here comes the Bullshit Express,' he said. 'Am I right? Is this the Bullshit Express?'

'Mikey, I . . .'

'Let me guess! You're begging forgiveness, and you're coming home. To get the crap kicked out of you by me and everyone else you left behind.'

'Mike, listen. I'm gonna make everything right. I'm gonna call Guy. Call your mother. I'm going to book a –'

Mike interrupted again. His voice rose high, higher. 'Really? You're gonna book a ticket? Well I haven't heard this one before, once or a thousand times.' Mike stood and shouted, pointing into thin air. 'I dare you to come back to Manchester. I DARE you. Go on. Do it! Hey, fuck it, I'll cancel my ticket to Moscow and we can all sit round and watch it together at mine, like one big happy – Christ, Dad, why not just admit that you wouldn't have the balls?'

Mike slammed down the phone, snatched up his keys and coat, and went out to the pub. He texted Guy on the way:

EMERGENCY DRINK, BRUV. NOW. I'VE GOT NEWS THAT'S GONNA MAKE YOU SHIT YOUR PANTS.

PENALTY SHOOT-OUT

GIGGS WILL TEAR YOU APART

'He who is afraid to roll the dice will never throw a six.'

Eric Cantona

Even when I really do want to do as I'm told, to have learned my lesson, it's hard to remember everything life's taught me all at once. My life makes sense in little jigsaw pieces, which don't always slide neatly together. Most times, like this one, here, now, if I close my eyes and concentrate, I can find a single jigsaw piece of my past, reach in and grab it. But the thing is, the wriggly fuckers, those memories, they don't wanna be caught. They hide out in faraway parts of your brain, while all these other lost things start spilling out instead, without permission. Before you know it you're weeping and wailing, beating your fists, rocking back and forward and begging to be put down. You're like those guys doing crazy shit for hypnotists who trick them onto the stage to make twats of themselves. On Blackpool Pier. At holiday camps. Sad bastards who crawl around on their knees and cry for their mums while people laugh like it's not the scariest fuckin thing you've ever seen in all your life.

That was me.

That's what I did, too many times. On streets, in gutters, in pubs, at home.

And I wasn't gonna let that happen again.

From now on I was gonna keep cool.

Cool.

No matter what.

Lying in bed late that night, on my side, I looked at that old wall opposite, for ages. There was nothing special about it. A couple of bumps, that's all – otherwise smooth. All right, it was a pretty fuckin grim wall – it was grey from top to bottom, and it was dirty, and I was bored of looking at it. But it was mine. It just stayed there, being a wall.

Holding the ceiling and floor apart. I loved that fuckin wall. I wanted to kiss it. Which probably wasn't a good sign. Once I finally did drift off, a few hours later, I had a TOP dream. I was flying over Old Trafford, and shitting on it from a great height.

REALITY AND FANTASY FUTURES

Imagine: after your last ever game, the last ever injury, the last pathetic attempt to get back to fitness and the eventual acceptance that you never will, the tired old habit is finally broken and in summer 2006 you make one more big attempt and promise yourself (again) that from now on the drinking STOPS. You're not certain – how can anyone be certain of anything? – but you really believe that this time you've stopped for good. You and Guy talk on the phone a lot these days, and when he asks, *What makes you so sure, Mikey?*, you think you have an idea. Two weeks later you're still sober, and the two of you are back in the good old Dog & Partridge. It's a threshold you haven't crossed for a while, but you tell Guy, *I'm ready. I don't need to drink to be there.*

It's World Cup time and Guy has a rare afternoon off daddy-duty to watch some meaningless game in the group stages between two countries neither of you could place on a map. When he arrives, Guy bends down and hugs you hard, making sure not to trip over your crutches or your leg in plaster. Guy's muscles make his T-shirt pull tight across his biceps. He looks tanned. (You remember now: he's been on holiday.) Guy looks younger than you these days, doesn't he? Sipping a flat lemonade, looking across at your big brother and his own soft drink (he won't drink in front of you any more), you cock your head at the screen and say, *World Cup time, everyone's a tactical genius.* Guy grins, one eye on the match. *Everyone thinks England are gonna win it.* Guy grins again, like the two of you are sharing a joke. *Better to save the United boys for the pre-season tour of South Africa next month, know what I mean?* Guy's still looking at the screen. He says, *I've really missed you.* Then another round of lemonades and bags of crisps are ordered, and the two of you devour them like they're tequilas and salt.

Everything about the way Guy is makes you want to cut the bullshit. So you tell him. *Everything's clear now*, you say, during a lull in the action. *I'm gonna make the right choices.* He nods. Both of you keep your eyes facing the big screen. You say, *I've been selfish, for years. I'm sorry.* There's a little silence. Then Guy turns his head and asks that question again, *What makes you so sure you can give it up?* And you tell him what happened with the doctor. You explain how, when you sat in her cold beige office after the examination, then pulled yourself up onto your crutches, feeling the soreness of the plaster against your shins after breaking the same leg for the third time, you asked her if you'd play again, and there was no doubt in her eyes. She looked at your leg, then at you, then gave you this weak little smile. *I finally fuckin got it*, you tell Guy. *About time, eh?* The two of you leave before the match finishes.

From then on it's the eighties all over again coz over the next couple of months Guy's back to throwing books at you and saying, *Read this, knobhead*, and *Don't be a dumb fuck for ever* and *Don't panic, there's no God in here, just practical advice*. You're up for hours at night again, just like when you were little, your flickering bedside light making those words glow yellow through the blackness. Only now there's not a communist or mass murderer in sight. This time it's *Seven Days to Change Your Life* and *Twelve Steps to Freedom* and *Alcohol: Beat It!* These books come from Sally's brother Danny's bookshelves. He's been sober ten years now; he wants to help a fellow sufferer. But it feels like they're written just for you. These books, they're things of beauty.

You get so consumed by the messages and lessons in the books that some days you forget why you ever wanted a drink. Find the thought of one sickening. Can't understand why anyone would ever have one. When you see people drinking, you pity them. It can last for hours at a time, sometimes days, but when you remember, you feel like cracking your own head open on a brick. Splitting it like an egg and feeling the goo bleed out. (Which is what you deserve.) But you don't, coz you're a MAN, coz real men SURVIVE WHATEVER SHIT'S THROWN AT THEM and coz there's LIFE out there to be sucked up – all the life you've missed out on, all those miserable years you've wasted (YOU'VE wasted, Mike), blacking out, battling, blaming other people when there was really only one person to blame.

(Do you believe that?)

The first thirty days sober are hell, and you nearly give up a hundred times. But after that your energy starts to come back. It returns in spurts, and it's then that you begin getting up early again, shaving every morning and looking through the paper for jobs, even taking down the ones you know you couldn't bring yourself to do. The same week, you decide to go back to the night classes. After standing outside the college building for ten minutes, nervously trying to summon the courage to go in the door, you do it, and do it as if it's no big deal. You swagger up to the reception desk and charm the same woman who watched you drop out before, telling her, *It's time for the two of us to move forward with our relationship*. After they accept you back (but what if you fail again?), you write to Gemma for the first time in a year. Not one of the crazy letters, or one of the angry ones. Not a demand. Not a threat. The message you slip through her door just reads, *I can do it now. Let me try. Please?* And she's wonderful. She's the best fuckin woman in the world. Coz she's done it herself and she knows how tough it is. When news filters through that you got the job at Sportswear Direction she sends a note back. *Well done, Mike. Keep going.* Which, in the darkest times, is just about enough to make sure you do.

It's always been the same: whenever you've managed to go more than a few days on the wagon, the dreams start up. You could have predicted that, Christ knows you've had fresh starts before. So many it feels like you've been having fresh starts back to back for the last fifteen years. But the old dreams about your debut, that tackle, and what you should have done different – they're in the past now. In these new dreams you see possible futures. And all this means (you understand in the dreams) that you'll live to see creases in the corners of your eyes, ruffled lines on your forehead. It means you'll live to see Little Ryan's eighteenth. In your sleep, you want to kiss the lines. The better real life is, the more one new dream reappears. And it reappears as a glamorous eighties American soap opera, like the ones Mum used to watch every afternoon. In this fresh start, when you curl up in one of the clean new duvets you bought for when Little Ryan comes to stay over again (IT'S GONNA HAPPEN SOON), you wonder if the next episode will be any different.

Okay, so this is what it looks like on set. Imagine: it's mid-afternoon in the summertime on a ranch in the Wild West somewhere, but the dusty sand all around, it's green. The ranch, it's a massive football pitch. It's the biggest football pitch in the world. (A nice, expensive aerial shot gives a sense of the size.) There's only one property on this pitch, only one farmer of the land, and that farmer is you. You built the foundations, the walls and the floors with your own hands. (Somehow you know this.) You have this tiny scar on your left thumb where you slipped with a nail on the day you were finishing the roof. (You know this too.) In your dream, it's cloudy but it's a bright day, all days are bright days here on the farm, and you're sitting out on your porch, in a rocking chair, supping an iced tea, which you've been chilling in the freezer for just the right amount of time. To your left, there's a short dirt track with your car parked in it, an old red Spitfire Mark IV, that (somehow you know) makes a satisfying gurgling sound whenever you start it up.

To your right, close by, is another chair, which a man is sitting in, rocking slowly back and forth. He's enjoying life's simple pleasures, this man, feeling the breeze on his cheeks and chewing some gum. He's wearing a cowboy hat, and cowboy boots that still have that new-bought leathery smell. Like you he's older now, and all right, he's put on a few pounds, but not much. He looks like he's enjoyed retirement, that's all. *Nice out front, ain't it?* says Ryan Giggs, tipping his hat in your direction and speaking in that soft Southern drawl that only makes sense in this place. *Yup*, you say, *it sure is*. Then Ryan says, *Hey, Mike. You recall that pass back in 1992? Well, I want you to know, I sure am sorry for any trouble I caused.* And it warms you to hear him say that. But on the farm, all is right, so you answer, *It's okay. Thanks, but it's over now. And, hey, I'm sorry too.*

Only you don't really have that conversation at all.

Each time you wake up, you remember you'll never play again, while the extension on the Ryan Giggs trophy room probably needs another fuckin extension by now.

Imagine: it makes you want to get wasted. To waste someone else.

Imagine: imagine what it's like. Can you?

Can you, Ryan?

Can you imagine what it would have been like for you to be me?

Ryan Joseph Giggs:

Officer of the Order of the British Empire (awarded 2007)
UNICEF representative (since 2002)
BBC Sports Personality of the Year (2009)
Awarded the Freedom of the City of Salford (2010)

I dunno what to say about it except that I when I wrote that letter, I meant every word. And I'm not ashamed. Why the hell should I be?

URGENT: FOR THE ATTENTION OF RYAN GIGGS.

13 May 2008

Dear Ryan,

Please help.

You know me. My name is Mike Wilson – we were together at United in 1991 and 1992. I did play for the first team once, against Oldham Athletic, but got injured and never made it back. You took me round OT when I was a kid. We played together. We met again recently. You were nice. It was good to see you again. You were always kind, I've always respected you. You've been my hero for twenty years now, I think you're the best United player ever and I totally love you. I love everything about you. I still follow the team and you're still my favourite player by a mile. You're not past it, like some of them say. I think you'll go on for ever. So it breaks my fuckin balls to have to write this. But I've tried every other option, believe me.

My letter is sort of about my United debut in a way, because it's kind of your fault that I'm in this situation. You've probably forgotten this now, and I don't blame you after all the games you've played over the years, and all your amazing achievements. But it was you who passed me the ball when I got injured going into a tackle on that day in November 1992, my debut day. Ryan, you're a star, you know I think that, but your pass was all wrong. You mishit the ball and it went way up the field, miles away from me. If you'd passed the ball right, just ahead of me so I could run onto it, then maybe I would have gone on and scored that day. It could have been the beginning of a great career, maybe even as good as yours. If you think about it, maybe I could have given YOU a shitty pass, YOU could have got injured and this could be YOU writing to ME now. I'm not trying to be funny, I don't want to be rude, but that's kind of how things are, don't you think?

I'm not asking for much. It's not like I'm one of those guys demanding damages or loss of earnings or anything like that. I'm not crazy! I just need – and I REALLY need this – you to talk to Gemma and Colum and explain something for me. Think of it kind of like a character reference. (Gemma's my ex by the way, and Colum's her husband.) If you popped round to their place to chat about our little situation, even just for a bit, and alerted the media, the attention could change everything. Just explain to everyone what happened. Tell them about me. You're the only one who can do it.

The thing is, since the early nineties, I've got myself in a bit of bother this way and that, and last month Gemma said I was on my last warning with her, as regards my son, and access to him. That's because I kept going round to their place, just standing at the other side of the street, watching them and thinking about what I might do. (Not even doing anything!) So when I went round again to see my boy the day United won the title (great goal by the way), she wouldn't let me in the house. I wanted to take him to Moscow but she said no, and when I started shouting and battering her car with my fists she threatened a restraining order. You see, since the injury I've had a bit of a temper. It comes on in a rush. It takes me over.

Ryan, in the last year I've done good things. I've done well in my job, paid off some debts, even taken some evening courses – one in sports psychology, and retaken basic English and maths too. (I'm really good at maths, I reckon that's all those years of looking at league tables!)

Also, I've been mostly sober since August and I've been trying to prove I can put my life back together – all for my son. I named him after you, Ryan Alexander Black, he's called, though I call him Little Ryan. I hardly know him. I miss him all the time. Actually, you know what? You don't even need to go round in person. You must be mental busy this week, what with the Champions League final and all. If you just wrote a letter to Gemma and Colum, a bit like this one, explaining how it's your fault what happened to me, and threw in a few autographed things, I'm sure they'd rethink the whole business. And I promise to never ever get angry again.

You see, my whole life has been totally fucked since 1992. My dad did a Houdini just before my debut. Uncle Si died soon after, leaving me without my stand-in dad as well as without the real one. That sent Mum into depression and Guy chucking himself into running Uncle Si's business, with Dad phoning me from fuck-knows-where, making me promise not to tell Guy anything. (Let's just say Guy didn't understand the pressures I was under. Wanted some answers I couldn't give.) And where does all this leave me, eh? Well, nowhere new. I've spent years going mental thinking, why me? And a few times I even thought I had the answer. But in the end I got it: it's not ABOUT me. It could have been anyone, this. And once you get knocked down, well, ordinary people can't always get up again. If you're already rich you can get away with pretty much anything, I reckon. Someone will try and hush it up, doesn't matter what you've done. Agents, managers, lawyers, that's what you pay those guys for. But if you're a nobody, you're fucked.

Look, I'm begging you. If you ignore this letter you're basically killing me, because I'll just top myself. I've tried it before and I'll make a better job of it this time. If they stop me seeing Little Ryan there's no point living – my boy is EVERYTHING to me. You understand that, right? You're a dad. If you help me, Ryan, if you help me just this once, I PROMISE I won't let you down. And I'll never ask for anything again.

With love and respect,

Mike J. Wilson
PS Please be quick!

As I was signing the letter I thought, He probably wouldn't even remember me. Giggsy might read this and think I was just some nutter who THOUGHT he'd been a United player once. And, fuck it, I'm man enough to admit the truth. At United, it IS as if I never existed. I held that letter in my hand and thought, I don't exist to anyone who COUNTS, do I? According to anyone who counts I was never there. You can check the megastore! Check the calendar! Check the DVDs and old videos and player biographies! I'm not in them anywhere, am I?

I almost didn't post the letter.

But I was there.

I WAS.

So I slipped it into the letterbox and prayed.

WEDNESDAY 21 MAY 2008
CHAMPIONS LEAGUE FINAL
LUZHNIKI STADIUM MOSCOW

ATTENDANCE: 67,310

Getting the ticket nearly bankrupted him, but as Mike thought, what true fan wouldn't do whatever it took to get there? After last time, even though there was no one there for company, he wasn't going to spend another historic day naked in the bath whining about Jesper Blomqvist. So when he met the man at the back of the Dog & Partridge, in the car park, and the man doubled the price, there wasn't time to resist. To make kick-off he was going to have to leave on Monday at the latest, as there were no more direct flights available. They'd all been bought already, by lucky fans and touts, or by so-called 'agencies' charging mountain-high prices. It was Sunday, the match was on Wednesday, and all his other avenues had turned into dead ends. Meanwhile, after the row that followed telling him about Dad, getting advice from Guy wasn't really an option.

'So, like we agreed,' said the man. He made a big show of bluffing, insisting they'd always agreed on the figure. 'The damn thing cost me this much,' he told Mike, counting notes. 'I only want my money back. I'm an honest guy. A working man. Like you.'

'For fuck's sake, comrade,' said Mike. 'Save it, will you?'

'Serious, man. I couldn't get hold of two tickets, and that's the only reason I'm not going. Coz if I can't take my boy then I don't wanna go at all.'

The man seemed to be expecting an answer. 'Hey, what was I supposed to do?' he asked.

Mike paid him half the asking price and finally said something. 'Well, if you want more, you'll have to wait for it.'

Later the same evening, Mike took out all the cashpoint would let him have, then stopped to make a private house call in Moss Side, explaining his predicament through a grille and agreeing to the rate of interest without a thought. (Dad used to say that if you ever needed to borrow money in Manchester, you always could. That was the kind of city it was.) He was sweating. He wished he could have spoken to Guy first. Maybe borrowed from him instead. When Mike met the man again to complete the handover, he took along his Swiss Army knife. He thought about stabbing him and stealing the ticket, but suspected it wasn't in him to do that kind of thing. Anyway, this man had a son. And who could do that to someone with children? Instead he thanked the man meekly, then ran to the bus stop, hoping not to be late for his shift.

It's tough doing any kind of shift job when you're dedicated to the team, isn't it?

Every day off has to be begged for, planned, swapped with someone who you then owe a favour you'll never be able to pay back coz there's always, always more games to come. It's a full-time commitment, this, if you're gonna do it properly. Sometimes, you need time off on a Sunday. (For the big Premier League games they show on the telly.) Sometimes, time off on Wednesday. (For Champions League games.) Sometimes, time off on Thursday. (For recovering from Champions League games or getting back after midweek away league matches.) Occasional Monday night off. (For more TV-sponsored Premier League.) Occasional Tuesday night off. (For Couldn't-Care-Less Cup, at least until United get knocked out, or for Tuesday Champions League matches.) Sometimes, even Friday off. (For getting to Saturday lunchtime away games.) So the only real free day is a Thursday, and even that can get cut into if there's an away game on a Wednesday night or you have to do an overnight down south for an early kick-off. (Or, God forbid, if United ever drop into the UEFA Cup.) Then there's friendlies. Pre-season. Testimonials. The rezzies. Of course, if you're following the best club on the planet, there's also European finals – and the off-season isn't long enough to pay back all the favours you owe. To cope with all the expense you need to work more, to get more money, to spend more on United. Which you need to get more time off for. Time to follow the team all over the globe, all the time leaking funds that might have gone on clothes, food, child support. United is your social world, your everything. Christmas, Easter, work nights out, parties, birthdays. Everything's lost if there's a fixture on. Existence has to be built around it.

These nine-to-fivers, these white-shirt-and-tie types, they don't understand that kind of dedication. Which is why you're thirty-two and answering to bosses younger than you. It's why your bank account hasn't seen the black for fifteen years. But that's all right, you tell yourself again and again, the mantra echoing in your head. That's all right. That's all right. You're doing better, that's what counts – *heading in the right direction*, as MumGuyDadGemBrianYourBoss say so often it gives you a headache to hear it. *Getting your life in order*, that's what they say. And you have been. And you don't wanna lose that. (You're hoping Gemma will drop the threats too, once Ryan saves the day. Maybe you can keep all this quiet. Pretend it isn't happening.) So this time you're gonna survive, get smart. No sudden handing in your notice, no tantrum, no disappearance, even though you're supposed to be standing in for the team leader for a couple of weeks while he's on annual leave. (*Great opportunity to prove what you can do, Mikey*, says Brian, his big hand firm on your shoulder.) Still, you CAN'T miss the final, can you?

On Monday morning, you make sure you're packed before you call. All polite, all sugar and syrup, you explain a nasty chest infection is gonna keep you off all week. *I'm so sorry, Brian*, you say, in your best throaty voice. *I know it's a bad time. And I don't want you to think I'm not interested in developing my career, because I want to be a team leader. I do. But I'm on strict orders not to get out of bed. I mean . . . I could come in, if you really need me . . .* Well, Brian's a good man. He's an old mate of Guy's – your always-to-the-rescue big brother who got you the gig in the first place, after all that scouting the papers led to Sweet Football Association. *Nah, it's all right, Mikey*, says Brian. *I don't want you infecting my workforce, especially not the ladies, know what I mean? Hey, take all the time you need. I know you wouldn't take the piss. We'll get someone in to cover from another branch. Just get yourself well again, okay? And DON'T WORRY.*

An hour later you're on your way to Manchester airport, whistling, collar up and sunglasses on, even though no one would notice you in that crowd, right? (Especially on a flight to Estonia. Which is where your connection to Moscow leaves from.) The airport is full of the Red Army on the move, half of them dressed up, chanting, boozing it up. The place is a madhouse, a good one, and you bounce, banter and sing along with all these friendly strangers at the queue for the check-in desk, at the security barriers, at the gate. (One bold old boy twirls a not-too-chuffed perfume girl around the floor of the duty free shop. A hundred men cheer.) You make some friends on the plane, where rumours are being chucked around about what team the Gaffer's gonna to play. Just like 1999, you couldn't guess it. Just like 1999, no one can know his mind. Which means Chelsea won't either. You text Guy from the plane, just as the air hostesses tell you to make sure all phones are off. You say: RED ARMY. What else is there to say? Guy could have come if he'd wanted to.

All around, while the plane's engines burr sweetly below, the chants begin again. (There's something comforting about how predictable football fans are.) You spot Ledley-from-the-Liverpool-game up ahead. He nods, letting on, but no more. Then he sits down, facing away, at the front of the plane. You think, Maybe I should have turned out for his team, after all. Played on one leg. Maybe you should have returned Terry's calls too, a few nights ago, when he left three messages, offering that drink again. At his. Maybe then he would have come with you and you wouldn't be on your own today, in this non-place between places, getting a text back from your brother that just says: Mikey, BEHAVE YOURSELF, OKAY? Like you're a fuckin baby or something.

After dumping your stuff in your (very expensive, last-minute) hotel and getting into full kit for the match (United top with WILSON across the top, United scarf, lucky United jacket with badges, lucky United cap), you head straight out to explore the city and watch it fill fast with colour. The weather is okay, so it's fine to walk around, and even though you're lost most of the time, you're never on your own with so many Reds around, and so many drinks to be drunk. (You make a deal with yourself to ONLY GET DRUNK WHEN UNITED ARE IN A CHAMPIONS LEAGUE FINAL. You set terms and agree them with yourself. Negotiations go smoothly.) You can feel the excitement on the streets and in the bars of

Moscow. On days like this, it isn't all about the game. If the game was postponed till next year, it wouldn't matter. It's about being part of the community, the big Red Army marching on Moscow, preparing for battle against the evil Russian Bear ripping apart the English national game, replacing old spirit (United) with new money (anyone else, basically), trying to buy itself glory. (United's spending, no matter how obscene, is exempt from critique.) But the Red Army aren't going to let the baddies win. Are we now?

The rest of Tuesday is a blackout, except for when you wake up about three a.m., desperate for a glass of water. You stumble to the bathroom, run the tap, gulp down the liquid and think to yourself, *What if I'd been a defender?* It's funny, thinking about how you almost were. You laugh out loud. In this half-moment, you imagine clearly the other existence that might have been. A solid career, with ten calm years as United's defensive rock, where you buy a big house in Hale Barns, have a fleet of cars you don't even use, get a Stretford End chant all of your own and a fan club in fifteen countries. You think about that for a while, then reach into the mini fridge in the hotel room and eat and drink everything in there. Then you fall asleep again.

On the day of the game, you get up mid-morning and pump the music loud and proud out of your hotel room direct to the good people of Moscow as you have a shower, a shave, a shit and a very large whisky. You whistle as you clean up last night's mess. You limit your playlist to the Holy Trinity of Manc bands. Bit of the Roses. Bit of Joy Division. Bit of The Smiths. Decent music, eh? None of that soft southern shite, or the rinkydink Russian liftmuzak that's everywhere in this place, and certainly no fuckin City-supporting OASIS. (Guy says all that's out of date now. That music. He says it's a bit of a joke.) You're educating the citizens, that's how you see it, doing the Manc monkey dance barefoot round your room. Couple of tins with breakfast, then you hit the streets. You wanna get in among the crowds before kick-off – climb into the soul of this city, find the Red bars and get a few frosty ones in. (Plenty of time for that. It's a late late start, this game – for the men in grey suits, who must ALWAYS COME FIRST.) You're walking through the city, gripping your precious ticket, following the Army towards the ground, when your phone rings. Probably Guy, no longer angry, now just concerned. Or maybe it could be Dad? You half expect him to say he's got a ticket too, and it just so happens to be the seat next to yours, and do you fancy meeting up for a beer?

You pick up the phone saying, nice and loud, *Man United Supporters Club, Moscow branch, how can I help you?*

Brian replies. *Well, Mike. You could help me by explaining why you lied.*

You stop in the street, trying to compute. Can you bluff it, pretend to be at home? Can you just brazen it out? Make for a quiet spot and deny all charges? Say you're in bed, watching the game on the TV? In the background a group of supporters sing *Giggs . . . Giggs will tear you apaaaart agaaaain.* As you're thinking of a way out, the song comes round once more, louder this time, but you can just about hear your boss say, *Enjoy the game, Mike – and good luck. Don't be asking for a reference.* For a few seconds after Brian puts the phone down, you're shouting. But nobody's listening.

The next few hours, I wandered about the city, between the streets and the bars, half numb. I explained what had happened to fans I met as I went round. Everyone told me work doesn't matter. Only football matters. In the bars and on the streets I met guys who had made real sacrifices – lots had told porkies to bosses, like me, in the name of the greater Red cause, faking a whole long list of illnesses they'd never have. In tonight's crowd, there were stomach ulcers and bronchitis sufferers and broken limbs and cases of gonorrhoea. Some had fresh-from-the-doctor cases of cancer and HIV. (Cases soon to be – hallelujah! – diagnosed as false alarms.) Some had lied to their wives, their children, their friends. One feller was supposed to be at his brother's wedding – he was gonna be best man – but when it came to it, he just *couldn't* abandon his true love. And besides, this was the *fourth* time his brother had got married, and only the *third* time United had made a European final. He said he had a contagious virus and couldn't be visited or contacted for three days. The feller reckoned his brother knew what was going on, but said nothing. *That's family for yer*, the feller told me. *That's the power of United. Hey, mate. Never mind your stinkin job. The world's FULL of jobs. Raise a glass! Forget about it!*

We're gonna be Champions of Europe! This stranger pulled me towards him and said, *Now let's go and watch the magic unfold, shall we?* He said it so softly, he must have been talking to himself.

At the ground I queued with the rest of the crowd and handed my ticket over. The guy at the turnstile looked at my ticket, looked up and shook his head. I don't speak Russian and the feller's English was pretty bad, but he'd learned some words well enough. Obviously had to say them a lot. *Fake, fake,* he told me. *You fake.* I don't remember much after that, but they say I pushed the people in front, trying to force my way inside. There was no way forward so I backed out, turning to find another route. When guards appeared from behind I threw a couple of sloppy punches, fell over, got up and limped away into the crowd – not quick, but quick enough. I could escape the law better than most, even with a dodgy leg. (I felt a throbbing in my knee.) It didn't hit me right away. What had happened. I just thought: Where will I watch the game? As I fought my way through the crowds facing the other way, adrenaline wearing away, I slowly realized I really wasn't gonna be able to get into the stadium, I really wasn't gonna witness it. I thought about Little Ryan. I wished he was close. Or anyone was. Just then, like he'd heard my wish, another message from my brother: U SAFE? is all it said. A few seconds later, another: U SOBER?

Mike realized he had to focus, and fast, or else miss the game entirely. He couldn't allow the old volcano to blow. So he got out his map of Moscow, headed towards a main road (feeling another twinge in his knee) and, using the international language of football, waving his scarf and making wild gestures with his arms, he just about communicated what he was looking for. Luckily, there were several places close by. Friendly locals directed him, also using hand signals. Soon he found a bar full of United fans. He stumbled in the door.

As the pre-match build-up began on the TV screens, Mike tried to forget what had just happened – being refused entry, accepting it so weakly. Why hadn't he fought harder to get in? In his mind, he imagined ways he could have beaten the security guards, danced between the stewards, evaded the police and somehow found a secret, safe viewpoint inside the ground. The more he tried to block it all out, the clearer it seemed. He blamed Russia. He blamed jet lag. He should have been there in the stands, cheering as each player's name was read out, but instead he was packed in among hundreds of other idiots without a ticket, each straining to see a fuzzy screen.

Mike let his head fall onto the bar, just a little too fast. He banged it, then tried to pretend he hadn't. A strange arm found its way round his shoulder and a friendly big red face spoke to him.

'All right, feller,' said the face. 'You got a fake too?'

Mike took the ticket out of his jeans pocket, held it up to the light and searched for what he knew wasn't there. 'Bastards,' he said, under his breath.

But the man with the red face didn't look unhappy. 'You can't let it beat you, my friend,' he said. 'It's gonna be a good, good day!'

Mike ordered a beer and joined his new friends, an unofficial group who called themselves the Dublin Reds, Northern Branch. Glasses were raised all round, toasts made to the team and Sir Alex, prayers offered to God (Sir Matt Busby, of course), followed by, on Mike's insistence, a rousing rendition of 'My Old Man Said Be a City Fan'.

The bar swelled fast. Evidently, the Muscovite landlord wasn't quite prepared for the avalanche of trade hitting his establishment, the Red Invasion, and was short of staff on what was surely his best day's business of the year. Maybe of his entire life. His expression while running back and forth was not that of a man making money, but of one losing it, second by second, with every extra pint he couldn't pour. Not enough people. Not enough pumps. Not enough space or time.

'Hey, Gorbachev!' shouted one thirsty fan. 'How's about some service over here, eh? Get a fuckin move on!'

The landlord grunted, wiped his brow, and slowly extended the middle finger of his right hand. It occurred to Mike to offer his services behind the bar. After all, he did need a job.

A little while later, you're trying to follow the back and forth between the men and women of the Dublin Reds (sitting with them now), but keep getting distracted, tuning in and out of conversations, remembering, remembering. To take your mind off the situation (OF ALL THAT WASTED MONEY AND THE SHAME AND THE DISGRACE), you tell the Dublin

Reds all about your trip, your life. *I used to play for United, you know*, you say. *Don't suppose any of you boys have heard of me?* The responses are polite. Someone thinks they have, then realizes they haven't. Another pretends, badly. Most don't bother. One old boy has been following United, he says, for fifty years. They call him the Computer. But even with a direct reference to your appearance date, and a suggestion of the circumstances, the Computer can only remember one Mike Wilson, and it's the other one. The Computer suspects you're bullshitting and the conversation moves on. Has anyone heard what the team is gonna be tonight?

The line-ups are just filtering through. Some are picking up the news on their phones. Others are passing the information round by word of mouth. *Has Giggsy made the team?* you ask Alec, one of the Dublin Reds. He laughs, puts an arm round you and says, *Doesn't matter, sunshine! Whoever plays, we've got God on our side! And God wouldn't let us come all this way to witness defeat. Now let's get you another fuckin DRINK, shall we?* This God must be a different one to the one Gemma's parents talk about (this forces you to think about Gemma), and the one Mum talks to (this forces you to think about Mum). You smile at Alec. Your mouth is sore. Alec says, *Sport brings people TOGETHER. Just beautiful, ain't it, brother? Don't you think?*

Game time: the players came out to the tune of the Champions League theme, every player's chin facing forward, every mind, United red or Chelsea blue, deep in contemplation. The first ever all-English final even had some Englishmen playing in it. One hundred million people were watching. Or a billion. For the first time ever, I felt a little bit proud to be English. The bar broke out into song, hundreds of arms out wide, lungs open, roaring blind fuckin loyalty – Reds from all over the world. Reds United. It was all peace love 'n' understanding, but I still couldn't believe it, you know? That I was in a fuckin sports bar, just like the ones I'd been into in London, in Madrid, in Milan. Christ, I could've watched it at home and been a team leader in a year's time. If I'd have played it smart – the last ten fuckin years – I could have been round at Guy and Sally's, sitting with Little Ryan on my knee, holding him tight to me, Gemma right there too. The line-ups flashed on the screen.

GK 1
VAN DER SAR, Edwin

CB 5
FERDINAND, Rio (C)

CB 15
VIDIĆ, Nemanja

RB 6
BROWN, Wesley

LB 3
EVRA, Patrice

CM 18
SCHOLES, Paul

CM 16
CARRICK, Michael

RM 4
HARGREAVES, Owen

LM 7
RONALDO, Cristiano

CF 32
TÉVEZ, Carlos

CF 10
ROONEY, Wayne

So there was the confirmation: Giggs hadn't made the starting eleven, but it turned out he had made the bench. Mike felt a sweet pleasure, and sour pain, in his gut. He didn't know which was stronger. Was Ryan going to miss out on a piece of history? Or was it set up perfectly for a grand finale? He thought about Ryan, who'd never replied to his plea. Ryan, who'd had a whole entire week to respond to what was clearly an urgent letter, and couldn't take five minutes away from his happy, successful, trophy-filled, perfect wife-and-two-kids life to pick up a pen or sit down at a computer to help the needy. Even if Ryan was sitting there right at that moment, on the substitutes' bench, dialling Gemma's number, it was probably too late.

They're never gonna let you see him again.
You know it.
And there's nothing you can do.

As Mike was watching the teams on the screen, lined up and listening to the Champions League theme tune, a brawl broke out in the bar, with two middle-aged men throwing vicious punches and kicks at each other, fighting like they were in it to the death. Mike asked Alec what the problem was, but he didn't know. Nobody seemed to.

'Come on, lads, we're all on the same side here!' Alec shouted, stepping forward to break it up.

Others were more direct. A big man forced his body between those of the fighters, and held them apart.

'Hey, dickheads, we're not animals!' he screamed, pointing at the flickering images of the two captains shaking hands. 'Have some fuckin RESPECT!'

And with that, as if a magic word had been spoken, both men came out of their spell, shuffled backwards and looked towards the screen. Another of the Dublin Reds offered to get them a pint each, and encouraged them to shake hands, just like the captains. All this, it could get to anyone. As Mike looked back up towards the screen he noticed it was getting fuzzier. A couple of times, the picture pixelated, froze, delayed. Players became slabs of red. The ball a square. Mike thought he smelled blood, and vomit.

You can hardly watch. The match takes no time at all. It takes for ever. You're looking but you're not. As the Dublin Reds cry out and sing and dance dance dance, you're back in October 1992, when your limbs were strong and the future was near. (Ronaldo scores, it's 1–0 to United, ohmyGod it's only set up by FUCKINWESLEYBROWN and the bar falls off its chair laughing.) But now it feels like it's finished, your life. You're thinking, as beers are spilled and cheers and screams deafen you, about how you're gonna have to put on a suit and go get a new job soon, on your own, and how nothing is fair. (United are playing well so far. It's looking good.) As these thoughts swirl about in your skull, you can feel a burning in your stomach. You recognize this burning, you know its name, and know you have to keep it down and (Lampard scores an equalizer just before half-time, against the run of play, the bar goes silent, you feel like you've been punched) and – and WHOSE

FAULT WAS ALL THIS ANYWAY? At half-time, Ryan troops off towards the dressing room with the rest of the substitutes, a look of grim concentration on his face.

As our maybe heroes and maybe zeroes went to get the hairdryer treatment one more time (Ryan still in his tracksuit, waiting for the call, powerless), I was just turning, turning, turning it over in my mind, thinking about the ocean of almost-legends who nearly made it in that promotion push but didn't, who just missed out on that crucial cup final where they might have been spotted by a top team. Good, sound, reliable players who got moved on after managers changed and whoever who brought them in was gone and already setting up somewhere else, maybe only a few months, weeks or even days after players he'd signed had hauled their families with them to Yeovil, to Darlington, or some other fuckin backwater they had to kid themselves they wanted to be. Thousands every year, in their early thirties, flair players and fringe players, the talented and determined, the unlucky, sitting down with their wives-or-girlfriends after the latest move that didn't work out, trying to think of what the hell they could do next with the shitty cards life had dealt them. (Or they'd dealt themselves?) Playing career dead. Unqualified for anything else. Kids to drag up. So what next? (The boys in the Russian box talked through the break, filling my head with sounds which I imagined meant: *It's a Champions League final of two halves, Sergei, and anything could happen here.*) Some players had dreams from when they were kids they wanted to make reality, like opening a restaurant or a pub. The ones with good connections and stacks of trophies could get media jobs and talk football for ever and ever – but not everyone gets that break. God knows there's only a few seats in the TV or radio studios need filling. And what the fuck do you do when you can no longer do the only thing you ever wanted to do? Painting and decorating? Building wells in Africa? In 2007, when I told Mum I wanted to go back to school, she burst out crying. *My beautiful boy*, she said, holding out her hands and touching my cheeks. *If only Gregory and Simon could see you now.* Only they wouldn't be proud, would they? Coz here I was, locked out of the biggest game of my life and broke from paying for the ticket, pissed again (another pint on the table in front of me, from the Dublin Reds, my new best friends), and it was finally official: I WAS A FUCKIN IDIOT. Standing in that bar in Moscow, bouncing around, surrounded by chatter, I thought, What if I could answer all my questions all at once? I was daydreaming, daydreaming. My mind was water.

'Welcome back to Manchester,' Mike imagined Debbie Carlsson saying to Gregory Wilson, as he stood on her doorstep, a bunch of flowers in his arms, suitcases either side of him. (In Mike's imagination his father had renounced football, and other women, to return home, as he'd promised on the phone.) 'I'm afraid I can't stop to chat, my husband and I are on our way out. Derek's taking me to a lovely new Italian in town – and who knows? Maybe a bit of karaoke afterwards. Sorry, Gregory, I'm forgetting myself. Mike's in Moscow watching the match, but perhaps you might want to go and see Guy? You're a grandfather now, you know. Several times over.'

Mike imagined his mum, her smile fixed, moving carefully, outwardly calm, writing out Guy and Sally's address on a scrap of paper and handing it over, wondering whether her ex-husband knew about the death of his brother. Then closing the door.

During half-time, you and the Dublin Reds line up shots and sink them. Every one in tribute to someone or something. Fuck knows what. Shouting, counting, banging the bar, you think, pretty fuckin predictable, this. Your fall. It was always gonna happen, right? That you'd crack at the first sign of a struggle. You stand there feeling absolute, total, all-consuming self-pity. And then, right there at the bar, you think that actually, you and Ryan, you're like twins. Like those ones glued to each other, born with one heart or head. One twin has to die, or be all fucked up, all mangled, so the healthier one can survive, thrive, grow up and be the Ultimate United Legend. You say to your shot glass: *I must pay the price for his immortality.* Then you knock it back and go for a slash.

As the second half kicked off, I looked up at the screen and noticed it was basically just a blur. I couldn't focus, and trying to focus made my eyes sting. It was easier to close them. That made me, made me . . .

made me what? I was calm, I think, and I could remember clearly how I tried to get into the casino the week after me and Guy had that first big win back in 1993, when I was still a United player. But this time I was on my own, and there was no one around to abracadabra the door open. (Big cheer all around the bar at the restart. Calls of MURDER EM and FUCK OFF *DROGBA* and CHELSEA SCUM.) The bouncers were different, and I wasn't dressed right – Guy wouldn't lend me one of his suits since I was sick all over the last one – so I couldn't get in. (Chelsea are bossing this final now, there's lots of *Ooh*s and *Aah*s and people hiding behind their hands. Essien shoots on fifty-four minutes, the shot goes over the top and some bloke up the back shouts BULL-SHIT-AAAAAHHHHIIIH.) Head spinning now, Mikey, isn't it? And on the screen at the game you can't be at coz – DON'T THINK ABOUT THAT – Drogba hits the post! (Ryan is warming up on the touchline. Ryan removing tracksuit.)

Neither team is breaking through, or looking like it, so it's gonna be extra time. (And here comes Ryan, just before the whistle, saddling up and getting ready to ride.) Guy texts you again saying: DON'T BE A DUMB FUCK ALL YOUR LIFE and those words take you right back to when the two of you shared a room and life was getting dangerous and images of *Eye Gauger* and *I'll Rip Your Face Off* and rotting bodies in heaps lived behind your eyelids at night. You miss Guy so much you want to reach into the phone and pull him through it to be with you. You miss Uncle Si, who would never have got in the mess you're in now, when mass murder and going on the run seem like an easy way out compared to returning home.

Then: the end of the ninety. Murmurs. Talk. The rush to the bar. I nodded when asked if I wanted another. In the break, I wondered what happened to Guy's collection of true crime books. And wondered, Whatever happened to the Eye Gauger?

In extra time, both teams had chances. Chelsea hit the underside of the crossbar. United legend Ryan Giggs had a shot saved off the line by the Chelsea captain's head, at which Mike Wilson clutched his own and called out, 'Destiny!' But now the clock was running down in a way that seemed, to Mike, and probably to Guy and Sally and Robbie, and the Dublin Reds, and Danny Tredwell, the Oldham defender whose career Mike had wrecked, and Debbie and Derek, to Gregory and his friends at the bar and to both team managers and all their staff, to be inevitable.

Nobody wants penalties.

You know as well as I do, Sergei, it's a lottery.

But until they come up with a better system . . .

United win the toss and go first, so Carlos Tévez (whose name will be forgotten) approaches the penalty spot, positions the ball, runs up and – SCORES – Čech dives the wrong way, it's 1–0 and Tévez clenches his fists as the BAR GOES MENTAL then goes hush hush quiet nervous waiting for the first Chelsea penalty which is taken by Michael Ballack (whose name will be forgotten) and he – SCORES – shot struck hard and confident and it's 1–1 as there are mumbles in this Moscow bar and thousands of others round the globe, the odd *we're gonna fuckin lose here* can be heard before big cheers swallow nervousness as Michael Carrick (whose name will be forgotten) steps up and Carrick – SCORES – it's 2–1 and *no doubt about that one* says the guy behind you as the BAR GOES MENTAL AGAIN then hush hush quiet nervous as Juliano Belletti (whose name will be forgotten) walks up and you try and will him to blast it high and wide but he – SCORES – with his first kick of the game though you wouldn't know it as the screen graphic flashes 2–2 and there are more mumbles in this bar but probably MASSIVE CHEERS in countless other places all over the planet from Chelsea supporters, some just-Chelsea-supporters-for-the-night from Liverpool and Barcelona and Edinburgh, some wearing T-shirts saying ANYONE BUT UNITED, all this as you wonder if Ryan's gonna take one, then big whoops all round as the big flavour-of-the-year and tonight's goalscorer Cristiano Ronaldo (whose name, despite everything, will be forgotten) steps up and does that cheeky fake stutter he does and – MISSES – Oh my God fuckfuckfuckfuck it's still 2–2 and there's an earthquake in your mind and it's obvious you're gonna lose now even though no one says it as before you know it Frank Lampard (whose name will be forgotten, thank God) is there and ready and he – SCORES – it's 3–2 Chelsea and a few people are already halfway to the exit as the guy behind you says *I wish he'd fuckin do that for England* and a ripple of nervous laughter goes round the bar as time speeds up and Owen Hargreaves (whose name will be forgotten) is next and balls-of-steel Hargreaves – SCORES – it's 3–3 and next it's Ashley Cole (whose name will be forgotten) and he – SCORES – too, 4–3, and all of a sudden it's all nearly over and Christ fuck bollocks it's down to Luis Nani (whose name will be forgotten), who gets a big groan as he walks up (you hope he can't hear it from where he is), but it's okay for now coz Nani – SCORES – only just mind, it's 4–4 and the bar braces itself for hell and a long night and a shitty trip home and months of paying back money spent on this shameful FAILURE when Mr Bastard Chelski himself, John Terry (whose name will be forgotten) places the ball, the Russian boys in the box are giving it the big intro which probably translates as *one kick till you're King of the World, Mr Abramovich* or some shit, but even they couldn't have predicted this coz even though United keeper Van der Sar (whose name will be forgotten) has gone the wrong way Terry slips and all of a sudden is on the floor and he – HITS THE POST AND MISSES! – HAHAHAHAHA and already the bar is celebrating HAHAHAHAHA like United have won as Terry is crouched on the floor wanting to die HAHAHAHA coz that kind of thing, it can only mean fate has already made her decision, but then, as one, the bar remembers that actually this isn't over yet and bloody hell we're into sudden death and panic panic panic spreads as Anderson (whose name you can hardly even remember) walks up to take his penalty, looking like this tiny little Brazilian boy who needs a cuddle and can't possibly be big enough for this situation and, you think, it's mental isn't it what minute details success and failure come down to in the end and Anderson – SCORES – lucky that almost hit the goalkeeper and bounced off but seemed to go through him instead, but it's 5–4, that's all that matters, and there are sighs of relief which last for just long enough for another baby boy, Salomon Kalou (whose name will be forgotten) to do that long lonely walk from the halfway line, place the ball and – SCORE – which means it's now 5–5 and it feels like this has been going on for ever, you can't remember anything before it or imagine any life after it but then planet earth stops spinning as yesladiesandgents Ryan Joseph Giggs (whose name will be remembered forevermore) steps forward – how could you not see this coming? – and he's walking, floating, flying to his destiny, blocking out everything around him and this is the calmest moment of your life coz you know that your soul and his are one, that everything's been leading to this, everything, and every second and millisecond of the last twenty years melts into the ground below you as the roar goes up in the stadium and in the bar when he takes his run up and of course he – SCORES – bending it into the corner of the net, it's 6–5, and if dreams were wishes and wishes came true then you'd be sitting on a cloud, Sir Matt lighting a fresh cigar for you coz, all right, none of these guys know it, but it's the WINNING PENALTY, and even though it's Anelka now to face the future and there are cries of *oh shit* from all around and *is this gonna go on all night?* and *my nan's up to take the next one* you have seen that this, right here, is the end, so when Anelka (whose name will be forgotten) – MISSES – Van der Sar saves, and United are the Champions of Europe and THE PLACE GOES FUCKIN MENTAL, you're not even looking.

You're on your way to the bar.

Might as well beat the rush, eh?

GIGGSY WATCH – LittleGiggsWilson says: Broke the record for United appearances. Scored the last United penalty on the night we win the biggest prize in football. IMMORTALITY HERE WE COME.

Average Fan Rating: 10/10

As the celebrations began, substitutes and trainers rushing onto the pitch while Chelsea players sank to their knees, Mike Wilson thought it couldn't ever get any better, for the team or for Ryan, the club captain, who didn't even *volunteer* to take a penalty. Mike thought of Terry, his Old Trafford friend, and of the samurai.

'God CHOSE Giggsy,' Mike said to one of the Dublin Reds, whose name he had forgotten. 'It's fuckin perfect.'

It was. And where do you go from perfection? Suddenly, Mike Wilson knew what he wanted to do. He knew what he had to do. He thought of what Guy often said: 'Love can't be explained, Mikey.' Well, he didn't need to explain anything to anyone. He only had to act.

On on on through the crowds, the madness, the chanting and swearing and the noise, which reminds you of that first game, years ago, your first visit to Old Trafford with Dad as a boy, when love was still uncomplicated. You press on through the raised beer bottles and swarming crowds, into the centre of it all. You're gonna find him. You're gonna find him. Don't know exactly how you're gonna go about it when you do get there (though you're working it out as you move), but you can't wait any more. It was never gonna end. It was never gonna end. Unless you did something, said something, reached out and changed history as you'd always known you could, then it was never gonna end. So you walk on, on. Everything is simple and clear and it's such a relief, this clarity.

You're gonna laugh, but when I think about it now, I mean REALLY think about it, my memory of those minutes, heading back through Moscow, back towards the ground when everyone else was flooding out: I was flying, like Ryan had done when he'd approached that penalty spot. Floating, like he had done that day in the bar, when he shook my hand and said it was nice to see me, and like he had done as he went up to take the penalty. I was floating like a cocker spaniel chasing a piece of silver paper in the wind. My leg didn't hurt any more. Running gave me no pain at all. I knew what I was gonna do and it felt right. So I flew through the crowd. Yes I did. Or maybe I didn't. Maybe my leg was throbbing, I was in agony, and the pain was making me giddy.

Mike Wilson slowed to a stop, panting, as he arrived at the Luzhniki Stadium. The press vans were out, with seas of journalists doing pieces to camera from every free spot, using words like 'momentous' and 'historic', as if a political dynasty was falling or being born, while earpiece voices reminded them to look like they could barely contain their excitement. Meanwhile, many of the fans were gone, off to enjoy a long night of happiness or sadness in the city's bars and restaurants. Only the hardcore United followers had chosen to stay to catch a glimpse of their heroes as they left the ground and headed for their hotel. The chances of attracting their attention were small. Surely the players would want to get away so they could celebrate freely together? But some fans were prepared to wait. Near Mike, a group of children gripped pens and United merchandise they wanted signed. Half an hour passed and their expressions hardly changed. Expectant but hopeful. Nervous but excited.

Finally the players appeared. Back in their club suits, but more casual now, each man began to file out of the ground, flanked by security guards. They climbed, one by one, up the two steps and onto the team bus and out of sight. *Rooney. Ronaldo. Tévez.* There were some grins. Some intense stares. Some players ignored the chaos around them, like there was nothing remarkable about this day, these photographers, these fans, standing there in awe, looking at their heroes. *Anderson. Van der Sar. Vidić.* Mike was keeping a lookout. Straining at the barrier, holding onto his place between two teenage girls. Waiting for the right moment.

Mike imagined what his mum and Derek might be doing at that moment.

Ferdinand. Hargreaves. Nani. Brown.

He imagined what his dad might be doing.

Scholes. Carrick. Evra.

He imagined what Guy and Sally and Robbie and Millie might be doing.

He imagined what Gemma and Colum and baby Alice might be doing.

He imagined what his son might be doing.

He imagined all these things, and they seemed real.

Then Mike saw him.

Mike saw Ryan Giggs, and he dived between two guards.

He lunged, reaching out, both arms extended.

His hands held Ryan's neck.

STAR STRUCK!

MANIAC EX-STRIKER ATTACKS HERO GIGGS AFTER DRAMATIC EURO FINAL

Timothy Davids reports

It was an amazing night already. One of the most successful club footballers ever, Ryan Giggs, 34, scored the last Man United penalty in the Champions League final, then lifted the famous trophy for the second time in his career. Giggs planned on partying the night away with pals and teammates – a party that surely even Sir Alex would have approved of. *But he nearly didn't survive the night at all.* And all because an obsessed stalker had tracked him down to Moscow with one thing on his mind: MURDER. Mike Wilson, a bit-part player in the United team of the early nineties (not to be confused with another, more successful Mike Wilson from the late nineties), went AWOL from his job in a shop in Manchester two days before the game and headed to Russia to prepare for his crime. The obsessed sicko had planned to watch the game before carrying out his twisted stunt, but early reports suggest he had bought a fake ticket and was turned away from the stadium. Last night, Russian TV channels were reporting a scrap between a security guard and a man fitting Wilson's description an hour before kick-off.

After the game, evil ex-striker Wilson, 32, headed for the players' exit to the stadium, where United heroes had stopped to sign autographs for fans before getting on the team bus. Wilson posed as an autograph hunter, then when Giggs reached out to sign his ticket, Wilson lunged at him as if he was going to strangle the star. Luckily, Russian security services stepped in just in time, saving his life. A Facebook group has been set up in tribute to those guards who saved the life of the United hero, and over 30,000 people have already joined. One comment on the site reads: 'Moscow, we owe you 4ever.' Another said: 'Whoever you are, thank u for saving Ryan. Just like Munich, we'll never forget!'

Workmates last night described Wilson as a 'bit of a

loner' and said he was 'obsessed' by Giggs, who he blamed for a sixteen-year run of bad luck. As for the attack, witnesses reported different versions. When asked if Wilson gave any warning, or spoke to Giggs before or after, one eye witness said he was heard to shout, 'I love you, now it's time to die.' One fan said that Wilson didn't speak at all. Another reported Wilson as saying, just before lashing out, 'Bring me the head of Ryan Giggs!'

The great man himself has not yet commented on the incident, though a spokesman has released a statement, saying: 'Ryan would like to take this opportunity to thank fans from all over the world for their overwhelming support during this difficult time. He would like to make clear that he wishes Mike Wilson well, and asks anyone who wishes to show their support to make a donation to the mental health charities stated on Ryan's personal website.'

Full Report, News, pages 4, 5, 7
Features, page 13, Arise Sir Ryan?
Opinion, page 34, The nearly men who hit the bottle instead of the back of the net

'In football, everyone has an unhappy ending. Only difference is, how long you take to get there. And whether, when it hits, you can turn it into a new beginning.'

From Mike Wilson's statement after being arrested in Moscow in May 2008

CAREER TIMELINE OF RYAN GIGGS

Full Name:

Ryan Joseph Giggs (previously Ryan Joseph Wilson)

Date of Birth:

29 November 1973

Place of Birth:

Canton, Cardiff, Wales

Height:

5'11" (1.80m)

Position:

Left-wing, centre-forward, right-wing, sometimes switched to centre-midfield later in career. Even played in defence when called upon, turning out at left-back on several occasions.

Heroes:

Sebastian Coe, Mike Hughes, Michael Johnson, Diego Maradona, Bryan Robson.

Hobbies:

Watching films in his home cinema, driving the cars stored in his four garages, enjoying the occasional drink in the Bridgewater Hotel bar, attending Salford Rugby Club matches, spending time with family.

Professional Career:

Manchester City 1985–87 (youth), Manchester United 1987–present

Club Honours:

- Premier League (12): 1992/93, 1993/94, 1995/96, 1996/97, 1998/99, 1999/2000, 2000/01, 2002/03, 2006/07, 2007/08, 2008/09, 2010/11

- FA Cup (4): 1993/94, 1995/96, 1998/99, 2003/04
- Football League Cup (4): 1991/92, 2005/06, 2008/09, 2009/10
- FA Community Shield (9): 1993, 1994, 1996, 1997, 2003, 2007, 2008, 2010, 2011
- UEFA Champions League (2): 1998/99, 2007/08
- UEFA Super Cup (1): 1991
- Intercontinental Cup (1): 1999
- FIFA Club World Cup (1): 2008

Individual Honours:

- PFA Young Player of the Year (2): 1992, 1993
- PFA Player of the Year (1): 2009
- FA Premier League Player of the Month (3): Sept 1993, Aug 2006, Feb 2007
- PFA Team of the Year (8): 1993, 1994, 1995, 1996, 1998, 2001, 2007, 2009
- PFA Team of the Century (1): 2007

Records:

- Most decorated player in British football history
- Most Premier League appearances for a player
- Only Premiership player ever to win twelve league titles
- Only player ever to score in twelve consecutive Champions League tournaments
- Oldest player ever to score in the Champions League
- Only player to score in fourteen different Champions League tournaments
- Only player to score in every Premier League campaign since its inception
- Only United player to have appeared in all four League Cup-winning teams
- Only United player to have played in both UEFA Champions League-winning finals
- Most appearances by any Manchester United player in history
- Never sent off
- Never received a yellow card for dissent

Orders and special awards:

- UNICEF representative since 2006
- Inducted into the English Football Hall of Fame in 2005
- Awarded OBE for Services to Football in 2007
- Awarded honorary Master of Arts degree from Salford University in 2008 for contributions to football and charity work in developing countries
- Featured in *The Simpsons* episode 'The Regina Monologues', set in England
- Won BBC Sports Personality of the Year 2009, age thirty-six. Giggs received 151,842 votes, beating the favourite, Formula 1 Champion Jenson Button, by 55,000 votes
- Received the Freedom of the City of Salford in January 2010, an award previously won by only three others: Nelson Mandela, Stretford-born artist LS Lowry and David Lloyd George, British Prime Minister 1916–1922. Giggs said: 'To be given the freedom of Salford, my adopted city, has to rank amongst the greatest honours I have ever received.'

Statistics correct as of 1 April 2012.

CAREER TIMELINE OF MIKE 'LITTLE GIGGS' WILSON

Full Name:

Michael Jonathan Wilson

Date of Birth:

25 May 1975

Place of Birth:

Hope Hospital, Manchester (now Salford Royal)

Height:

6' (1.82m)

Position:

Centre-forward

Heroes:

Sir Matt Busby, Sir Bobby Charlton, Sir Alex Ferguson, Ryan Giggs.

Hobbies:

Reading sports autobiographies and true crime books, playing *Football Manager.*

Career:

Manchester United 1991–93, Plymouth Argyle (loan) 1993–94, Salford City FC, occasional (1994–99), variety of local amateur teams, occasional (2000–08)

Club Honours:

Only medal was as a fringe player in the famous FA Youth Cup-winning team of 1992, though Wilson did have an impressive, if brief, record as a trainee. After a short spell playing in the academy team he played thirty-seven times for United reserves, scoring twenty goals, a record return at the time. Impeccable disciplinary record – no yellow cards or red cards in reserve games. Only appearance for first team was United v Oldham Athletic, 21 November 1992, notable for lasting just 133 seconds before a challenge on promising young defender Danny Tredwell, which eventually ended both men's careers.

Individual Honours:

None

Recovery/Retirement:

After breaking his leg in 1992, took six months to recover, then re-entered United reserves. Went to Plymouth Argyle on season-long loan in 1993. Failed to impress in the reserves, featured on the bench for the first team several times, but was never used, and broke his leg again in training, keeping him out of action for another few months. Returned early after walking out of the dugout during a match. Released by Manchester United in 1994, and retired from professional football shortly after. Broke his left leg for a third time in 2006.

Family Background:

Father, Irish Catholic, mostly absent since 1992, though he did watch Mike play for Plymouth Argyle once, in secret, and returned to Manchester on the day his son was arrested. Still owner of a residence in the Algarve, Portugal, in a resort close to Faro, where he used to live full time. Mother, also Catholic, observant, from three generations who worked in the textile and engineering industry in the North of England. Now remarried, and running her own online jewellery business.

Post-retirement Career:

After spending several years battling alcoholism and gambling addiction, Wilson re-entered education in 2000, studying sports psychology at Stockport College, then attempted to qualify as a football coach in 2002. Abandoned courses part-way through after showing initial aptitude for both. Spent a further year claiming benefits, before entering a series of menial office jobs which never lasted for longer than a few weeks before resignation or sacking. This pattern lasted until 2006, when he was employed at Sportswear Direction, training to be a team leader. He remained in this job until 2008.

Criminal Record:

Occasional minor misdemeanours and petty crimes when Wilson was a teenager, mostly theft. But he will best be remembered, if at all, for a failed attack on United legend Ryan Giggs, after the 2008 Champions League final. Dragged from the scene by police, Wilson was handed over to the UK authorities after talks between British and Russian officials. Wilson currently resides in Strangeways Prison, Manchester.

Acknowledgements

Thank you to:

My agent, Jenny Brown, who has supported me since the start.

My editor, Luke Brown, and Alan Mahar, Emma Hargrave, Melissa Rudd and Rikhi Ubhi, for making this book happen.

Creative Scotland, whose generous Writers' Bursary was essential throughout the writing process.

The University of Strathclyde, where I wrote most of the novel as the Keith Wright Creative Writing Fellow, 2008–10.

Cove Park, where I finished it, in 2011.

Alan Bissett, Mark Buckland, AJC, Tim Glass, Kirstin Innes, Anneliese Mackintosh, Paul Martin and Adrian Searle, for caring about the details.

A NOVEL IS A JOINT EFFORT

About the Author

Photo: Ross Wood

Rodge Glass grew up in Cheshire in a family who've held Manchester United season tickets for over fifty years.

He is the author of the novels *No Fireworks* and *Hope for Newborns*; and *Alasdair Gray: A Secretary's Biography*, which won a Somerset Maugham Award in 2009. Recently, he was co-author of the graphic novel *Dougie's War: A Soldier's Story*, nominated for several awards. He lives in Glasgow, where he is a lecturer at Strathclyde University and associate editor at Cargo Publishing.

For more information visit: www.rodgeglass.com